**"Gray!" I wasn't even embarrassed about the panic in my voice.**

"Yeah?" He said as he emerged from the basement.

"Bring your light over here. Shine it on my arm."

He did so. "You scratched yourself."

I shook my head. "That's the drip."

"But it's–"

I nodded.

He swung his penlight, and the beam picked out a red puddle on the floor, drops plummeting from above to splash in the viscous pool. A footprint repeated across the floor, getting fainter and fainter with each step until it was almost nonexistent when it stopped at my left shoe.

He trained the beam overhead, and a woman's pale hand appeared, flung out over the opening. Gray and I looked at each other in dismay, knowing that where there was a hand, there was a body attached.

**GAYLE ROPER**

has always loved stories, and as a result she's authored forty books. Gayle has won the Romance Writers of America's RITA® Award for Best Inspirational Romance, repeatedly been a finalist for both the RITA® Award and the Christy Award, won three Holt Medallions, the Reviewers' Choice Award, the Inspirational Readers Choice Contest and a Lifetime Achievement Award as well as the Award of Excellence. Several writers' conferences have cited her for her contributions to the training of writers. Her articles have appeared in numerous periodicals, including *Discipleship Journal* and *Moody Magazine,* and she has contributed chapters and short stories to several anthologies. She enjoys speaking at writers' conferences and women's events, reading and eating out. She adores her kids and grandkids, and loves her own personal patron of the arts, her husband, Chuck.

# GAYLE ROPER

# SEE NO EVIL

Steeple
Hill®

Published by Steeple Hill Books™

STEEPLE HILL BOOKS

Steeple
Hill®

ISBN-13: 978-0-373-44229-4
ISBN-10: 0-373-44229-7

SEE NO EVIL

www.SteepleHill.com

**Printed in U.S.A.**

"For I know the plans I have for you,"
declares the Lord, "plans to prosper you and not to
harm you, plans to give you a hope and a future.
Then you will call on me and come and pray to me,
and I will listen to you. You will seek me and find
me when you seek me with all your heart."
—*Jeremiah* 29:11–12

To Chuck,
my own personal patron of the arts,
for all the years of your stalwart love and support

# ONE

"Anna Volente, keep your mind on your work."

How many times in the past had I heard those words from my dad or mom or one of my teachers? Even from Glenn, now that I thought about it, though I tried to think of him as little as possible. Of course I knew I should be concentrating on the project at hand, the hanging of the window treatment I held.

But how could I ignore the strange man skulking in the backyard of the unfinished house kitty-corner from the backyard of the completed model home I was working in?

He wasn't one of the construction workers. I was certain of that. They had all gone home a couple of hours ago, lunchboxes and thermoses in hand, leaving me alone to finish my work in the warm, sultry August evening. The prowling man wasn't dressed right for building anything either. He wore khakis and a red short-sleeved polo shirt hanging outside his slacks. I couldn't tell from this distance if the dark mark he had over his heart was an alligator or a pony or a spot of dried gravy from his dinner.

I studied him. His clothes might be ordinary, but there was something not quite right about him, though I couldn't decide what it was with the lowering sun shining so brightly in my eyes. I raised my hand to shield my eyes.

Was he just moving awkwardly, like someone who had a sprained ankle, or was he really skulking? Either way, as far as I knew, at this time of day no one should be anywhere near any of the houses in this very new, very upscale development. I excluded myself, of course.

From high on my ladder at the tall back window of the living room which ran the depth of the model house, I eyed the interloper. If I'd been hanging one of the front or side windows, I wouldn't have seen him. If I'd been standing on the floor, I wouldn't have seen him. The fence across the backyard and the plantings artistically fronting it, especially the weeping cherry, would have blocked him from view.

I frowned. Should I tell someone about him? Call someone?

*Oh, Mr. or Ms. 911 Person, there's a man walking around in the backyard of one of the houses in Freedom's Chase.*

*And what is this man doing?*

*Walking around in the backyard of one of the houses in Freedom's Chase.*

*That's it? Call me back when he does something illegal, okay?*

*But isn't trespassing illegal?*

Then again, what if he was just looking around with the idea of buying a house here?

"How much longer will you be?"

The question, asked from behind me in a very male, rather abrupt voice, startled me, and I almost lost my precarious footing. I put a hand out and caught the upper sash to steady myself. With my sudden movement and less firm grip on the material, the heavy window treatment I held began to slip from my grasp. The slick silk flowed south with determination, a fabric Mississippi heading for the wooden Gulf of Mexico.

"No!" I couldn't let that wonderful fabric get all wrinkled, maybe even damaged, not after all the hours I'd put in working on it. I lunged for it, the man outside forgotten, the man inside ignored.

Then the curtain was forgotten too as I belatedly realized that you can't lunge when high on a stepladder. Maybe, I thought desperately as I flailed my arms, I could sort of step backwards and find the floor without falling flat on my back or stepping on the precious material. Of course that would be quite a step; the floor was several feet down.

"Watch it! You're going to fall!" the man behind me yelled helpfully.

Tell me something I don't know!

I scrunched my eyes shut as I felt myself plummet in a graceful sort of slow motion, at least until gravity got hold of me. Then it became full speed ahead.

*Lord, don't let it hurt too much!*

How would I ever finish my decorating job if I broke my leg—or broke anything, for that matter? And then there was school, which started Monday. How could an art teacher ever manage one hundred and fifty-plus intermediate school kids and all the supplies for their various projects while on crutches? I could barely hold my own on two feet.

Suddenly strong hands grabbed me none too gently about the middle. The man they belonged to staggered under my weight, not the most complimentary thing that ever happened to me, but he didn't go down. Thanks to him, neither did I. No broken legs after all. Just wounded vanity.

He set me unceremoniously on my feet. Yards of glorious Scalamandré fabric billowed about us. I watched as it settled on the floor, burying my sneakers and his dirty workboots.

"Be careful," I cried. "Don't move. Don't get that fabric dirty! It costs a fortune."

He snorted. "Tell me about it. I got the bill yesterday."

I carefully lifted the drapery off his boots, laying it over one of the plaid slipper chairs. I examined it minutely and couldn't see any dirt on the pale-cream background. Relief washed over me.

I turned to my rescuer. Now that I could spare him a glance, I saw he was what Dad always called a man's man: big, physically fit, ruggedly handsome with dark eyes and wavy dark hair that needed a haircut. He wore jeans and a white T-shirt, and he had a phone clipped to his belt and a pair of sunglasses hanging from the neck of his T-shirt.

All in all, very impressive, but I'd given impressive men a wide berth since Glenn. Once burned was more than enough.

A pad of lined paper filled with notations and a black leather carrying case holding what I assumed was a laptop lay on the floor where he'd dropped them when he grabbed me.

"That would have been a nasty fall," he said, picking up his tablet and case.

I nodded. Of course I wouldn't have fallen at all if he hadn't scared me to death, but I decided not to mention that little fact. "Thanks for the rescue."

He grunted, frowning at me. "What are you doing standing on something as unstable as that ladder? It looks like it's going to collapse under you at any moment."

"What's the matter with my ladder?" I looked at the paint-splattered contraption. It was my father's. He'd used it for all his home projects for years, as had Granddad before him. It bordered on family heirloom.

Dad had loaned it to me almost ten years ago when, to help pay college expenses, I began sewing curtains, slipcovers, pillows and anything else a customer wanted for her home.

I was now long out of college, but the ladder was still with me, as was my part-time business, Anna's Windows Plus. When I'd picked that name years ago, I'd never given Bill Gates and his Windows program a thought. I didn't get *too* many calls about malfunctioning computer programs.

"What's the matter with your ladder?" He looked amazed I would ask. "You're kidding, right? The brace on one side is broken. It has more potential splinters on it than a porcupine has quills."

Yowzah! The guy spoke in poetic images.

"In short, it's an accident waiting to happen, and when you break your neck, I'll get the blame."

I blinked. "Why would you get the blame?" But I was pretty sure I knew since I'd just figured out why he looked so familiar.

"Because I'm the contractor, and Freedom's Chase is my project."

"You're Edward Grayson." Just as I'd thought. I'd seen his picture in the *News* often enough. I'd guess everybody in the Amhearst area knew his name, probably everybody in Chester County, if not Philadelphia and the whole Delaware Valley. He built wonderful homes like the one we were standing in and sold them at outrageous prices, though rumor had it he didn't need the money. His family was supposedly drowning in Texas oil or something.

Maybe that's where he got the financial backing for the massive renovation of downtown Amhearst he had planned and which City Council had just approved after much dispute. All the deteriorating buildings in the four-block area that had once been a thriving shopping and business district were to be torn down, and condominiums and apartments built, with all the facilities such a community would need.

I had followed the newspaper reports about the huge

project every step of the way. I loved Amhearst, and anything that would make it a more healthy community had my support.

"You're younger than I thought, Mr. Grayson." Not too much older than I was. Mid-thirties to my late twenties, I thought. Young for such responsibility.

"That's Mr. Edwards, not Mr. Grayson," my rescuer said. "My name's Grayson Edwards. Gray Edwards."

"You're named after a color." As an artist I liked that idea, though gray wasn't the color I would have chosen for him. Nothing so soft, so muted. Black maybe. Strong and powerful. Or Green, a deep, forest shade. Too bad I'd never been asked my opinion. I looked at Gray Edwards. Like he'd ever want my opinion.

What if I were named after a color? I could be Rose Volente or Violet Volente. The thought made me grin.

"I am not named after a color." There was enough pique in his voice to indicate he'd dealt with this comment before. "Grayson is my mother's maiden name."

Mom's maiden name was Rasmussen. Thank goodness she had realized there wasn't any possibility of a first name for her only daughter to be found there. Suddenly *Anna* looked very good indeed.

"As I was saying before you interrupted—" he said.

I frowned at him. I'd hardly classify my comment about his name as an interruption. He frowned back.

"—this is my project." He waved his hand, tablet and all. I understood he meant not the living room in which we were standing but Freedom's Chase with its mini-mansions under construction, each house all but overflowing its mere quarter-acre lot. There'd never be much call for a lawn service around here. There weren't any lawns.

"If you fall and kill yourself," he said, "your survivors will doubtless sue me for all I'm worth." He looked as put upon as if the suit were already in progress.

Thinking he needed to lighten up a bit, I asked oh-so-sweetly, "And you're worth how much, Edward? Just so I can tell the family an amount to ask for if the unthinkable comes to pass."

He stared at me, dark eyes narrowed. "Cute." .

I grinned. "Thank you."

He shook his head and reluctantly grinned back. My heart went pitter-pat as if I were sixteen, and the star quarterback had deigned to smile at me.

"Will you be much longer?" He glanced at his watch. "It's eight o'clock. Past time to go home." He practically vibrated with impatience.

I turned to the fabric, carefully lifting the beautiful, pricey Tuscan Vine. The large clusters of aubergine grapes, the green leaves and the brown vines were embroidered on cream silk. I loved the pattern. I glanced at him over my shoulder. "I'm not sure how long I'll be. It depends on whether I have the peace and quiet I need to do my job."

"Ha-ha," he said.

I searched for and found the top edge of the drapery. "You don't have to wait for me, you know." I pointed to the other long windows. "I managed to hang those all by myself. I'm sure I can manage this one, too."

He flicked a glance at the windows I indicated. As he did, the sofa caught his eye. "The couch is purple!" He sounded offended.

"Aubergine," I corrected, glad I wasn't the one who had picked the color. The interior designer who had subbed out the windows to me had made that selection. I decided not to mention that I thought it went well with the grapes in Tuscan Vine and the purple in the Sinclair plaid on the slipper chairs.

"It's purple. Bright purple."

"It's not bright purple," I said patiently. "It's aubergine."

He sniffed, walked to it, and ran his hand over the seat. "It's slippery!"

"It's taffeta."

"Taffeta? Taffeta is for dresses, not sofas." He suddenly looked uncertain. "Like evening gowns, right?" At my surprised expression, he said, "I have four sisters."

"Huh," I said eloquently. "I have four brothers. I'm youngest."

"Oldest. And you can call purple aubergine until you're blue in the face, but it's still purple."

"Deep purple. Eggplant. In fact *aubergine* is the French word for eggplant."

"Semantics. And you need to pack up. I'm not leaving until everything is locked up tight. We've had some nighttime thieves recently, and I'm not taking a chance with this model home."

I stopped fussing with Tuscan Vine and its clusters of grapes. "You've had thieves?"

"Storage shed broken into, tools taken, nails, lumber. Nothing has been vandalized, nor has anything of great value or quantity been taken. Still, I've hired a night guard to patrol the development."

I frowned. "I saw a man walking around one of the houses on the next street." If he was the thief, that would explain his skulking air, and if he was the guard, I guess he was sneaking around trying to catch people.

Gray stiffened. "The guard doesn't come on until midnight. When did you see this man and at what house?"

"I was watching him when you startled me. And that house." I pointed out the back window.

He walked over and looked. He immediately relaxed. "It's

all right. The Ryders bought that house, and Dorothy Ryder comes out practically every day to see how the work is progressing. Drives my men crazy. Ken must have decided to come with her today, so they came later, after work and dinner."

Relieved, I nodded. Thank goodness I hadn't called anyone.

Gray turned from the window and sat in one of the plump armchairs covered in Scalamandré's plum Bali pattern, and began ticking mysterious things off the lists on his tablet. His cell rang, and he silenced it, checking the readout. He made another note on his pad.

He looked good in the chair.

Of course, that was solely because the chair looked good. The whole house was being done in fabulous fabrics from Scalamandré, the high-end company that did one-of-a-kind orders for clients like the White House and limited quantities of hand-loomed fabrics for the wealthy. I'd never cut and sewn such expensive material in my life and probably never would again. I calculated over and over to be certain of my measurements, and every time I cut, I hyperventilated. The thought of ruining material worth three to four hundred dollars a yard tended to do that to a person.

While Gray checked things off on his list, I repositioned my ladder.

He looked up suddenly. "Our first official Open House is Saturday." He nodded toward the partially draped window. "You will be finished by Saturday?"

"I will be finished by Saturday," I agreed. "Absolutely."

"Today's Tuesday. You only have three working days left."

"How convenient. I only have less than three days worth of work left," I said, the very soul of reason. I didn't mention that several pillows and the round table skirt, aubergine taffeta like the sofa, weren't yet cut out, let alone sewn. Neither was the square table topper of Sinclair tartan in soft green, mauve and aubergine on cream.

I put a foot on the first rung of my ladder.

Gray jumped to his feet. "What are you doing? Don't use that ladder!"

I mentally rolled my eyes. "I have to use the ladder." I climbed the first two steps. It swayed drunkenly. "How else can I hang the treatments?"

"Look—" He halted. "By the way, what's your name?" He actually appeared interested.

"Anna Volente."

He nodded. "Look, Anna, get a decent ladder."

"I am not going to go buy myself another ladder. My father gave me this."

"Your father—" He stopped abruptly, wisely thinking better of saying whatever he was thinking. "This is a building site. We have plenty of ladders."

"And they would be where? Oops, not here."

He muttered under his breath. "I'll get you a decent ladder. Just get off that thing before it collapses under you." He stalked to me, grabbed me by the wrist and pulled me gently but decisively off. He indicated a point at my feet. "Stand there. Don't move. I'll be right back."

I raised an eyebrow. "Do I look like a cocker spaniel or something?"

"No, though the hair's about right for an Irish setter. Stay." With a grin and a hand held up to emphasize the command, he left the room.

I stared at the doorway through which he'd disappeared. I looked at the spot at my feet. With calm deliberation I took my first step. Then my second, and soon I was at the front windows where I had already hung Tuscan Vine. I worked with the folds of the heavy silk fabric, adjusting them to drape just so. I stepped back and eyed the overall effect. I nodded. They looked good, if I did say so myself. Apparently *he* wasn't going to say so.

Gray returned, lugging a stepladder that was taller than mine and obviously much sturdier.

"Now you won't have to stand on the top step, so you can lean into it to keep your balance. No more falls." He folded my old standby and set up his ladder in its place. It looked strong enough to hold both of us, an unexpectedly cozy thought.

"Now get up there and let me hand you this heavy thing." He indicated the Tuscan Vine lying on the chair. "Or better yet, let me hang it."

"That's all right," I said as I climbed quickly. I recognized potential disaster when I saw it. "I know what I'm doing."

He didn't say a word, merely gathered the fabric in his arms and stood there radiating energy and cooperative spirit. He handed me the top of the panel, and I began attaching it beneath the swag I'd hung earlier. I had to admit that the task was going to be easier now that I didn't have to both hold the material and attach it.

Movement outside caught my eye. I glanced again at the house kitty-corner from the one I was decorating. The man I'd seen earlier stood at the opening for what I guessed was one day to be the kitchen door. He jumped to the ground. I squinted. What was it about him that was so strange? As I watched, he unscrewed something and stuffed part of it in his pants pocket. The rest he stuck in his waistband at the small of his back, pulling his red shirt over it. After wiping the back of his wrist across his forehead, he peeled flesh-colored gloves from his hands, balled them, and stuffed them in his other pocket. I frowned.

"Gray." I motioned for him to come look. "The man's back. He just took off some gloves like the ones doctors wear."

"Gloves? Why is he wearing gloves in August? And why that kind?"

Like I knew. Shrugging, I moved as far to one side of the ladder as I could so he had room to climb. It vibrated under me as he took the first two steps, then stopped.

"Move to the center," he said. "I think it will be better if I put one foot on either side of you. Otherwise we'll be unbalanced."

I nodded absently and slid to the center, concentrating on the man outside. I blinked in disbelief as he suddenly pulled what could only be a stocking from his head. His features leaped into focus.

"No wonder he looked so funny. He was wearing a stocking over his head."

"What?" Gray stood on the step below me and tried to peer around me. "Can't quite see yet." He slid one foot beside mine, looking down to be sure of its placement. He began to raise himself to slide the other foot in place.

I froze as the man in the yard swiveled his head and looked directly at me. I knew I was highly visible with the westering sun streaming over me, just as he was clearly visible to me, blond hair, hook nose, mustache and all. I'm not very fanciful, but I could feel the malevolence of his stare across the distance and felt goose bumps spring up on my arms.

"What's wrong?" Gray asked, straightening to peer over my shoulder.

"He's—" I'd been about to say that he was looking at me, but the sentence changed when he pulled something from the waistband at the small of his back "—got a gun!"

# TWO

"He's got a gun!"

At least that's what I meant to say. What came out sounded more like I was gargling with a particularly offensive mouth-wash. I hurled myself backwards, away from the window, away from the danger.

I slammed hard against Gray who made his own gargling sound. Together we tumbled to the floor, a wild pinwheel of arms and legs. I thought I also heard a particularly heartfelt grunt from Gray when we struck the unforgiving floor. Over the crash of the falling ladder and the terrified beating of my heart, it was hard to discern one sound from another.

There was a brief moment of silence as I lay on my back, breath squished from my lungs by the bone-jarring impact. I stared at the ceiling and the little circles of red dancing across it. I gave a mighty gasp, and oxygen rushed into my depleted system. The red circles disappeared.

A gun! The man had a gun! I had never seen a handgun like that in real life before, and the hairs at the base of my neck twitched as I remembered how one looked pointed directly at me. I rolled off Gray, who had unintentionally buffered my fall, and scuttled on my knees to safety in the front hall.

"Out here should be safe, don't you think?" I crouched, curled into a ball, and hugged the wall. "He can't see us here."

Of course he could decide to walk over to the house and in the unlocked front door that I was staring at. I groaned at the thought, crawled to the door, and turned the lock.

"There!" I pulled myself into a tighter ball. "My phone's in my purse across the room. You'll have to call 911."

Gray didn't answer, and he didn't punch numbers. All I heard was a peculiar gasping sound.

"Gray?" I turned, surprised to find he wasn't in the hall with me. I'd thought he was right behind me. "Gray?" I crawled back to the doorway into the living room and peered in. I clapped my hand to my mouth to stifle a scream. It leaked out anyway.

Gray lay on his back where he'd fallen, his mouth open, his eyes closed, his face covered with blood.

"He shot you!" I crawled toward him. Why, oh why hadn't I decided to be a nurse rather than an art teacher? "You're bleeding!"

Gray made that gasping sound again. At least he wasn't dead.

"Don't move!" I tried to remember the first aid class I'd taken as part of my health requirement in college. What did you do first? Staunch the blood! That was it. All I had to do was find where the blood was coming from. I put a tentative hand to his head, burying my fingers in his thick hair.

Gray pushed my hand away none too gently, rolled to his side, and pushed to his hands and knees.

"You shouldn't move." Gently I tried to push him back to the floor. "Everyone knows you don't move when you're shot."

He resisted my push with a growling sound that reminded me of our neighbor's ill-tempered schnauzer, Daisy. He gasped again, his back arching like he was doing the cat stretch exercise. Blood poured onto the hardwood floor.

Thank goodness the soft green rug wasn't being laid until tomorrow.

Gray snaked out a hand to grab the Tuscan Vine, its unattached end sagging from the rod so that a large puddle of silk lay on the floor. His intent was obvious.

"No!" I leaped to my feet, gunman or no gunman, and snatched up the fabric. "Don't get that material bloody!" I pulled it as far from him as I could without ripping the already attached end, flinging it over the plum chair, for once mindless of wrinkles. "It costs two hundred and twenty-five dollars a yard."

"Bake dat three hundred and fifty," he muttered in an odd voice. He began pulling his T-shirt from his waistband.

"Don't use your shirt either," I told him. "You'll never get the blood out. There are some towels in the kitchen. I'll get them."

I ran to the back of the house and grabbed the designer towels laid artistically beside the sink and raced back to Gray. I found him sitting cross-legged on the floor, his head tilted back, his T-shirt bunched under his arms and wadded against his face.

I dropped to my knees beside him and handed him the towels. "Where did he shoot you?" My heart hammered. What if Gray's handsome face was scarred for life? What if he'd taken a bullet in the eye? Of course, reason told me, if he'd taken a bullet in the eye, he wouldn't be sitting up holding his nose.

His nose.

"Are you having a nose bleed?" I demanded as my fear and relief transmuted to irritation.

He lowered his head enough to glare at me. "Yes, I'mb having a dose bleed, doe thanks to you."

"Me? It's not my fault heights give you nosebleeds."

"Heights, by foot. Id was your hard head."

"My head?" I lifted a hand to the back of my head and hit

a sore spot. I realized suddenly that I had a miserable headache, one I'd been too frightened to notice before.

"Firs' you gib me a header, den you dock me flad on by back—and id's a wonder I didn't break id—and den you fall on me and dock my breaf out of me so I thought I'd neber breafe again."

"Well, you don't have to get so testy about it." Tears filled my eyes. "I thought you were shot!" *Thank You, God, that he wasn't!*

"Shod? Me?"

"By the man with the gun. The man in the yard over there." I pointed toward the Ryders' house as goosebumps once again raced up and down my arms.

Gray blinked. "He had a gund?"

"You didn't see?"

"I din't ged a chance. I god attacked first."

"Attacked?" I was torn between guilt for hurting him and indignation that he'd think I did it on purpose. Then I noticed the little upward quirk of his lips where they were visible below the towels. "Beast," I muttered.

He grinned as he pulled himself to his feet and walked cautiously to the window, towels in place, head still tilted back to stem the flow.

I caught at his arm, trying to pull him back. "Don't, Gray. He might still be there."

"I doubt it. He'd either be here—"

I shuddered.

"—or be gond."

The squeal of tires taking a corner too fast and the snarl of a pedal pressed to the metal made me jump. I rushed to a front window and saw a flash of black disappear down the road bordering Freedom's Chase.

"See? There he goes," Gray said. "Id's safe."

"How do you know it's him?"

"When I drove through the develobment for my last check of the evening, I din't see anyone."

"No black car anywhere? What'd he do? Hide it in a garage?"

"He was driving a black car? What kind?"

I threw up my hands. "How should I know? They all look alike."

He gave me that guy look. "They don't, but that's beside the point."

"It was just black, and what is your point?"

"My point is that there couldn't have been anyone other than him hanging around. I'm not that blind."

I decided that his flawed logic wasn't worth a comment. Still, I did agree with his thought that the man would either be here ready to do us further damage or be gone. Since he wasn't here, and since I'd heard that car take off like a proverbial bat trying to escape a very hot place, I relaxed.

"We deed to report this to the police," Gray said.

I nodded. "He pulled it from his waistband." I whipped my hand up to illustrate.

Gray nodded as he looked out the back window toward the Ryders'.

"You can't see much of anything but the roof unless you climb the ladder. Remember?"

"Id's my nose that got creamed, nod my brain. I bemember."

"Well, you don't have to be all snippy about it."

He looked down at me from his awkward head tilt. "I think I'mb entitled to be a liddle snippy."

I sighed. Maybe he was. All he'd wanted to do was to lock up and go home, probably to take some beautiful woman—his wife?—to dinner. Well, it wasn't my fault that man had a gun and that I was scared of men with guns. Everybody was scared of men with guns.

Holding on to the ladder with one hand as he held the towels to his nose with the other, Gray climbed one rung at a time.

"He's not dere now," he said as he searched the area, head swinging from left to right. "We're right. He's gond." He started back down the ladder, froze momentarily, then leaped back just as I had. Somehow he managed to make that giant step to the ground look easy, landing neatly on his feet.

"What?" I looked from him to the window. "What'd you see?" Then I saw it, a small hole in the glass near the top on the right. "G-gray." I pointed.

"Yeah," he said, his voice no longer peeved or teasing but thoughtful. He looked at me. "I think he'd have missed you even if you hadn't ducked, bud id's probably a good thing you did."

"And that's supposed to make me feel better?" The man in the red shirt had shot at me! Me, Anna Volente, intermediate school art teacher and registered coward.

I stepped closer to Gray. My hands started to shake, and my stomach felt dangerously unsettled. I swallowed several times to make sure things stayed where they were supposed to. Blood on the floor was enough of a mess. I took another step closer.

Gray pulled his cell phone from his belt and held it out to me. "Call 911. I'mb afraid to take the pressure off my dose."

I hit the digits and spoke to the voice at the other end, ending with, "No, neither of us was shot. No, we can't see him any more. We think we heard him drive away. Yes, we'll wait."

When I disconnected, I rubbed my cold arms. "But he saw me, Gray. And he knows I saw him. What if he's now out to get me?"

"I wouldn't worry." Gray started walking toward the kitchen. "He's long gone. He had to know we'd call the cops, and doe one hangs around waiting for the cops to show."

"But what if he comes back?"

"You won't be here. You'll be home, tucked safely in bed."

I followed him to the kitchen, glancing uneasily over my shoulder at the hole in the window. "Where are we going?"

"Here." Gray leaned his body over the sink, then slowly withdrew the towels from his nose. He stood unmoving, head still slightly tilted upwards. "I'mb not bleeding any more, amb I?"

I looked at him carefully. "No, but you look like you've been in the war." I grabbed one of the towels and wet a corner not covered with red. "Look here."

Gray stood impatiently as I began the delicate job of swabbing his face and neck without hurting him further. After a minute of my tentative swipes, he reached for the cold water, turned it on full and threw handful after handful over himself, scrubbing his cheeks and neck after each wave. Then very gently he scrubbed beneath his nose.

He turned to me, dripping onto his bloody shirt. "How's that?"

"Pretty good." I reached up and wiped at a patch of red beside his nose. He grimaced, whether from pain because I hit a tender area or from reluctance to have me touch him, I couldn't tell. He lifted an arm and dried one side of his face on a shirtsleeve. He repeated the operation with the other sleeve.

I eyed his shirt. The blood was turning rusty around the edges of the stains.

He looked down and shrugged. "Can't do too much about that. I'll just toss it." He started toward the back door. "I won't be long. I need to check the Ryders' to make certain there was no damage done by our armed visitor. Don't leave before I come back. I want to walk you to your car." He looked back at me and grinned. "And don't stand in front of any windows."

I stared at him. Was that last line supposed to be funny? Because it wasn't. "I thought you thought he left."

"I do. You don't need to worry. You'll be fine."

"You can't know that."

He nodded agreeably. "You're right. I can't. Let's say you'll probably be fine."

That settled it. "I'm coming with you."

He raised his eyebrows at me.

"It isn't safe for you to be alone either." I tried to sound as if I was selfless, full of concern about him. I didn't want to admit out loud that I was reluctant—admit it, kid, you're downright scared—to be in the house by myself.

"Don't want to stay here alone, eh?" His smile was only slightly teasing, very understanding.

I felt my cheeks flush. Sometimes intelligent men were a burden.

We struck off across the newly sodded backyard, around the back fence and into the Ryders' backyard, me practically skipping to keep up with Gray's long stride.

I stared at the unfinished house wrapped in Tyvec. The holes where the windows would go stared back at me like black, empty eyes in the gathering dusk and gave me the creeps. I looked instead at the scale of the house.

"Why do people buy places this big?" I thought of the small, two-bedroom apartment I'd lived in before I moved in with Lucy and Meaghan. The whole thing would fit into the great room of the model, and this house didn't look any smaller.

Gray shrugged. "Americans like big."

"Even if they can't afford to furnish half the rooms? Even if they can't go on a vacation for years because they're house-poor, or put money aside for their kids' braces and educations because they have to pay that astronomical mortgage every month? Even if they both have to work to stay afloat financially, leaving the kids to raise themselves?"

I blinked. Where had all that come from?

"Easy there, Anna," Gray said mildly. "I just build 'em. The Realtors and the buyers handle the money issues." He started around the side of the house.

I hurried after him, unwilling to get too far from his comforting presence. It was a good thing I had no aspirations of being Nancy Drew or even Stephanie Plum, let alone Kinsey Milhone or Sidney on Alias. I obviously didn't have the constitution for dealing with bad guys with guns. Dealing with rebellious schoolkids was more than tough enough for me. "Where are you going?"

"I want to walk around the house to make certain everything outside is okay before I check inside."

"Shouldn't we just wait for the police?" I glanced over my shoulder as I followed him into the front yard. "What if we mess up footprints or something?"

He stopped and looked down at the parched dingy orange subsoil studded helter-skelter with stones and pebbles of all sizes. Then he looked at me.

"Yeah, yeah," I acknowledged. "Too hard for prints." I glanced over my shoulder again.

"He's gone, Anna. He was just a penny-ante thief looking for whatever he could get his hands on, maybe even the guy who's been robbing the site."

"Wearing gloves and a stocking mask? Shooting at innocent people? I don't think so." I studied him. "And neither do you."

He smiled slightly as we rounded the last corner and found

ourselves in the backyard once again. Gray went to the back-door opening. Ignoring the lack of steps, he pulled himself up and into the house.

"Don't you dare leave me out here alone." I reached to pull myself up, but he turned and grasped my hand. He lifted me effortlessly.

"It's dark in here." I'm very good at stating the obvious.

"Darker," he corrected. "Let your eyes adjust."

Dusk sent its silver light through the many window openings, and I had to admit Gray was right. It wasn't as dark as I'd first thought. Soon I could make out the rooms, the studs dividing them awaiting the electricians and plumbers before the insulation and drywall went up.

We looked carefully around the kitchen, the great room, the den, the bath, the pantry, the dining room and the living room. Aside from a couple of sawhorses, an aluminum extension ladder lying on the kitchen floor, several plastic-protected windows stacked in each room, a litter of nails and sawdust, and a ladder leading to the basement, the place was empty. The eerie silence pulled at me, making me shiver in spite of the fact that the temperature was still well above eighty.

I cocked my head as I heard a soft plop, plop, like the dripping of a faucet with a bad gasket. "Is the plumbing finished upstairs?" I pointed to the black opening to the second floor.

Gray tilted his head and listened. "That's strange. It's not even begun. I'm going to check the basement, and make sure nothing's dripping down there."

I watched him step onto the ladder propped against the hole where the cellar steps would go. Talk about dark and eerie. I shuddered. No way was I going down there. Bad as alone was, it was better than black and scary. "I'll just wait here." I motioned to the front hall where I stood.

He nodded and, pulling a penlight from his pocket, stuck it between his teeth. "Be right back." Slowly he disappeared.

I walked to the front door and looked out. The police were nowhere in sight. I looked at the rapidly darkening sky, the only light the faintest of rosy glows in the west. I felt the gloom behind me deepen and press.

I turned and looked back at the front hall. It was spooky without Gray's company, especially since the mysterious drip, drip, dripping echoed gently in the silence.

Frowning, I walked slowly around the hall, trying to find the source. I was convinced it wasn't in the basement. Sure, sounds echoed in an empty house, but this was too loud to be coming up from downstairs. I jumped when a drop struck me on the outside of my left upper arm. I felt liquid run down and drip off my elbow. Another drop hit me.

I stepped to the side and looked up. I was beneath the place where the hall stairs, when they were built, would end at the second-floor landing, but it was too shadowy up there to see anything.

"Gray," I called down the cellar steps. "I found where the drip is coming from."

"Be right there."

I went to the front door where the last remaining light showed the dark trail running down my arm. I dabbed at the wet stuff, then sniffed. My stomach pitched. There was no mistaking that sweet metallic odor.

"Gray!" I wasn't even embarrassed about the panic in my voice

"Yeah?" His head appeared, followed by his shoulders and torso as he emerged from the basement.

"B-bring your little light over here. Shine it on my arm."

He did so. "You scratched yourself."

I shook my head. "That's the drip."

But it's—"

I nodded.

"Where did it come from?" He used the tail of his ruined shirt to wipe my arm clean.

I pointed. "I was standing there."

His swung his penlight, and the beam picked out a red puddle on the floor, drops plummeting from above to splash in the viscous pool. A footprint repeated across the floor, getting fainter and fainter with each step until it was almost non-existent when it stopped at my left shoe.

"Oh, no! I stepped in the blood!"

"Yeah, but the question is whose blood?"

He trained the beam overhead, and a woman's pale hand appeared, flung out over the opening. Gray and I looked at each other in dismay, knowing that where there was a hand, there was a body attached.

And the drip, drip, drip of the blood continued.

# THREE

"We've got to get up there!" I cried. "Maybe she's still alive." Though remembering the man with the gun, gloves and mask, I doubted it.

Already, Gray had grabbed the ladder lying on the kitchen floor and after extending it, leaned it against the opening at the end nearest the front door, away from the hand. He climbed quickly, and when he stepped off onto the second floor, I started up. I swallowed frequently, terrified of what I was about see.

*Help us, Lord, if we can help her. And help me to hold myself together.*

I found Gray on his knees beside the body of a woman wearing shorts and a yellow knit top. She lay on her stomach with her head slightly turned, one arm flung over her head, the other curled at her side. If it weren't for the pool of blood that spread from her head across the plywood subfloor to the opening where it dripped, she might have been sleeping.

Gray had his fingers on her carotid artery, seeking a pulse. He looked at me and shook his head.

"Did you try her wrist?" I swallowed several more times against the sights and smells. And to think, I'd always prided myself on my cast-iron stomach.

He nodded. "Nothing there either."

"Maybe we should turn her over to check some more?"

Gray stood. "No. We'd be tampering with a murder scene if we did."

I shuddered. Murder scene! Shades of CSI. *Lord, I teach intermediate school. I don't do murder.*

Gray and I climbed down the ladder in silence. In the front hall Gray placed our second call to 911. The mention of blood and a body brought help much more quickly than a report of a departed masked man. Officers descended, lights flashing, radios squawking, climbing from several cars. Even though Gray stated clearly that the woman was dead, an ambulance was part of the full response team as was a fire engine, even though there was no fire.

"She's on the second floor," Gray said. "Right by the stairwell opening. We left the ladder we used in place for you."

The EMTs headed to the house immediately, equipment in hand. Two policemen followed. Other officers checked the grounds of not only the Ryders' house but nearby sites. Two others, one an older officer clearly in charge, the other a young woman, stopped to talk to Gray and me.

"I'm Sergeant William Poole, and this is Officer Natalie Schumann." He peered at Gray with interest. "What's that all over your shirt?"

"Nosebleed."

I felt the officers' skepticism. Somewhere I had read the axiom that the police always assumed everyone lied to them. So many people did, even over foolish things, that the blanket reaction was to paint everyone with the same brush.

It made me nervous to think they might not believe Gray or me. "Really," I said. "I saw it. The nosebleed, that is, not the crime. In fact I caused it." I put my hand to the still tender back of my head. "The nosebleed, I mean."

Sergeant Poole acknowledged my comment with a nod. "Did either of you touch anything near the victim?"

"Nothing except her wrist and neck to check for a pulse," Gray said.

"Nothing except the toe of my shoe." I held out my foot. "It got in the puddle of blood in the downstairs hall before I knew it was there. I—I didn't see it in the dark."

The sergeant nodded. "Schumann, get their personal information." He didn't say, "Keep an eye on them," but I thought he might as well have, given his demeanor. He started for the house, then turned back. "Please don't leave. I'll need to talk with you more later."

I looked at Gray as Officer Schumann pulled out her notebook. "Do you think we're suspects?" I whispered.

"Of course you're not suspects," Officer Schumann said with the sly lift of an eyebrow. "You don't have to worry about that until you're Mirandized."

"What?" I stared at her. Was Schumann going to whip out a little card and start reading, "You have the right to remain silent...."

Officer Schumann put up a hand. "Just a little police humor. You are not suspects."

I clearly heard *yet* hanging in the air.

With professional efficiency, Officer Schumann took our names and addresses, work information and reasons for being at the murder site. "Now let's move over here and stay out of the way," she said, not impolitely. "And don't talk about the crime."

"Where's Sipowitz?" I muttered to Gray as we watched another female officer in uniform begin to string yellow crime scene tape by winding a strip around the large oak that sat near the edge of the Ryders' corner property. Unrolling tape as she went, she had just disappeared around back when a truck arrived with high-intensity lights that were lifted by ropes and pulled through window openings to illuminate the second-floor interior. Frequent flashes of light indicated pictures being taken of the victim and the crime scene. "I want Sipowitz."

"Two problems," Gray said, deciding to sit while he waited. He dropped down, resting his arms on his raised knees. "This isn't *NYPD Blue,* and this is real life."

The real life part was underscored as the coroner arrived in his black van.

I sat beside Gray, legs bent, knees tucked under my chin, arms wrapped around my shins, watching the procession of people going in and out of the house. The female officer with the crime scene tape appeared on the far side of the yard, looking vainly for something to attach her tape to. Finally she set the tape down, walked to a pile of building refuse two houses away and rooted, her flashlight beam leading the way. She returned with two boards, one of which she began trying to force into the dry, pebbly dirt, using the second as a hammer.

Sergeant Poole jumped out of the house and walked over to us. He stood with his back to the house and pulled out a notebook. Automatically Gray and I stood, facing him. Officer Schumann left to help the yellow tape officer with her hammering.

How clever, I thought as I told myself I wasn't nervous. Our faces are lit by the spill from the house. He can see our expressions, watch for any lies that way. Not that we have anything to lie about. At least I don't. And I wouldn't lie anyway, being a Christian and all.

"Let's begin with you telling me why you're here tonight," Poole said, his voice mildly curious. He looked at Gray.

"I'm the contractor on Freedom's Chase," Gray said. "Grayson Edwards."

"The downtown guy?"

"The downtown guy. I was getting ready to go home around seven-thirty, eight, when I realized that Anna was still here, working in the model house. Since we've had some thefts recently—"

Poole went on alert. "What kind of thefts? Have you reported them?"

"Just lumber, nails, stuff like that. And no, I haven't reported them. They weren't significant enough to involve you, just bothersome, not even enough for an insurance claim. Anyway, I wanted to be certain everyone was gone before I left. I went to the model house to see how much longer she'd be."

"And what were you doing there so late?" Poole looked at me.

"I was hanging window treatments," I said. "The model opens on Saturday, and I've got to get everything finished before then."

The sergeant nodded. "Did either of you see the victim arrive?"

I shook my head, as did Gray.

"What happened to bring you from the model to this house?" The sergeant's pen was poised to take down our answer. "By the way, I'll want you to come in tomorrow to give a more complete statement."

"Okay," I said, and told Sergeant Poole about standing on the ladder and watching the man with the gun.

"You saw him clearly?" Poole asked, his craggy face intent.

I nodded. "And he saw me. He shot at me. That's when I hit Gray in the nose and made him bleed."

Poole stared. "He shot at you."

"But that was after he took off the stocking mask and the gloves."

"We called it in," Gray said. "911."

"So even though a man with a gun shot at you, a man who had been wearing a mask and gloves, you came over here where you'd seen him and just happened to find the victim."

It was hard to see Sergeant Poole's face because of the way he stood, but I was pretty sure that if I could, I'd see disbelief. And put the way he put it, our actions did sound the height of folly. Well, we weren't cops. We were just regular people who didn't have much experience with gunmen. At least I didn't, and I doubted Gray did. So we'd taken what probably looked like a foolish risk, like someone who came home to find his house robbed and went from room to room before the police arrived, just to be certain the burglar was gone.

"We heard him drive away," Gray explained. "We figured it was safe."

"And it took us a few minutes to mop Gray up," I added.

Gray slid his hands into his jeans pockets. "There was no way I could leave Freedom's Chase until I was certain everything was all right over here."

"I came along because I wasn't going to stay in the house alone, not with that bullet hole in the window." I shivered at the memory.

Sergeant Poole grunted. "Point out the window."

I looked toward the model house. "You can't see it from here. You have to be out back."

The sergeant started for the backyard, and we followed. When we rounded the corner of the house, I pointed.

"See? Right up there."

Poole studied the window, the top third of it visible. "So you were standing on a ladder, hanging curtains—"

"Window treatments," I corrected.

"—when you saw this man twice. Then you decided to

come over here to be certain he hadn't done anything to damage the property."

Gray nodded. "That's when we found Dorothy."

"So you recognized the victim?"

Gray rubbed a hand over his face, wincing when he hit his nose. I winced with him. "Dorothy Ryder," he said softly.

"And you knew her because?" Poole asked.

"Two reasons. Dorothy was a partner in Windle, Boyes, Kepiro and Ryder, the accounting firm. She handled my business. Also, she and her husband Ken bought this house." He nodded toward it. "In fact, it was the first sale in the development. Dorothy liked this lot because it's on the corner and has three big trees that we left when we cleared the land." He indicated the trees that had enabled the woman officer to put her tape up at least partway around the house. "Dorothy would stop by almost every day to see how much more work had been done."

Sergeant Poole was quiet for a moment. Then he looked at me. I gave him a nervous smile. "Can you describe this gunman?" he asked.

My smile became real. "I can do better than that, Sergeant. I can draw him." At the surprised looks from both him and Gray, I reached for Poole's notebook. "I teach art." Look, Dad, it does come in handy!

I quickly sketched the man in the red shirt while Gray held his penlight for me so I could see what I was doing. I drew the man as I first saw him behind the house, burly body moving stealthily. Then I did two head sketches, one profile, one full on. The man's dark blond hair hung over his forehead as it had done when he pulled the stocking off. I closed my eyes for a minute, letting him come to life in my mind's eye. I studied my drawing and quickly added a couple of strokes to the bushy mustache that sat on his upper lip like a light brown wooly caterpillar. His rather beaky nose jutted out in the profile, and strong dark eyebrows arched over his eyes. I studied the sketch, strengthened his cheekbones, then studied the sketch again.

"That's him." I looked at Gray, then Sergeant Poole. "I don't know what color his eyes were. Too far away, though I got the impression of dark. As to the hair, the stocking mask may be responsible for it falling across his forehead. He had to have been sweating in it." She handed the tablet back. "But that's him."

"Wonderful." Though Poole appeared pleased to have the drawings, I guessed from his lack of reaction that he didn't recognize the man. "This will be a great help. Now I want you both to come in tomorrow morning to give a detailed statement and make another sketch."

I blinked. "It'll look just the same."

"And that will be just fine." He turned and started back to the house.

"Does that mean we can go?" Gray called after him.

"No, you can't go yet," Poole's voice floated back to us. "But it shouldn't be much longer."

Sighing, I turned to Gray. He was eyeing the yellow crime scene tape with distaste.

"Bad PR. And it'll still be here on the weekend, I bet. Who wants to buy into a development where there's been a murder?"

"Maybe it'll bring more people because they're curious," I said, wanting to help. He looked so discouraged.

"Yeah, curious to look but unwilling to buy."

"Well, this house may be hard to sell, but if the others are anything like the model, they'll go fast, Gray. Americans like big, remember?"

On that happy note, we fell silent. I wondered how much

longer we'd have to stay here, and if I was allowed to call Lucy and Meaghan. I looked at my watch. Ten-thirty. It would probably be another half hour before they began to worry seriously about me. Besides, I realized, my cell was at the model house with my purse.

Finally the sergeant returned, Officer Schumann trailing him. "Thank you for mentioning that you stepped in the blood, Miss—" He checked his notes. "—Volente. It saves us spending a lot of time trying to trace the footprints."

I beamed, happy I'd helped, certain he'd now perceive my innocence.

"I'm afraid I'll have to take your shoe, though, just as I'll have to take your shirt, Mr., uh, Grayson."

"Edwards," Gray said.

The sergeant looked at him blankly.

"It's Grayson Edwards," Gray said patiently. "Edwards is my last name."

"Gotcha. I still need your shirt."

I narrowed my eyes. "Surely you don't think Gray—"

"Do you often suffer from nosebleeds, Mr. Edwards?" Poole was eyeing the bloody shirt again.

Gray shook his head. "Never."

"Tell me again how this one occurred."

"When Anna saw the man had a gun, she jumped back and her head—" With one hand he made as if to squish his nose.

The sergeant flinched. "Painful."

Gray nodded. "Very."

I felt bad all over again. Guilt, a woman's most faithful companion.

Sergeant Poole held out a large plastic bag. Gray pulled his shirt off and dropped it in.

The officer turned to me. I pulled off my sandal and put it in another bag, trying not to think of the painful hike over all the little stones and rocks on the way back to the model house.

The sergeant handed the bags to Officer Schumann. "Seal these, Natalie, and tag them." He turned to me. "Were you working alone?" He jerked a thumb toward the model home.

"Until Gray showed up."

"When?"

"About eight o'clock or so."

"And why were you still there at that hour?"

"I stayed at the shore an extra week with Lucy and Meaghan." Both men looked at me strangely.

What? Was I suddenly speaking Farsi or something? "I got behind on my sewing when I stayed that extra week, so I had to work late."

Both men's faces cleared, and Poole asked, "Who are Lucy and Meaghan?"

"Lucy Stoner and Meaghan Malloy. I share a house with them, and we all teach at Amhearst North. I teach art."

"I can vouch for Miss Volente, Sergeant," Officer Schumann said. "I believe she has taught my younger brother, Skip."

Schumann. As in Skip Schumann? "Sure, I know Skip." Can you say thorn in the side? "I don't think art is his favorite subject." I hoped I didn't sound too sarcastic.

Officer Schumann just smiled.

"And where were you," the sergeant asked, turning to Gray, "when she hit you in the nose?"

"I was climbing the ladder behind her."

"The same ladder?"

Gray nodded. "It seemed a good idea at the time. Then he pulled his gun, she jumped back, and I—" He shrugged.

Sergeant Poole made more notations in his notebook. I noticed a bright blue Honda CRV pull to the curb. A woman with spiky brown hair and a determined attitude climbed out.

"The press has arrived," Schumann muttered to Poole.

He glanced at the reporter who was bearing down on us as she pulled a small digital camera and a tape recorder from a large bag hanging over her shoulder.

"Merry Kramer." The sergeant looked resigned but not distressed as the woman stopped in front of us. "Give me a minute, Merry, and I'll be with you."

"Sure, Sergeant." The reporter gestured to the house. "Can I go in?"

"Can I stop you?" he countered.

"Well, sure you can, but I'm hoping you won't."

"Just stay out of everyone's way, and don't—"

"And don't touch anything," she finished for him. "I know." With a little wave, she headed for the scene of the crime. Halfway there she paused and took several quick shots of the house and the people milling around.

Poole watched her with a little shake of his head. Then he turned back to Gray and me. "Schumann, give these people receipts for the shoe and the shirt."

"Right, sir." She handed us already written slips of paper.

"And you two, don't forget to come in tomorrow."

"Right," I said as a black BMW screeched to a stop at the edge of the road.

A slim man climbed out. His face was creased with concern as he eyed the yellow crime scene tape, the emergency vehicles, and all the people, many in uniform.

"What's going on here?" he demanded of anyone who would listen. He caught sight of Gray and homed in on him. "Gray, what's happening?" He strode across the barren yard toward us, though he was obviously searching for someone else. "Have you seen Dorothy? Is she all right"

My mouth fell open. Was he who I thought he was?

Sergeant Poole stepped forward. "And you are?"

The man blinked. "I'm Ken Ryder."

My breath caught. I looked helplessly at Gray, and saw a reflection of the same discomfort and uncertainty I felt. What could he possibly say?

Ken Ryder turned back to Gray. "I was supposed to meet Dorothy here about seven to seven-thirty, but I got held up at work." He started for the house. "Is she inside?"

Sergeant Poole put a hand on Ken Ryder's arm. "Stay here, please, Mr. Ryder."

Ken frowned vaguely at the sergeant but kept talking to Gray. "I called her on both her cell and the home phone, leaving a message that we'd have to come here another night." He shrugged. "I knew I was disappointing her, but I couldn't help it. When I got home about a half hour ago, she wasn't there, and she'd left no note like she usually does. This is the only place she planned to go this evening, so I'm here even though I can't imagine she'd still be here."

He took a breath, then kept talking. Nerves? Why? Did cops make him feel guilty too?

"You know how she loves to come check on the progress of things, but it's so dark. How can she see? There's no electricity in the house yet." He looked confused as he glanced at the well-lit house. "Is there?"

"Where do you work, Mr. Ryder?" Sergeant Poole asked.

"Chester County BMW. I'm sales manager." He reached in his pants pocket and pulled out an empty key chain with a green plastic tag which had white printing on it.

"Ride with Ryder?" Poole read.

Ken Ryder nodded. "My slogan. I guess she didn't get my message, though why she'd still be waiting for me here, I don't know."

His voice trailed off as he seemed to see the coroner's van for the first time. "What's that for?"

No one said anything though the reporter held her tape recorder out in anticipation.

"Where's Dorothy?" This time there was a note of panic in his voice. "I want to see Dorothy."

Just then a gurney with a body bag lying on it was lowered out the front door opening.

I watched Ken Ryder's face as he added two and two. "That's not—"

Gray put out a hand and clamped it on Ken's shoulder. "Easy, Ken."

Ken ignored him and started toward the gurney, his movements jerky. "It can't be!"

Sergeant Poole grabbed him by the arm. "Not now, Mr. Ryder. You just stay here with me. We need to talk." He kept a firm hold as Ken Ryder tried to pull free. He stepped between the man and the gurney. "Mr. Ryder, I'm sorry for your loss."

Ken Ryder turned horror-stricken eyes to the sergeant. "My loss!" He swung back toward the body bag. "No. You're mistaken. You have to be. Not Dorothy!" His face crumpled as the gurney was lifted into the coroner's van. "Not Dorothy!"

# FOUR

Gray and I walked back to the model house in silence, Sergeant Poole, Officer Schumann and the police photographer following. They wanted to see the evidence of the shot. The reporter trailed along, too. I had been right. It did hurt to walk barefooted on this stony dirt.

As I limped along, I couldn't get the picture out of my mind of the distraught Mr. Ryder all but collapsing as they wheeled away his wife's body. I rubbed my arms to get rid of the emotional goose bumps, but they weren't the kind I could rub away.

Gray saw the motion, and he looked from me to my old Caravan.

"Why don't you just go on home, Anna?" he said. "It's been a hard night. I'm sure the sergeant wouldn't mind if I showed him what he needs to see."

I sighed again. "I wish I could just leave, but I've got to go inside. My purse. And I've got to finish hanging that treatment before it gets too wrinkled."

"Okay, get your purse, but then go. It's after eleven. You've got to be beat. Finish the window tomorrow."

"I can't. I've also got to pin the drapes up off the floor so the rug can be installed tomorrow."

Gray frowned. "I'm not much of a decorator, but wouldn't it have been easier to wait until the rug was in to hang the things?"

"The rug was originally laid yesterday, but the interior designer—"

"That would be you."

"No, not me. The woman I work for. She took one look at the rug and screamed, 'It's the wrong color green! Too yellow. Too yellow. Get it out of here!' I was hanging the treatments in the master bedroom at the time and heard the whole thing."

"So a new rug in a different shade of green arrives tomorrow."

"Yep, and since I don't know what time, I have to leave everything ready tonight."

Gray nodded. "Let me get another shirt from my gym bag, and I'll help." He reached behind the seat of his silver pickup, parked behind my Caravan, pulled a black nylon bag out, and rooted around until he found a gray T-shirt. He pulled it over his head.

He wrinkled his nose. "A bit ripe. I wore it to play basketball today at lunch, but at least I feel decent. I'd advise you not to get too close though." He smiled, and in spite of the emotional intensity of the evening, my toes curled.

Oh, for goodness sakes, Anna, get a grip!

We walked to the house and went inside. We found Sergeant Poole in the living room, staring at the ceiling. I looked up, and there was a hole where the bullet had struck. I hadn't noticed it before.

"See it, Schumann?" Poole bellowed.

Schumann's voice floated down the stairwell. "It's lodged in the side of a night table."

Rather the night table than me. I walked to the Tuscan Vine draped over the slipper chair.

"Let me hold the material for you." Gray reached out a hand. "I promise not to bleed on anything."

"What are you doing?" Poole asked, his gaze suddenly fixed on me.

I stopped, startled, one foot on the ladder. "I need to finish hanging this treatment."

The sergeant shook his head. "Not tonight. The crime scene guys need to go over the room first."

Gray made a noise of distress, then held up a hand as Poole glared at him. "I understand, Sergeant, but it does make things difficult for me and for Anna."

"They shouldn't be too long in here. Just pictures and the removal of the slug. Oh, and scrapings of the blood for analysis. I'll let you know when the coast is clear."

"There's a rug being laid tomorrow," I said.

"Not until we're finished here there isn't."

"And the model house opens to the public Saturday."

"Probably."

Recognizing an immovable object when I saw one, I nodded at the sergeant and carefully laid the lovely silk fabric over the slipper chair again. This time I took care to smooth it.

"Go on home, you two," Sergeant Poole said. "We'll make certain the place is locked when we're finished."

I grabbed my purse. As Gray and I walked out of the room, the sergeant called, "By the way, the place looks very nice."

"Thanks." *Nice.* We had been going for a lot more than *nice.*

Gray walked to my Caravan with me. I smiled at him, uncertain how to end the evening. On one hand, I'd just met him. On the other, we'd shared a pretty intense experience. Before the situation became too awkward and for want of a better idea, I stuck out my hand to shake good night. "I'm glad you were here. I'd have hated to go through all this alone."

He waved my thanks away. "I'm going to follow you home to make sure you get there, okay?"

I was impressed and felt warmed right to the cockles of my heart, wherever those were. "You don't have to do that."

"I know. I'd just like to." He paused. "You don't live, like, miles and miles away, do you?"

"No, about ten minutes." Which, out in western Chester County, was nothing. "Really, I'll be fine."

"I'm sure you will be. Still, I won't sleep unless I know you're safe. It's a guy thing."

"Protect the ladies?"

He shrugged. "What can I say?"

My stomach growled, and I flinched. So feminine and becoming.

He laughed as I pressed a hand against my middle. "Me, too. I never did get any dinner." He checked his watch, something he'd been doing off and on all evening. "I think the only place that's probably still open besides Wawa or Turkey Hill mini-marts is the Wendy's window. Is that okay with you?"

I nodded, unreasonably glad I'd get to spend a bit more time with him. "We can pick something up and take it to my house."

Gray climbed into his truck and followed me to Wendy's and then to the three bedroom brick ranch I shared with Lucy and Meaghan in a modest neighborhood set on a hilltop. On the way we passed my favorite house, a beautiful and unique place that was part restoration of a great historic barn and part new construction with lots of windows and gables. Somehow it all worked, and as I stared up the long maple-tree-lined drive, I grinned. My window treatments hung in that house.

I pulled into the drive of our ranch, a far cry from the mansion I admired from afar, but a whole lot more user-friendly. I parked in the turnaround, the place designated for my Caravan since it was by far the worst of our three vehicles, and the weather couldn't possibly do it any harm. Gray pulled up in front of the garage door.

I climbed down from the van, glad he was with me. The strips of woods between the houses might be a welcome privacy screen most of the time, but tonight they looked like menacing hiding places for assassins looking to take out witnesses. I walked quickly to the front door of the dark house, Gray right behind me.

"Looks like everyone's in bed," I said as I unlocked the door.

We had just stepped into the entry hall when the bedroom hall light flicked on. A very tousled Lucy appeared in her Girls Rule, Boys Drool sleep shirt, talking as she came. Her red curls corkscrewed wildly about her head, and her big black cat Tipsy lolled in her arms.

"And just what took you so long, Miss Anna?" she asked. "I was getting worried about you over there in that unpopulated place all alone." Then she saw Gray. An appalled expression on her face, she darted back out of sight.

"That's Lucy," I said around a laugh. "And the furry monster in her arms is Tipsy. Luce, this is Grayson Edwards."

"Hi, Ed," Lucy called, and Gray rolled his eyes. "What a shame Anna can't keep you, 'cause you look nice enough, the little I saw of you, tall, handsome, but you've seen me looking yucky, so you've got to go."

Now it was my turn to roll my eyes. Lucy was an original, and she said anything that popped into her mind, often in one long run-on sentence. Gray looked a bit thunderstruck, though he was smiling.

"Go to bed, Lucy." I gestured for Gray to follow me to the kitchen. "I'll tell you and Tipsy all about it tomorrow."

"Yeah, I guess I'd better before I embarrass you more."

"What makes you think I'm embarrassed?"

"Hah! I know you, kiddo. Good night, Ed." Her bedroom door clicked shut.

"Is she a teacher too?" Gray asked, his eyes dancing.

I nodded. "We all teach at Amhearst North Intermediate School. Lucy teaches English."

"I bet her classes are a riot."

"This is sixth to eighth grades we're talking. All classes are a riot if you don't watch out."

"Didn't you say there was a third one of you?" he asked.

Just then a snore echoed down the hall.

"That's Meaghan. She has sinus issues. And when she falls asleep, nothing wakens her, except maybe her own snoring."

"And what does she teach?"

"She's the guidance counselor," I explained as we unwrapped our fries and square hamburgers at the kitchen table. "Want a soda?"

He nodded and waited while I got two cans from the refrigerator and two glasses from the cupboard.

"Don't dirty a glass. I'm fine with the can," he said.

"This is an all-girl household." I poured the sodas and handed Gray his drink. "We use glasses for company."

"Waste of a clean glass."

"I bet you usually drink your milk right out of the carton."

"Unless my mother's visiting. Then I put my manners back on so she thinks she did a good job raising me." He took a swallow. "And I usually also say grace whether Mom's around or not. Do you mind if I say it now for both of us?"

"Please do." As I bowed my head, I glowed inside. Handsome, successful and Christian?

"So," I said after his amen, "did your mom teach you to pray too?"

He nodded. "Janet Grayson Edwards is the queen of prayers. 'There's nothing too big or nothing too small to talk to the Lord about,'" he said in an obvious quote.

"Sounds about right to me," I said.

Gray unwrapped his second burger. "Well, I can tell you, I don't remember ever praying as hard as I prayed tonight when the shots started flying—"

"Shot," I said automatically and wanted to shoot myself. I could hear my frustrated father saying, "Anna, you don't have to correct every little thing." I breathed more easily when Gray didn't seem to notice.

"—at least not since I took my tests to be licensed as an architect."

"The worst part was the look on Ken Ryder's face." I was suddenly no longer hungry.

Gray fiddled with a fry, swirling it around and around in a blob of catsup. "Not finding a pulse was pretty bad too."

I made a sympathetic noise. "Was she a good friend of yours?"

"Not really. Business acquaintances, both of them, though I knew Dorothy better than Ken." He set the fry down. "And I liked her. She was pleasant. Nice. Very good at what she did. Knew just what she wanted in the house. Only changed her mind every other day."

A thought hit me, filling me with horror. "Do they have kids?"

Gray shook his head. "Thankfully, no. She's all business-woman. You got another soda?" He held up his empty glass.

When I walked him to the door a half hour later, he took my hand in his, sort of a shake but not quite. "You did great tonight, Anna," he said. "It's been a pleasure meeting you."

Warmed by his compliment, I watched his truck back down the drive and disappear into the darkness.

*Lord, they don't come much hotter. What do You think? Better than Glenn?* I rolled my eyes. *Of course he is; almost everyone is. We both know that, right?*

When I heard no celestial *He's yours, girl,* I sighed, flicked out the lights, and headed for my bedroom. I wasn't sure I wanted him or any man anyway. I still had too many bruises from before. I wasn't even halfway down the hall before Lucy was right behind me, Tipsy prowling at her feet.

"Okay, Anna, give," she demanded. "Where did you find him?"

"You're supposed to be asleep," I told her. I glanced at the cat weaving through her legs. "You, too, furball."

"With a handsome, unknown dude like Ed in the house? No way. I want details."

So I recounted my evening yet again, finishing, "I thought my heart would break for him. I can't imagine what it would be like to have someone you loved murdered."

For once Lucy was dumbstruck. She stared at me, emotions flitting across her face. Finally she said, "I can't decide whether I'm more appalled at what you went through or more excited that Ed was there so you didn't go through it alone."

"Gray." I pitched my one remaining sandal into the closet. I pulled my T-shirt over my head and tossed it at the hamper.

"Whatever. You know who I mean." Lucy looked thoughtful. "I wonder what it's like to be named after a color."

I pulled on my sleep boxers and top and headed for the bathroom to brush my teeth. Lucy followed and said, "At least his mother's maiden name wasn't magenta or chartreuse. It'd be hard on a guy being named Chartreuse."

I paused in the middle of brushing and just looked at my housemate.

"Well, it would."

I mumbled through the foam, "I'm sure you're right."

Lucy's face crumpled suddenly. "Oh, Anna, you could have been killed. Right this very moment Meg and I could be having broken hearts over losing you." She threw her arms around me, foam and all.

"Easy, Luce. I'm fine."

"I'm not." She gave me a hard squeeze. "Lord, thank You for keeping her safe!"

I rinsed, turned, and gave Lucy a hug in return. One of the best things that happened to me four years ago when I began teaching at Amhearst North was that Lucy, a veteran of one year, took me under her wing.

"Don't stand too near Mrs. Meanix, the English teacher, when she's excited," she'd told me the first day in the teachers' lounge. "She spits, sort of like a llama. And watch out for old Mr. Simmons." We both looked at the skinny old man who taught math and should have retired ten years ago. "He's got roving hands." When all I could do was sputter, Lucy nodded vehemently, her eyes dancing. "I kid you not. And whatever you do, don't smile until after Thanksgiving."

"What?"

"My father's advice," Lucy said. "He's a teacher, too, though in New Jersey. 'Remember you are not their friend, Lucy,'" she mimicked in a deep voice. "'You are their teacher. Don't smile till after Thanksgiving. Don't send your discipline problems to the office. Take care of them yourself. And whatever you do, don't take off one day every month like so many women.'"

Lucy turned big brown eyes to me. "I'm afraid to get sick except on weekends, but I don't want to get sick then because I'll miss all the singles' stuff at church. So I have a policy never to get sick." She grinned. "You have to come to church with Meg and me. You'll love it."

Lucy introduced me to Meg. The three of us clicked, and soon I found myself living with them, enjoying the third bedroom and as unwilling to get sick on weekends as Lucy and Meg. There wasn't a day that went by that I didn't thank the Lord for these special friendships.

But tonight I was more than ready for solitude and a good sleep. I knew Lucy would be happy to stay and talk until all hours, so I shooed her with a flick of my hand and a smile on my face. "I've got a lot to do tomorrow, girl, so good night."

Lucy paused in my bedroom doorway. "Be sure you dream of Ed."

Right. Last time I dreamed of a man, he left me. Boom. Gone. Pain. Still, there was something about Ed. Gray.

I eyed my bed and the black furry boneless creature filling half of it. "Luce, you forgot Tipsy."

I put a hand under the cat and pushed. "Off, buddy." Moving not an inch, he turned his great head and showed me his fangs. I pushed harder.

The cat smiled, I'm positive, as Lucy gathered all twenty pounds of him close.

Moments later, snuggled under the floral print Martha Stewart sheets and summer blanket from Kmart, I found I couldn't sleep. Every creak of the house, every chug of the refrigerator's motor, every snore that came from Meaghan's room, every hum of the air-conditioning system going on or off made me go rigid.

He's not here, my practical self assured me.

How do you know that? my irrational self countered.

He doesn't know who you are or where to find you.

But he saw me. How spooky is that?

Very. Now go to sleep!

I wish.

The whole situation was preposterous. I was an art teacher, for goodness sakes, the original good girl. I painted on the side, and not even all that well if the truth be told, though I'd never admit it to my father. I sewed curtains and drapes for people for extra cash. I made fabric pictures— "fabric mosaics" Lucy called them—for the fun of it. I spent more time at church than I did at the mall. Any previous dealings with bad guys were absolutely nonexistent, any run-ins with law-enforcement authorities almost nonexistent. Almost.

Once I'd called in a child abuse report about one of my students. Once I'd gotten a ticket I couldn't afford because of my penchant for being heavy-footed. Once when I'd glanced at my watch and seen I was going to be late for a date, I'd accidentally walked out of a store with a pair of gloves in my hand. I'd rushed right back in to pay for them, probably passing the store detective coming after me to arrest me.

I'd committed one of my two serious offenses when I was six years old. I lifted a chocolate bar at a Wawa mini-mart. When I climbed into the car eating it, Dad marched me right back to the store and made me apologize. He paid for the candy, then made me work off the price by helping him with his annual garage cleaning. He made certain the task took all day.

You'd think that between the mortification and the sore muscles over the chocolate-bar incident I'd have learned my lesson, but I guess I'm just slow. Once, as a teen, I kept too much change at Kmart, using the undeserved five dollars to buy a colorful scarf. I still had the scarf, but I had yet to wear it. I kept it to remind myself of the fine line between evil and good, guilt and grace. I'd returned the five dollars as soon as I'd gotten my next babysitting job.

That was about as close as I ever came to lawbreaking and lawbreakers, Skip Schumann excepted, if mouthiness and disrespect were breaking the law. Evil people, really bad guys, couldn't usually be bothered with ordinary goody-goody people like me. They thought we weren't any fun, and we sort of thought the same about them. We went our separate ways.

Until tonight.

I squeezed my eyes shut again and tried to get comfortable in my very comfortable bed. Lucy sneezed, Meaghan snored and I sat bolt upright, trying to see through the darkness. I told myself over and over that it was only Luce and Meg, but my nerves, busy jitterbugging up and down my spine, didn't seem to grasp that truth.

Light. I needed light. If he came after me, I wanted to see him, rather than be taken unawares. I reached for my bedside lamp. As soon as I snapped it on, all the shadows dissipated, and all my fears quieted. Just seeing that everything was normal made all the difference. With a sigh that was a combination of relief and fatigue, I slid down and pulled up the covers. I was asleep in seconds.

I was up at eight the next morning, down at the police station by nine, and down in my basement workshop by ten. Lucy and Meg left to run errands, and I sewed. If I was lucky, I'd have almost everything done today. The rug should be down by then, assuming the cops were finished, and I could run to the model and work before the development became deserted. I was not staying there alone ever again.

Praise music rang from my boom box, and I sang along, almost drowning out the muted roar of the sewing machine. In a momentary pause of both the machine and the CD, a muffled, "Anna, open this door," sounded.

What in the world?

"Anna!" A fist beat rhythmically on the front door.

The music started again and I lunged for the off switch.

"Anna, come on!" The doorbell rang and rang, and knocking continued unabated.

I hurried upstairs. It sounded like Gray, but why was he banging on my door in the middle of the day?

I caught sight of myself in the mirror in the front hall. Yikes! I quickly combed my hair with my fingers and stuffed it back in the red rubber band I found in my shorts' pocket.

"Anna!"

"I'm coming! I'm coming!"

I threw the door open to find Gray, today wearing a black T-shirt and jeans, looking like an August thundercloud about to hurl lightning bolts at anyone within range. He had the day's Amhearst *News* in his hands.

He stalked into the house. "Look at this!" He shoved the paper at her.

Staring at me from the front page above the fold was a picture of Ken Ryder, looking stricken. Standing beside him, hand on his shoulder, was Gray, and standing beside Gray, looking heartbroken, was me.

"Ken Ryder, husband of victim Dorothy Ryder, being comforted by friends Grayson Edwards and Anna Volente," read the caption beneath.

"I didn't even know the picture had been taken," I said. "That reporter must have done it."

Next to the picture were my head sketches of the red-shirted man. Beneath his picture were the words: "Do you know this man? Wanted for questioning in the murder of Dorothy Ryder."

I put my forefinger on the face of the red-shirted man. "The drawings reproduced well."

"That's not the only likeness that reproduced well," Gray muttered. He dragged a hand through his hair.

I stared at him. "What?"
He pointed to my face, then to the caption beneath.
I went cold all over. "He knows who we are."

# FIVE

Dar Jones was not a happy man, but he also wasn't a particularly worried one. He just hated that the job hadn't gone perfectly. He prided himself in being the best hands-on for-hire killer in New Jersey, maybe the whole Northeast. Maybe the entire country.

He wasn't one of those prima donnas the movies were fixated on, the guys who used rifles and scopes and elaborate scenarios. He was a good, basic craftsman. Hire him, and your intended target went down quickly and cleanly. No prints. No clues. No DNA. No nothing but a dead body, done up close and personal so there was never any doubt.

So this time a woman saw him. Granted it irked him. After two weeks of casing the development, he knew that everyone was gone way before seven. Last night was the very first night someone other than the Ryder woman was there at that hour. Who could have guessed?

But so what? It wasn't like the woman in the window was a threat or anything. He hadn't looked like himself. So what if she saw the man with the light brown hair and the bushy mustache? She'd never finger him, not in a million years.

He ran his hand back over his naturally black, poker-straight hair and smiled to himself as he looked out his oversized window at the Atlantic Ocean rolling relentlessly onto the Seaside, New Jersey, beach. Even that red shirt with the little pony over the heart was a disguise. He'd never wear one of those preppy rags. He'd go naked first. And khaki slacks? He shuddered.

Basic black was his color. Black jeans, black T, black athletic shoes and socks. If he had to get dressed up, like for a funeral or to eat at some fancy-schmancy restaurant, he had his black cashmere sports coat. When winter came, he had his black leather bomber. If it was unbearably cold, there was the black down jacket.

The Man in Black. Just like Johnny Cash. Too bad he couldn't sing like Cash, but then Cash, if he was still alive, couldn't kill like him. Dar grinned. To each his own.

He could still see her horrified expression when she saw his gun. His grin broadened. She probably thought she was very fortunate to have escaped with her life. She probably spent the night thanking her lucky stars.

He laughed out loud. Like he'd ever miss. If he'd wanted, she'd be as dead as the other one. But all he'd needed to do was scare her so he'd have plenty of time to drive away.

Even if she'd seen him leaving, he'd been driving the black Taurus with the Pennsylvania plate with the scene of the old square-rigged warships fighting on it. The numbers and letters on the plate were impossible to read because they blended so well with the picture. Everything was beige. The plate was registered to Jon Paul Jones, just like the false registration and insurance papers, all with a phony Pennsy address. If anybody ever tried to trace the address, they'd end up at the credit union in South Coatesville.

Dead end.

The Taurus was tucked away in New Jersey, in Tuckahoe in a garage behind the house of a little old lady who was as daffy as they came. Every month an automatic bill payer sent her a check under his phony name, Jon Paul Jones. He kept just enough cash in the account in a Tuckahoe bank to pay her.

He turned from the window and slipped on a pair of black flip-flops because in August, the beach was too hot to walk on barefooted. He already wore his black swim trunks. He grabbed his black beach towel, draped it around his neck, and let himself out. He carried Lawrence Block's latest Bernie Rhodenbarr book. He loved reading about the thief, and he got some good ideas too.

Today he was rewarding himself for a job well done. He'd already put the ten thou for completing last night's job in the bank, joining the ten grand he'd gotten when taking the contract. Today was a day for sun and sand and the blissful relaxation of the well-satisfied. This evening he'd take himself to Moe's, his favorite hole-in-the-wall seafood restaurant, then head for Atlantic City. Maybe he'd even splurge and allow himself a hundred dollars for playing the slots. He'd never be foolish enough to head for the high-stakes tables. He'd worked too hard for the dough, and as far as he was concerned, real gambling was too much like dumping your money into a shredder.

He had two other hit jobs in the queue, but they could wait a day or two. Neither had a time aspect, like some hits he did where a witness had to go before the trial date or something. These two were the plain I-hate-the-target-kill-him type.

Forget the woman who'd seen him. Besides, if she made any trouble, he knew where to find her.

# SIX

I perched on the front of the love seat in the living room and read the article in the *News* very carefully. I stared at the picture of Gray and me again. "It doesn't say anything about me seeing the killer. That's good, huh?"

"If he doesn't see the paper," Gray muttered, clearly unhappy.

And if he did? "I suddenly feel like I've got a bull's-eye painted on my back." I shivered.

Gray was slouched on Meg's blue-and-cream striped sofa, ankles and arms crossed, head thrown back, eyes closed. My heart was beating faster than a repeater weapon could spit out shells, and he was completely relaxed? For some bizarre reason, his composure irritated me. I liked him better when he was beating on the door in concern for my safety.

"What's with you, Edwards? You rush over here to tell me I'm going to be murdered, and now you're talking a nap?"

He cracked one eye and just looked at me.

I flushed. "Sorry. That wasn't very gracious when you were so nice. I'm usually quite good-humored. I'm just not used to being fingered for a killer." I gave him a weak smile. "It makes me anxious."

He closed his eye. "You're sure you don't have a history

of being chased by bad guys? Maybe that innocent, dedicated teacher bit is a cover for nefarious behind-the-scenes stuff."

I all but sputtered. "Come on, Gray. I don't even know any bad guys unless you count Skip Schumann, and he's only thirteen, and he's not really a bad guy. He's just too full of himself and doesn't like me."

"Huh."

I glared at him. He looked so at ease! "What about you? Don't contractors have to deal with the Mafia and all? I bet you know lots of bad guys. Did one come looking for you because you didn't pay your protection this month and decide for some perverse reason to take out Dorothy instead?"

This time Gray opened both eyes, and they flashed with annoyance. "You've been watching too much TV and reading too many novels. Contractors are just as honest as any group of people, and I, being a Christian, am among the most honest of all. I value my good character too much to compromise it with questionable associations."

I'd offended him. Well, he'd offended me. I rubbed my forehead. The afternoon was not going well. Maybe if I went to bed right now and made believe the day was over, things would get better. My eyes fell on the newspaper. No, they wouldn't. *He* was still out there.

Gray sighed and held up a hand. "Hey, I'm sorry. For some strange reason, I'm a bit touchy today. This mess is interfering with my schedule like you wouldn't believe."

"It's not doing mine any good either," I shot back. Here we were being fingered for a murderer, and he was worried about a few missed meetings?

He took a deep breath and sat up. "Let's start over."

I stared at him grumpily for a minute, then nodded. I was supposed to *teach* intermediate school kids, not act like one. "Okay."

"Okay." He sat up. "Since we're agreed we're both missing too much work and we both hang out with nice people, Skip Schumann aside, apparently we only have to worry about this one man."

We? "You don't have to worry about him at all." My voice was tart. "I'm the one he saw."

I leaned back into the love seat. I'd brought it from home and reupholstered it in steel blue to go with Meg's striped sofa. Tipsy, sleeping on the other half of the love seat, looked at me with resentment. "It's called sharing," I told him as I pushed his stretched-out hind legs back onto his side. "And stay on your own space."

He showed me his fangs.

"We're in that picture together." Gray flicked a hand at the *News*. "We're in the mess together."

I looked at him. "I think your comment's supposed to comfort me, right?"

He shrugged. "I sort of hoped it would."

"Well, it sort of does, and I thank you, but I'm still the only one he shot at. What if he's got friends who'll help him get me? Bad guys have friends, don't they? Well, don't they?"

When Gray didn't bother to answer, I said, "The Mob. That's what they've got. I know all about Tony Soprano and Don Corleone."

He actually had the nerve to smile. "Don't overreact or anything."

I glared at him. "Fine. Make fun. Go back to your meetings. I'm going to keep sewing while I think about this whole mess and try to figure out a way to keep from being killed."

"Let me know when you have any good ideas," he said and pulled his PDA from the clip on his belt.

I studied him, watching his total absorption in whatever

was recorded there. He was definitely a good-looking man, sort of a young Sean Connery without the Scots accent and with wavy hair. Somehow his mere presence made me feel less vulnerable.

But how in the world could he concentrate on something as mundane as work in the middle of this crisis? I felt as wired as if I'd drunk a whole case of super-caffeinated cola.

"Have you got anything cold I can drink?" he asked, startling me.

"I thought you were concentrating." His eyes were still on his PDA.

"Always something to do, something to check up on, but a man still gets thirsty."

"Soda, iced tea and lemonade."

"Lemonade would be good."

I got to my feet, and Tipsy immediately stretched his legs out over the cushion I had vacated.

"I saw that," I hissed at him.

He curled his furry lip.

I started for the kitchen. Gray hadn't yet looked up. He muttered something under his breath. I was surprised when he slipped the PDA into its holder and pulled himself off the sofa. He followed me to the kitchen, the newspaper under his arm.

He sat in the same chair he'd used last night, a fifties red vinyl seat and back with legs and frame of chrome. The red Formica table with chrome legs matched the chairs. The set was one of Lucy's "treasures," picked up from an estate sale at an old farmhouse.

Frankly I thought most of Lucy's treasures were tacky Elvis-on-black-velvet sorts of stuff, but I liked the bright, cheery feel of the red kitchen set. The week after she brought the table and chairs home, I'd made red-and-white checked curtains for the window over the sink and the glass-paned back door.

Gray studied a watercolor on the wall beside the red table as I pulled the pitcher of lemonade from the fridge. The painting was a typical Chester County scene, a covered bridge and stream with a dramatic cloud-strewn sky bathed in the setting sun.

"Yours?" he asked.

I glanced up from pouring and nodded. I'd painted it during my representational Peter Skullthorpe/Richard Bollinger phase, though my abilities were far less than those of the men I emulated.

"Nice. Looks good up there."

"Thanks." The sad thing was that *nice* was the best that could be said not only of this painting but all my paintings. I had technique and a good color sense, but I didn't have that indefinable something that made a true artist rise above the many who painted. This picture hung over the table because it looked good in the room, not because it was good.

I spent a lot of time talking to the Lord about my art, and on cynical days I knew it was all my parents' fault.

"Look, Daddy," I used to say when I was little. I'd hold out another of my pictures for him to see when he came home from work. The kitchen table where I was working was my studio, littered as it was with markers, a shoebox full of broken and stubby crayons and dreams. "I'm going to be an artist when I grow up."

"Don't try to be an artist, Anna," my father always told me as he surveyed my pictures. "They never make any money. Maybe teach art, but don't make art your career."

"Now, Tom, let her alone," my gentle mother countered. "She's only five." Or eight. Or twelve. "And she's good."

"Yeah, but good isn't enough, Maggie. Not with art."

While still a kid, I vowed to myself that I'd show him I was good enough. I would become the world's greatest artist, and I'd get rich from my masterpieces. I never swerved from that goal. I took art lessons all through junior high and high school, and I majored in art at college. Dad complained about the costs of something he thought a waste, but he couldn't refuse his little girl, and I knew it. Besides, I minored in education to make him happy.

Mom died when I was sixteen, a terrible blow to all of us as we watched her waste away with ovarian cancer. Just before she died, before the pain was overwhelming and the morphine made her too unaware to think clearly, she spoke to each of us kids privately. I don't know what she told my brothers. Being male, they never shared. But I never forgot what she told me.

"Anna, God has given you great talent. You are an artist. Don't ever forget that."

"I won't, Mom."

"Promise?" She held my hand, hers so thin I marveled I couldn't see through it. "Don't let anyone talk you out of it."

I knew she meant Dad, though she'd never say so. "I promise."

"Say it for me, Anna, love. 'I am an artist.'"

I was crying so hard, I could barely speak. "I am an artist."

"Never forget that, sweetheart. It is as much a part of you as your heart for God. Serve Him with your art, and you will find joy."

I looked at the scene hanging on the kitchen wall above Gray and knew that I was still trying to keep my promise and prove to Dad that I was the artist Mom had thought me. The only things missing were the talent and the joy.

*God, I can do it,* I often prayed in frustration. *I know I can, especially if You just help me. Make me an artist who touches*

*people's hearts, who turns them to You. Lord, make me really,
really good!*

The rest of the prayer, buried deep in my heart, was, *So I
can find joy.* I didn't have the courage to say this out loud
because it sounded selfish and demanding. Of course, I knew
God knew this wish because, after all, He knows everything.
I think not saying it made me feel less shallow, less needy.
But, oh, how I wanted the joy my mother had talked about.

Through the years I continued to turn out "nice" paintings
that all my non-artist friends thought wonderful. My artist
friends were usually kind enough to keep their thoughts to
themselves.

Too bad I became more morose every time I picked up a
brush.

My eyes fell on the newspaper at Gray's elbow. Now the
issue seemed to be not whether I was good enough to paint
well, but whether I'd even live long enough to paint another
mediocre picture.

"So what do I do now?" I put a tall, ice-filled glass of
lemonade in front of Gray and sat across from him with my
own glass. He drained his in one long gulp.

I rose and put the pitcher at his elbow. "Help yourself."

He did.

"So what do I do now?" I repeated.

"You mean about trying to not get killed?" He downed the
second glass almost as quickly as the first.

I nodded, studying the photo in the paper again. "The only
good thing about this mess is that my father doesn't know."

"Protective, is he?"

I rolled my eyes. "You might say that. My brothers are
just as bad."

"Maybe I should give them a call, enlist their help," Gray
said. "They could be your bodyguards."

I shot him a horrified look. "Don't you dare!"

"Where do they live?"

"Ohio. And we're going to leave them there. All of them."

"How'd you end up in Amhearst?"

"I went to college nearby and stayed in the area after graduation. I love my family, but..." I shrugged. He smiled at me.

"Don't worry. I know that family, no matter how loving, can sometimes be overwhelming. You should see my sisters try and fix me up with women." He shuddered. "It's like the attack of the good fairies. 'You need to settle down, Gray, and we know just the woman. You'll love her. She's wonderful.' Or beautiful. Or gorgeous. Or my favorite, intelligent."

"What's wrong with intelligent?" I couldn't believe this gorgeous man was dumb enough to like dumb women.

"Nothing. I like intelligent women. I find them very appealing, and they certainly make for interesting conversation. But if that's the only adjective used, it's a sign to stay away."

I laughed. "You're as bad as my brothers."

He shrugged, completely unrepentant. "I don't have time for a woman anyway. My work takes all day every day. I finally moved to Amhearst from Philadelphia three weeks ago, and I'm still taking my clothes out of cardboard boxes every morning. No time to unpack."

"Do you have furniture?"

He seemed insulted by the question I had thought appropriate. After all, I'd seen my brothers' apartments before they got married.

"Of course I've got furniture."

I raised an eyebrow and waited.

"I've got a table and four chairs, a great recliner, a plasma TV, a Bowflex, a first-rate sound system and a bed."

I didn't bother saying that a wall-mounted TV, a sound system and an exercise machine weren't furniture. I knew that was a male/female definition thing. "Does the bed have a headboard, a footboard and a box spring?"

He became very interested in refilling his glass. "It will. Eventually. When I have time. Like I said, I'm very busy."

"So what are you doing drinking lemonade in the middle of the afternoon?"

"Good question." He looked at me for a long moment, then seemed to choose his words with care. "I don't want to scare you, but I don't think you should be alone right now, even here at home."

I went all warm and melty inside. He was concerned about me.

"I certainly don't want you alone on the site. The last thing I need is another murder."

Ah, a bucket of realistic cold water. It was Freedom's Chase that he was really concerned about, not me. "Yeah. Bad for sales."

He frowned. "That didn't sound quite right, what I said. You know I didn't mean it that way."

"Don't worry." I gave him what I hoped was a frosty smile, though I don't do frosty well. "I understand just what you meant."

He looked at me, clearly exasperated, but he chose not to pursue the issue. "How about your friends?" He nodded toward Lucy's and Meaghan's rooms. "Where are they?"

"Meaghan's at school locking horns with the new principal, and Lucy's getting food for the final weekend down the shore before school starts. They're leaving for Seaside tomorrow."

"Are you going with them?"

I nodded. "But I probably won't leave until Friday when I'm finished at the model."

"Home alone for a night?" He didn't look happy.

"Maybe I'll sew quickly and be ready to go with them tomorrow."

"Much better. Where do you stay?"

"Lucy's brother James has a house right on the beach at Forty-Second Street."

Gray looked surprised. "Does Lucy come from money or something? A house on the beach is worth millions."

Trust him to think in terms of real-estate values. "James made millions with a dot-com company of some kind. He sold out just before the bubble burst, and now he's a novelist who can write exactly what he wants because it doesn't matter whether he makes money or not."

"Is he any good?"

"Actually he is."

"Huh." But clearly Gray's mind was somewhere else. "So Lucy, Meaghan and James can keep an eye on you down there."

Meg and James, maybe. But Lucy? I tried to picture her as bodyguard, flack vest, protective helmet and all. Somehow she ended up looking a lot like the biblical David, laden down with King Saul's armor just before he decided to confront Goliath with only his slingshot.

I heard the front door open and Lucy yell, "Ricky, I'm home."

"In the kitchen," I called back.

"Ricky?" Gray asked.

"It's her little bow to *I Love Lucy*. That's what happens when your mother names you after a TV person. It's almost as bad as being named after a color."

Gray grinned. "Ha-ha. Well, she's got the red Lucy hair." He poured himself some more lemonade.

"Maybe I should run to the pound and get a very vicious pit bull."

"That's not a bad idea."

Actually it was a very good idea. I wondered what Meg would think of a dog in the house. A big one with teeth, but one who was smart enough not to eat one of us for dinner if I was late feeding him.

At that moment Tipsy entered the kitchen and ambled to his water dish. He slurped indelicately.

"Tipsy won't like a dog," Gray said.

I eyed the huge black beast who eyed me back with great golden eyes that never seemed to blink. "Tipsy doesn't like anything."

"He likes me," Lucy said as she came into the room with a bag of groceries. She set them on the counter and gathered the cat in her arms, cradling him like a baby. "Don't you, sweetheart?"

"Of course he likes you," I said. "You feed him."

"Are you sure he's got a backbone?" Gray eyed the animal doubtfully. "He's as limp as spaghetti."

Lucy adjusted him in her arms. "He may not have any bones, but he's got plenty of fat."

As if he understood and knew the comment was derogatory, Tipsy turned and stared at Lucy who stared innocently back.

"You'll never win a stare-down," I said. "Tips doesn't blink."

Lucy kissed the black monster on his nose and, bending, dumped him on the floor. She turned to the groceries and began stuffing them in the refrigerator.

Gray tore a corner off his napkin and wrote a phone number.

"We've got real paper you could use," I told him.

He shrugged and pushed the napkin corner toward me. "This works fine. I'd give you a business card, but they're all in the truck, and I don't have time to go get one. I've got to get back to the site. Here's my cell number. I want you to call me immediately if there's any problem. Immediately!"

"Before or after 911?" I said, trying to defuse the anxiety building in me over his intense concern.

He reached over and placed his hand on mine where it lay on the table. "Anna, I'm serious."

"About what? The danger? The dog? Calling you?"

"Yes."

Goody. I smiled weakly. "I'll be okay. I've got Lucy." Who had gone to get another bag of food from her car.

"And lock all the doors when I leave."

I nodded, but I was all too aware that locked doors wouldn't keep a determined killer at bay. They never did on TV. It was enough to make you wonder why you had locks to begin with.

Gray stood and pulled me to my feet. Only then did I realize that somehow I had turned my hand over and that I now clasped his. Or he clasped mine. He seemed as surprised as I was, staring at our meshed palms.

At that auspicious moment, Lucy came back into the kitchen. Her eyes widened when she saw our hands. With what could be seen as insulting speed, Gray released me.

I trailed him as he walked to the front door, wishing for the comfort of his grip again. "What about you, Gray? Who's going to keep you safe?"

Gray paused with a hand on the doorknob. "He doesn't want me."

"Oh. Right." How could I forget that little difference in our situations?

When he drove away, I locked the front door and leaned against it. I shuddered as I heard the drip, drip again and saw the bright pool of blood in the beam of Gray's penlight. I tried to imagine how a man could shoot someone willfully and in cold blood.

Life was precious, not something to be done away with

at whim. As long as life continued, a connection with God the Father might be made through Jesus the Son. Then when life ended, there was heaven. Snuff out a life prematurely, and a person might never have the opportunity to make that choice for God.

I wondered about Dorothy Ryder. Had she known God? Had she even thought about Him? Not that anything could be changed now. Her opportunity to decide for God was gone. She'd either made that decision previously, or she'd never make it.

*Lord, take care of Mr. Ryder. Comfort him. And help the authorities find the guy who did it—without me getting killed, too, okay?*

Maybe I should call Sergeant Poole and ask the police to assign someone to guard me. I shook my head. Amhearst didn't have a big force, and I suspected there weren't extra cops lying around to take on a duty like that.

I went to my room rather than down to the cellar to work. As I walked in, my eyes were drawn to the fabric mosaic over the bed, and I smiled. It was a three-foot-by-four-foot whimsical depiction of the Ark with its animals, sewn from hundreds of little pieces of material of different hues, textures and patterns to get the shadings of color I wanted. It had taken me a year to finish it, but every time I looked at it, I felt better, no matter how bad my day had been.

A pair of giraffes held their heads high, each spot several tiny scraps of rusts or ecrus, their manes brown embroidery floss. The smiling lion's mane was several shades of gold and bronze yarn packed tight and cut into eighth- to quarter-inch lengths. His lioness was a tawny collage of beige and amber calicos. The elephants were strips of varying shades of gray, gathered to create their wrinkles. The porcupines squatting on the roof had their laid-back quills made from the straws of a new broom.

Meg kept urging me to take part in high-end craft shows or at least sell my mosaics on eBay. "You could make a fortune, Anna. Your stuff is so beautiful."

"I just do this for fun," I always answered.

Last Christmas I'd given Meg a mosaic of a single rose in myriad shades of pink, rose and crimson, the leaves made up of more greens than a spring meadow. I'd made Lucy a whimsical red-headed cat, its color slowly darkening until its tail was a deep, almost black crimson. Two years ago I'd given my father a pair of cardinals, male and female, sitting on a snow-laden pine bough. I'd loved the challenge of the slender needles and the fluffy snow, the subtle shading of the feathers.

I turned from my masterpiece-to-date and settled myself against the headboard of my bed. I reached for my Bible. I wanted the comfort of others who had lived through danger and adversity and had written about God's faithfulness in their dark nights. I wanted to be reminded that God was ever faithful. I turned to Psalm 66, one of Mom's favorite passages during her illness.

> You let men ride over our heads;
> We went through fire and water,
> But you brought us to a place of abundance.

I put the Bible back on the bedside table.

*Lord, not too much fire and water? Not too many men riding over my head? But I'll take that place of abundance whenever You send it my way.*

# SEVEN

Thursday morning Dar walked in the back door of his home on the beach. A grocery bag crackled in his arms. Freshly ground coffee, half and half, a loaf of cinnamon raisin bread and a beautiful, thick filet mignon to grill for tonight's dinner. This afternoon he'd run up the road to a produce stand for some fresh Jersey beefsteak tomatoes. He'd grill them with the steak. He'd also get some fresh peaches, sweet and succulent, for dessert with some of the vanilla ice cream stashed in the freezer.

He stretched, pleasantly tired after a night in Atlantic City celebrating his kill. And what a lovely celebration she had been. What was her name? Kimba? Nola? Some cartoon animal thing. Bambi! That was it. Not that it mattered. He'd never see her again.

He wandered into his bedroom and stripped off his black T-shirt and black slacks. The bed looked very welcoming. A few hours sleep, and he'd be as good as new. He took a quick shower to wash Bambi away, and as he lay down, he still felt the satisfied afterglow of a hit well done. It was wonderful to love your work this much.

Four hours later he pulled on a pair of black shorts and a black T-shirt. He straightened his black sheets and summer-weight blanket and pulled up the black comforter. He padded barefoot into the kitchen and made himself a cup of coffee. As he leaned against the black granite countertop waiting for the brew to drip through the machine, he saw yesterday's newspaper lying on the kitchen table.

He pulled it over. Day-old news wasn't usually all that interesting, but maybe there would be something about the Amhearst job. Granted the *Atlantic City Press* didn't carry much Philadelphia area news, but you never knew.

He flipped the paper open and blinked. There he was on the front page, staring up from a pair of drawings, one full face, bushy mustache carefully in place, the other profile. He wasn't nervous that anyone would recognize him from the drawing. Between the wrong hair and the mustache, he was unidentifiable.

But whoever had done these drawings had gotten the nose. Not good. He ran a finger over the prominent bump. He studied the drawings some more. They were very good and had the words "Do you know this man?" beneath. They were no IdentiKit things either. They were closer to portraits.

He swore. It was that girl. It had to be her. No one else had seen him.

And there she was in the photo. He read the caption. Anna Volente. It said she was a friend of the victim's husband, she and that guy beside her.

Huh.

He filled his coffee mug and walked out onto the deck overlooking the beach and the Atlantic. A slight breeze blew off the water, rumpling his uncombed hair. He sat on the rail and thought.

When he came back in an hour later, he pulled the filet from the refrigerator and slid it in the freezer next to the vanilla. He had some important things to attend to, and with the trip to Tuckahoe for the Taurus, he doubted he'd be back in time for dinner.

# EIGHT

"Dad." As I heard his voice over the phone Thursday morning, I felt the familiar mix of love and frustration. "How are you?" I tried to sound bright and perky. Not a care in the world.

Lucy sat at the red table downing an alarming number of Lorna Doones, grinning as she unabashedly eavesdropped. She and Meg still hadn't left for the shore which surprised me.

"Who cares how I am?" Dad thundered. "How are you, and how did you get mixed up in a murder?"

"Um, what do you mean?" How did he know anything about the killing? I hadn't planned to tell him about it until the murderer was behind bars, and I could make the whole thing a big joke. He had hovered over me, "my little chick in a barn full of strutting roosters," my whole life. After Mom died, he'd been worse than ever. If he knew I'd actually seen the murderer, he'd have apoplexy.

"I read about you in the paper."

"I was in the Ohio papers?" Who would have thought?

"Page six," said the man who only read the headlines and the sports section with occasional glances at the comics. "I missed it myself, but I go to work this morning, and the guys say, hey, Anna was in the paper yesterday. Then they show me. I mean, wouldn't you think my girl would tell me about something so important?"

I heard the disappointment in his voice.

"I'm sorry, Dad. I didn't want to worry you." Or have you drive down here and sit on my front porch with your loaded hunting rifle. "Um, what's the newspaper say?" Hopefully no more than the *News*.

I heard him rattle the paper.

"There's a picture of this guy who's the killer, and there's a picture of you and two guys, one the husband of the murdered lady. How do you know people that get themselves murdered?"

Like it was Dorothy's fault?

"I don't. I was putting up some treatments in the model house and I just saw—" I caught myself before I spat out the part about seeing the killer. "—I saw all the emergency vehicles, you know?"

Lucy's grin widened at my evasion. Well, I did see them. I wasn't saying anything untrue. I was just bending the time frame a bit. I scrunched up my shoulders, waiting for the providential lightning bolt to strike me for my semi-prevarication.

"Who's the other guy?" Dad demanded. "This Grayson Edwards person?"

"He's the contractor in the development where I was working and the woman was killed."

Dad grunted. "Sounds like a man you should avoid if things like that happen on his job sites."

"He's a nice man, Dad."

"Is he ever," Lucy muttered.

I rolled my eyes at her. "He had nothing to do with Dorothy's death."

"And you somehow know this for sure?"

"I know this for sure."

Dad grunted, clearly reserving judgment. "And you're certain you're okay?"

"I'm fine, Dad." *Lord, may that continue. And please don't let him come here. We made it safely through last night, and I'm sure we'll be fine tonight, too.*

"You want I should come?"

I heard the worry in his voice. "Dad, I'm okay. Really. You don't have to come."

"I will, baby. In a moment if you need me."

"I know."

"And the boys, too."

"I know." My eyes filled. He might drive me crazy at times, but I never doubted he loved me.

"Or you can come here. Just until they catch this guy," he said quickly, like he knew I was going to protest.

"Thanks, Dad, but I can't. I'm going to Seaside with Lucy and Meg for the weekend, and school starts on Monday."

"Already? What's with this starting before Labor Day? They never used to start before Labor Day."

"They do now, and I need to be there."

"It makes no sense. The kids go to school for a coupla days, and then they got a three-day weekend."

Reprieve! He was off on another topic. But my relief was short-lived.

"If you're scared this guy might come back, you can miss a few days of school. I'll even write you a note." I had to smile at his attempt at humor. "Dear Mr. Principal, Anna missed school this week because her father didn't want her in the same town as a killer. I'm sure you understand, probably having a daughter of your own who hardly ever listens to your advice."

"Oh, Dad." My rebuke was mild.

"Are you still painting?" he asked, jumping topics faster than I could blink.

Here we go. "Of course."

"Are you still planning to be a famous artist, lauded by the world for your extraordinary talent?"

Hardly, though I'd never admit it to him. Still, I had to keep trying.

*"Anna, you are an artist. Don't ever forget that. Promise?"*

*"I promise."*

Not that Dad knew about Mom's final words or the pact I'd made with her. They were too precious, too personal to share with anyone, even this man who loved me so. "My World-Famous Artist certificate comes in the mail next week."

"Smart aleck. But you're still sewing?"

"You should see the fabulous fabric I'm working with on this job. It costs three hundred dollars and more a yard."

"Some people have more money than brains. But that's not what I meant. Are you sewing?"

I knew very well what he meant. Was I doing my fabric mosaics? "I'm working on one for a gift." If I didn't fall in love with it and keep it myself.

"Anna, work on them all as your gift from God."

"Yes, Dad." I put my hand over the mouth of the phone and hissed, "Lucy, go ring the doorbell nice and loud and long."

Shaking her head in laughing sympathy, Lucy headed for the front door.

Dad sighed. "Is it that you love painting even though you're not so good at it, or that you won't admit that your father has been right all these years?"

The doorbell sounded, and I heard voices in the front hall. Meg was home—unless Lucy was having a conversation with herself in different voices. With her anything was possible.

"Whoops, the doorbell's ringing. I've got to go, Dad. Thanks for calling. I'm fine and I love you. Don't worry." I hung up.

I stood with my forehead against the wall. He did it to me every time. Every time. I knew he meant well, but the questions always left me feeling inadequate, as if I were disappointing not only Dad, but Mom as well. I pictured her in her radiant robe, one among thousands sitting at Jesus' feet, shaking her head. I knew theologically that there was no sorrow in Heaven, but I still saw Mom looking distressed.

I took a deep breath and straightened as Lucy and Meg walked into the kitchen.

"Guess what?" Lucy said as she grabbed a couple of more Lorna Doones from the almost empty wrapper. "We aren't going to the shore today. We decided to wait until you can come with us." She waved a cookie at me. "We don't think you should be alone."

I looked from one woman to the other. "You're missing two days at the beach for me?" Can you say friends?

Meg shrugged. "We're not completely altruistic. We've got stuff to do to get ready for next week."

"Besides, how often do we get to play bodyguard?" Lucy offered her depleted cookie bag first to Meg, then me. "Your father might not realize you saw the killer, but we do."

Meg poured some lemonade into a glass. "Not that we're likely to scare anyone away, but being alone when things are hard is the pits."

I saw, as I often did, that shadow in Meg's eyes. Some time, somewhere, she had been in trouble alone, and the experience still haunted her. But close as we three were, she never alluded to whatever had happened. Lucy and I had speculated a time or two, but all we knew for sure was that whatever it was, it had occurred before we knew her.

"You guys are the greatest." I hugged Meg, then Lucy. I hesitated a minute, then said, "Gray and I had an idea."

Lucy all but clapped her hands. "You two? This is bound to be good."

"A dog."

Meg and Lucy looked at each other and grinned.

"Big?" Meg asked.

Lucy nodded. "With lots of teeth."

"We were going to suggest it to you." Meg rinsed the empty lemonade pitcher.

I laughed. "You sure you don't mind, Meg? It's your house, after all."

"Don't think twice about it." Meg sliced a lemon to float in the new pitcher of lemonade she was making. "You're much more important than unscratched doors or hairless clothes."

"Hairless clothes we never have anyway, courtesy of Tipsy," I pointed out helpfully.

"What do you think about a Doberman?" Lucy asked, ignoring the slur on her cat's grooming. "They snarl really well."

"This is going to upset Tipsy," I warned. Personally, I suspected the spoiled thing could stand being upset a bit.

"Some things are even more important than Tipsy." Lucy gave me a teary smile.

I smiled back, touched. "I have to take some more stuff to the model this afternoon. The police called and told me it was okay. Maybe we can meet at the pound at four-thirty, and both of you can help me pick our dog?"

"Will you be at the model alone?" Lucy asked.

"I'll be all right. It shouldn't take me long. I just need to unpin and arrange the drapes, cover the table, and put out the pillows I've finished. Then I need to take some pix for my portfolio."

"I think we should keep you company." Meg poured us each a glass of lemonade. Lucy nodded. "We can unpin stuff for you. That doesn't take much talent."

I looked at them with affection.

"Let us know when you're ready to leave," Meg said, "and we'll go along."

"We could take Tipsy as our attack cat." Lucy picked up the black beast who had been rubbing against her ankles with exactly that hope.

"Puh-lease." I reached out and scratched his ears. He blinked at me. "I don't think he even knows how to growl, let alone attack. All he ever does is show his fangs."

Meg put the new lemonade in the fridge. "I vote we let Tips have one more afternoon of peace before the attack dog arrives. Drink up and let's go."

I went down to my basement workshop, taking care to close the door at the top of the stairs. We'd discovered to my chagrin that while Tipsy didn't particularly like me, he loved my sewing projects. He'd climb onto them and sleep, leaving his long, silky, black hairs behind. Sometimes he'd burrow into the material, wrinkling it and forcing me to iron all over again. Fortunately, as an indoor cat, he was declawed, or I'd shudder to think of the damage he could do. Solution: keep him upstairs.

I gathered the pillows and tablecloth I'd finished. I had four sewing machines down here, a Pfaff that had cost me more than fifteen hundred and could do everything but stand on its head, two heavy-duty industrial machines I'd bought at a great price when a clothing factory in Philadelphia closed down, and a machine for serging. Each was a far cry from the Singer most women owned.

For my cutting surface I had taken over the Ping-Pong table that came with the house when Meg bought it. I'd sanded the edges myself and refinished it with several coats of urethane to make certain there wasn't any possibility of splinters catching in the material I placed on it. The last thing a client wants is pulls in her drapes.

As I gathered the pillows and fabric, I looked with longing at the mosaic I was working on. It was going to be a diptych of a breaking wave. I'd been inspired during that longer-than-planned shore visit with Meg and Luce a couple of weeks ago, and if truth be told, this fabric wave was as responsible for my last-minute rush on things for the model as was my extended stay.

I'd already sewn together tiny strips of varying shades of dark navy for the underside of the wave. They'd be placed on an angle to create the feel of the water being pulled toward its breaking point. For the rush of sleek water topside I'd begun sewing a random pattern of small squares of glossy navy satin intermingled with tiny white and pale yellow pieces, the latter to depict the sun jewels dancing on the water.

I hadn't begun to sew the foam of the breaking wave yet. I still played mentally with the effect of everything from quilted cotton or eyelet for texture to cotton batting for a three dimensional effect. Maybe some lace for the foam at the very crest where it began to cream. Maybe I'd use multiple fabrics to convey the wave breaking on the diagonal. This trip I needed to get a better sense of the subtle shades of the creaming wave. Whites, creams, pale aquas, pale lavenders?

My fingers itched to work on this project some more, but I turned my back on the waiting fabric. I would be strong. I would do my work. Gray was depending on me. Meg and Lucy were waiting for me.

Twenty minutes later, using my key, I let us into the model. I had half expected to see yellow crime scene tape lapping this lot, just as it did the Ryders' where it hung limp under the afternoon sun. Fortunately for Gray, the model's exterior looked just as it had when we left the other night, lovely and welcoming. I went inside, wondering what I'd find there.

I was still in the front hall when I saw a square drawn on the living room ceiling, marking the bullet hole there. Lucy and Meg stared open-mouthed.

"That sure makes it real," Meg finally said. She slung an arm over my shoulder. "Thank God he missed."

We stared at the bullet hole a few moments more. Would the police be coming back to cut the square of ceiling out? Or were pictures of the hole enough? Would Gray—or one of his workmen—be allowed to merely spackle the hole over and repaint that little spot, or would he end up with a hole four inches by four inches to fill? And how soon would he be allowed to repair whatever the police left him?

We knew we weren't in the house alone by the little noises coming from the living room. It wasn't the rug guys. I could see the plush green floor covering from here, so they'd come and gone. We peeked around the corner and found a glazier on a stepladder replacing the window pane that had the bullet hole in it.

He glanced at us over his shoulder. "Hi, ladies." He grinned, eyes settling on Meg. "Well, well. The day is definitely looking up."

Meg made believe she didn't understand his comment. She looked around the room as if he wasn't there. "How come you got a purple sofa?"

"It's aubergine," I said.

"Looks purple to me, too," the glazier agreed.

I managed not to snarl.

"Are you putting glass in or taking it out?" Lucy asked him.

"The cops took this one pane, and I'm replacing it," he said in a voice filled with importance. "I don't know why they took just this pane but I'm glad to help out. I mean, a lady died over there. Murdered!" He gestured toward the Ryders', then looked bemused. "I just don't know what a pane of glass in the model house has to do with anything."

"They must know what they're doing," I said.

"Ya think?"

"I think."

We dumped my pillows, and I gestured to the girls to follow me. We went upstairs and down the hall to the master bedroom suite.

"Wow." Lucy sounded awed. "What a great room!"

"The bedside table's gone." I pointed to the empty space beside the big poster bed with the blue toile quilt and hangings, all of which I'd sewn. "That's what the bullet lodged in."

The pewter bedside lamp with its colorful Tiffany shade lay tucked among the bed's many pillows, all of which I'd also made. All were of the blue toile fabric except one, a small envelope pillow in blood red with one white button.

Polly, the interior designer, had had me make curtains with the toile fabric, too. I'd also covered the top half of the walls with it, stretching it over thin cotton batting from the ceiling to the off-white wainscoting. The lower wall was painted the blue of the print. The rug was that ever-practical shade, off-white. Spectacular to look at, I had to admit, but I hoped Polly had lots of clear plastic runners to put down for rainy days.

We went back downstairs, and I called Polly. "You need another night table in the master bedroom. The police confiscated one."

"What? Why? Where will I ever find another before Saturday?"

"If anyone can do it, Polly, you can."

In the living room, the new green rug was a wonderful match for the greens in Tuscan Vine. Polly had been absolutely right to order the new shade. After the glazier climbed down from his ladder, folded it, and disappeared with a lingering look at Meg who studiously ignored him, I opened the sturdy stepladder Gray had brought me the other night. With Lucy's help, I finished hanging the back window, all the while eyeing Ryders' back door as if I expected the man in the red shirt to appear there again.

The final window finished, I propped my pillows artistically on the sofa and chairs, taking care not to squash their hyper-expensive fringe. My favorite fringe had little jade monkeys hanging amidst the eggplant and ecru tassels. Real jade, unique and very lovely if you didn't mind little bumps in your back when you leaned against it.

While I draped the circle of aubergine taffeta over the round table between the green slubbed overstuffed chairs and laid the Sinclair tartan topper, making certain it came down an equal amount all the way around, Meg and Lucy began unpinning the tacked-up window treatments. I stepped back and looked critically at the room. When Polly got finished adding the decorator items, all too large to be carted off by light-fingered, potential Freedom's Chase homeowners, it would look spectacular.

I dropped to my knees and began removing pins, too. I worked at the windows across the front, making certain the treatments draped just so. While I fiddled with the fabric on the last window, Lucy took pictures of the room with my digital camera.

"I still think you should be in them," she said. "People in pictures add life."

"It's to sell my work, not me, to future clients."

The front doorbell rang. I glanced at my watch. Almost four-fifteen. I'd called Gray to tell him we were going to be at the model and that we were going to get a dog. Maybe he'd decided to come with us. Of course, as he reminded me, it would mean leaving the job site early, apparently an unpardonable sin.

"Hey." Lucy lowered the camera and grinned at me. "Ed's here."

I dropped the curtain I was working on and peeked discreetly out the window, telling myself I wasn't really hoping, hoping it was him. After all, we girls could pick out a dog just fine by ourselves.

There was nothing in sight but my Caravan and a black car a couple of doors down. "I don't see his truck." I told myself I was not disappointed.

"Then it's someone interested in buying a house. Maybe you can sell one and really impress Ed."

"Right." I walked to the front door and opened it. A man with black hair combed straight back stood on the porch. He wore a black T-shirt and black jeans with one hand slipped into a pocket. If the black car was his, he sure liked black.

"Hi," he said, a pleasant smile warming his face. "I was wondering if I could come in and take a look around. The wife and I are moving to Amhearst in a few weeks, business transfer, you know, and I was wondering about this development. I thought that if I could take a quick look, I could tell Rhonda about it when I got home."

I hesitated. None of the Realtors who would be working out of the converted garage were here. "The model's not officially open until Saturday."

"But I won't be here Saturday." He gave me that charming smile again.

"I guess it would be all right, Mr.—?" Hesitantly I stepped back.

He didn't give his name but stepped forward, his hand going to the small of his back. His smile remained in place, but it suddenly seemed more feral than charming.

"Oh, let him in, Anna." Lucy stepped into the hall, waving her arm at him. "Come on in. The place is gorgeous. You'll love it, and so will Rhonda."

Meg peered into the hall. "Lucy's right. You'll love it."

The man paused, startled by my housemates' appearance.

"I'll even take your picture." Lucy raised my digital and aimed it at him. "The first visitor to the model home." She glanced at me. "Ed'll love it."

The man in black took a quick step back. His hand came up to brush his upper lip. He looked disconcerted. "Well, I've got to go." He turned just as the camera flashed. He all but ran down the walk, almost colliding with Gray who was walking up it. His silver pickup was parked behind my Caravan.

"I take it you don't want to look around after all?" I called after the retreating man.

"Weird." As usual, Meg hit it succinctly.

"Rats!" Lucy looked at the camera. "It takes so long for these things to actually *take* the picture that I missed him. Well, I didn't actually miss him. It's just not good."

"Who was that?" Gray asked as he came into the hall.

"Some guy who said he wanted to see the model, then changed his mind." I started to close the door, wanting to shut out the moist August heat.

"Wait!" Lucy stepped out on the porch and took a picture of the strange man as he opened the door of the black car parked down the street. "This is for you, Ed, so you can see your first almost-customer." She looked at the viewfinder and grinned. "Got him." She held the camera out to Gray. "Just don't hire Anna to sell these mansions. He ran as soon as she asked him in."

"But she sews well, so we forgive her a lot," Meg said. "Hi, Gray. I'm Meg."

"Let's see what you got, Lucy." I peered at the camera.

She held it out, and I stared at the profile of the man in black as he bent to enter his car. His shirt was neatly tucked in except at the small of his back where it hung loosely. My blood chilled. "Show me the other picture."

"It's no good either. I'm going to erase both." Lucy put her finger on the delete button.

"No!" I grabbed the camera.

Lucy jumped. "Anna!"

I flicked the back button and stared at the first picture Lucy'd taken. The man in black had his hand over half his face, and he'd been turning away when the shutter clicked. Once again his profile, at least the top half of it, was clear.

I threw the door open and ran onto the porch. The black Taurus was gone.

Lucy and Meg came onto the porch and stood beside me.

"Anna?" Meg looked at me with concern. "What's wrong?"

My hand shook as I held out the camera. I pointed to the image visible in its little square. "It's him. I'd recognize that profile anywhere."

# NINE

"It's him," I repeated. My mouth was so dry I could hardly get the words out.

Gray looked over my shoulder at the picture. "You mean from the other night?"

"*Him?*" Lucy squeaked. "As in the bad guy?"

I nodded.

"We invited him in!" Lucy was appalled.

"How do you know?" Meg the ever practical asked. "He doesn't have blond hair or a mustache."

"No, he doesn't, but he has the nose." I touched my own nose, then pointed to the feature in question in the pictures. "A nose like his is hard to disguise. You can make a small one bigger, a straight one look crooked, but a hooked nose like his is an outstanding physical characteristic."

Meg nodded calmly. "Your artist's eye."

"Oh, Anna! What if we hadn't come with you!" Even Lucy's curls seemed to sag at the thought, but she perked right back up. "A German shepherd, and you keep him with you like a Seeing Eye dog, only he's a Seeing Gun dog. Just no pit bulls. They scare me, and I want to be able to hug the mug without worrying about losing some important body part."

"Tipsy will never let you near whoever we get," Meg told Lucy as she quietly gave my hand a comforting squeeze.

"He'll just have to learn to share." Lucy had the door open and was halfway across the porch. "Come on. To the pound."

I looked at Gray. "He put his hand to the small of his back just before Lucy came into the hall."

His eyes widened; he knew exactly what I meant. He pulled me close in a comforting hug. "Don't think about it." He gave me a couple of awkward pats on the back like a new father burping the baby for the first time. "Which is a foolish piece of advice if ever I gave one."

I laughed in spite of the fact that I was shaking in reaction— to the man in black, not Gray, though come to think of it, I was probably reacting to Gray too. I pulled out of his comforting, too comforting hold. "We've got to call Sergeant Poole."

Five minutes later, unable to get hold of the sergeant, I hung up. "You're not going to believe this, but he and Officer Schumann are out of town at a special, daylong class on search and seizure being given at the state police academy. They aren't due back until about midnight."

"Is someone else coming?" Lucy asked.

I shook my head. "They're working on very short staff, but the dispatcher's going to report the incident to the state police who will respond as soon as they can."

"What does 'as soon as they can' mean?" Lucy asked.

I shrugged. "I told them we were leaving here and would be at home shortly. They'll send the officers there. In the meantime they want me to e-mail the pictures so Sergeant Poole will have access to them first thing tomorrow."

Lucy's eyes went big. "Then we're all in danger tonight, aren't we? Because we all saw him." She shivered. "I even took his picture. Twice."

"I don't think you need to worry, Lucy." Gray indicated

her, Meg and himself. "We three can't place him at the scene of the crime. Only Anna can do that."

"Whew!" Lucy's shoulders slumped with relief. Then she straightened, a funny look on her face. "Not that I want you to be in danger either, Anna."

"I know what you mean," I assured her. "Now let's go get us a dog."

We left the model, locking it behind us.

"Want to ride with us in the Caravan?" I asked Gray.

Gray eyed his pickup. "How about if I follow?"

He probably thought I hadn't noticed him checking his cell while I was talking to the police or seen him pull his PDA out a couple of times. He was probably dying to return calls and do whatever it was his PDA told him to do.

"Fine." I got in the Caravan with Lucy and Meg, and he got into his pickup.

"You could have sent us home and gone with Ed," Lucy said.

"What? No way. This is going to be your dog, too. You've got the right to help pick him."

"We wouldn't have minded, would we, Meg?"

"Not at all. First things first."

"Look, guys, not that I don't appreciate you trying to help along my non-romance, but I want you to remember two things. One, I think it's in very bad taste to drop your girlfriends for some guy."

"You wouldn't be dropping us," Lucy said earnestly. "We'd be waiting to suck all the dirt from you when you got home."

Meg leaned forward from the back seat as far as her seatbelt would allow. "Yeah, sort of like gossip vacuum cleaners."

I had to laugh. "What I mean is that we planned to go get

a dog, the three of us girls. Just because Gray decided to come along doesn't mean I don't want you guys along too."

Lucy looked unconvinced. She turned to Meg. "Well, it's not like the pound is romantic or anything."

"And my second point is that I don't want any plotting here." I shook my index finger as I talked. "If the Lord wants something to develop between Gray and me, it'll happen without any subversive machinations."

"Subversive machinations," Lucy repeated as if awed. "You got no worries, girlfriend. I don't even know what they are."

"Sure you do. You teach English."

"Yeah, but only seventh grade. They don't learn subversive until eighth and machinations until tenth."

We pulled up before the Chester County SPCA and stood waiting for Gray for about five minutes while he played with his technological friends. Finally we left him and started for the door.

"See? It's the three of us." I pulled it open. "Girl power."

His cab door flew open as we filed inside. "Hey, wait for me!"

The dogs greeted us with a welcoming din. We moved from cage to cage, and my heart broke. Poor things, living in such small quarters. No matter how well-treated, and they were well-loved and cared for, it wasn't like living with people who loved you and took you for walks or gave you a backyard to run around in. I wanted to take all of them home, especially the new litter of Great Danes with huge feet and floppy ears.

Gray caught my arm and pulled me away from the puppies. "The idea is to get a big dog, remember? One that will scare people away today, not six months or a year from now."

Lucy was sitting on the floor holding a conversation with

a white cockapoo who actually seemed to understand what was being said. The dog's answer was immediate, staccato and somewhat shrill, and Lucy nodded solemnly. I wondered if Tipsy was about to get a brother or sister. Since Tipsy and the dog were of a size and weight, it would be an interesting struggle for dominance.

Meg was scratching an elderly hound with graying jowls and the saddest canine face I'd ever seen. The old dog had his eyes closed in ecstasy.

"Anna, there you go." Gray pointed to a fawn boxer who sat with his nose pressed against the chain link fencing of his cage. He watched us with total concentration and pulled back slightly as we approached. When we stopped and spoke to him, he began to grin. His whole body vibrated from the tip of his cropped tail to the points of his cropped ears.

I knelt and held out my hand. "Hello, boy. How are you?"

The boxer, a young adult, leaned into the fence and looked at me with liquid brown eyes. I poked a finger through the links and scratched his back. The dog sighed in delight.

I was a goner.

When we came outside, it was raining, a hard summer storm, the kind that usually knocked the humidity down for a couple of days. We raced through the downpour, the dog galloping happily beside me on his new leash. When we stopped by the Caravan and climbed in, he was clearly disappointed. He wanted to run some more.

Then my dog—boy, that sounded nice—shook all over us as he shed the rain. Not that it mattered since we were already wet, but we still ducked and yelped. Reflex. Then the animal refused to sit in the rear where I'd put him. He jumped the middle seat and squeezed between the front bucket seats. He climbed into my lap, not easy to do with the steering wheel in the way, and collapsed against me, his head lolling on my shoulder.

I hugged him. "You are a big baby! You're supposed to be a vicious watchdog."

He lifted his head and kissed me.

"If you want him to stay in the back seat, you're going to have to get him a seat restraint," Lucy said.

"A seat belt for dogs?" What would they think of next?

"And maybe with all the trips to the shore you should get him a life jacket."

I tried to imagine stuffing the boxer into a bright orange life vest. "How do you know about all this stuff?"

She grinned. "I watch Animal Planet."

"What are you going to call him?" Meg asked around her laughter.

"I don't know." I scratched the dog's ears. "It has to be just right."

"I know, I know!" Lucy raised her hand. "Rocky. He's Rocky the boxer."

The dog lifted his head from my shoulder and looked at Lucy.

She leaned over and kissed him. "See? He knows."

Rocky? I wasn't certain. I couldn't help wonder how many boxers there were in America named after the celluloid Philadelphian. "Rocky?"

He turned and gave me another kiss.

"It's good, Anna," Gray said, leaning in the still-open driver's door to pet the animal. Crystal droplets sparkled in his hair, and his wet T-shirt clung to his chest. "Hey, Rocky, guy."

I gave up. "Rocky it is."

Tipsy took one look at Rocky when we brought him into the house and had a hissy fit. His back arched, his fur rose, his lips curled and he spat fury. Rocky bounded forward to greet his new housemate and was startled and highly offended when Tipsy slugged him in the snout. The dog stood, stunned, giving Tipsy time to swat again, which he did. This time Rocky turned tail and hid behind my legs.

"My hero." I reached back and scratched his ears.

"The wars have begun," Meg said through her laughter. "My only rule is that if they break anything fighting, whichever one does the breaking, his owner has to replace the broken item."

"Agreed," both Lucy and I said.

"Keep a running total, ladies. I want to know who wins." Gray had followed us home to be certain everything was all right at the house. Now he dropped to his knees and rubbed his hands up and down Rocky's back. If Rocky'd known how to purr, he'd have done so. "Okay, let's check the basement."

I led him downstairs, making sure Rocky stayed upstairs behind the closed door. I didn't think he'd be as gauche as Tipsy and sleep on my expensive fabrics, but I couldn't take the chance.

"You've got some workshop down here, Anna." Gray sounded impressed as he surveyed the ordered chaos. Bolts of material leaned in one corner, with more in the closet under the stairs. Clear plastic tubs full of remnants were stacked in the closet too. Spools of thread of all colors were arranged in rainbow fashion on a long narrow shelf that Dad had hung for me shortly after I moved in. My ironing board and the special iron that glided on a mesh metal plate so the hot footplate never touched the fabrics sat in another corner.

I wished madly that I'd known earlier in the day that Gray would be down here because I'd have swept. Lint, pieces of thread, snipped off pieces of material, straight pins, and more littered the floor. And of course there was my mosaic wave and all the quilting supplies and frames for that work heaped on a card table, overflowing to more plastic tubs stacked along the wall.

Gray stared at the narrow navy strips for the underside of the wave and frowned. He looked at all the little squares of satin.

"It'll be a wave," I explained. "A fabric mosaic."

"Huh." Clearly he had no idea what I was talking about, and I couldn't blame him. At the moment it looked like nothing so much as scraps waiting to be tossed.

"I'll show it to you when I'm finished." I wondered if he'd even remember who I was by the time the wave was finished several months down the pike.

In the far corner by the sliding door to the backyard I had my easel and painting supplies, but there wasn't a picture in process. The sewing for the model and the beginnings of my wave had taken all my time and energy recently. Sometimes I wondered why I kept the brightest area of the basement for the activity I did least, but deep inside I knew.

*"Never forget, Anna. You are an artist."*

"You need some kind of an anti-theft bar in the track of this door." Gray started looking about the room. "It's too easy to break open a slider."

"Oh." I'd always thought of the door as a source of light, a welcome conduit for sunshine, not an easy entry point for dangerous men.

Gray pointed to the metal pole attached to the ironing board, the one that held the iron's cord out of the way. "Let's use that until you can get to the store to get something tomorrow."

I released the pole and handed it to Gray who slid it into the door's track. He opened the door until it bumped the pole. He studied the width of the opening.

"I think someone might still squeeze through here." He started looking around again.

"Wait! I know." I grabbed my three-foot metal ruler. I had one six-foot one, too, but obviously that one was way too long.

We took the iron's pole out of the track and stuck the ruler in. It just fit, and the door wasn't opening at all with it there. I felt amazingly secure as I stared down at it.

We went back upstairs to delicious smells coming from the kitchen. Lucy usually cooked, and she was very good at it. Meg and I took turns with the clean up.

"Want to stay for dinner, Ed?" she called. "I'm doing chicken basted in teriyaki sauce on the grill. Caesar salad and rolls, too."

His cell must have vibrated just then because he glanced down at it and frowned. At the same time his stomach growled.

"You've got to eat." I gestured to his truck. "Go get your laptop. You can work in the living room until dinner's ready."

He barely hesitated. "Okay, I'd like that." He raised his voice. "Thanks, Lucy. I'm taking you up on your offer."

I had been petting Rocky as Gray and I talked. He clung to my side like a nettle on knit, casting a fearful eye at Tipsy who glowered in the kitchen doorway. He lifted soulful eyes to me and whimpered.

Gray and I looked at the cowering dog and laughed. Then we looked at each other. He reached out and ran a hand down my arm from shoulder to elbow. I hoped he couldn't see the goose bumps his touch raised.

"You doing okay?"

I was at the moment. Big-time. "Sure. I've got Rocky here. What more does a girl need?"

Gray looked at the dog. "I've been passed over for a canine pugilist."

As if Rocky would take priority over the most interesting man I'd met in years, if ever. As if he meant his comment as anything more than a little joke.

While Lucy finished getting dinner, I e-mailed the

photos of the man in black to both the Amhearst police and to the state police. I studied the second picture as it filled the screen of my PC. Using my photo program, I enlarged it several times and, presto!, the license number on his car—it was a Taurus—appeared, fuzzy but readable. Three cheers for Lucy!

Rocky slept at my feet as we ate, and I decided that even if the dog was afraid of Tipsy, he was a great comfort. Besides, I understood; I was half afraid of Tipsy, too.

After dinner we saw Gray off, and the three of us settled in the living room to watch *Bringing Up Baby,* the old Katharine Hepburn/Cary Grant comedy. The screwball humor was just what we needed, and seeing Cary Grant running around in a woman's negligee with ostrich feathers at the neck, still dignified down to his toes, never failed to make me laugh.

The movie was almost over when the doorbell rang.

"Sergeant Poole." I hoped. I hurried to answer.

But it was Gray, freshly showered and wearing jeans and a royal blue T-shirt. He had his laptop in hand.

"I got thinking about you girls and Rocky and probably no cops until morning, and I decided to see if you'd mind if I slept on your couch."

Yowzers! A workaholic knight in royal-blue armor.

"I even brought my toothbrush." He pulled it out of the pocket on his T-shirt.

I was much too touched by his thoughtfulness for my own good. "Come on in. Susan's about to wreck the dinosaur."

"What?" But he followed me into the living room and watched the final scenes of *Baby* with us.

It was eleven when I turned out my light, feeling very secure with Gray down the hall tapping on his laptop and Rocky sleeping on the floor beside my bed. I didn't jump at every sound as I had the last two nights, and I didn't mind the darkness. Besides, the rain had stopped and the moonglow shining through my window made the furniture familiar friends.

I was almost asleep when Rocky decided he was sharing my bed. He jumped up and curled at the foot as if he'd done it every night of his life. I wondered about his former owners. They must have let him sleep on their bed too. So why had they given him up?

When he sighed with contentment, I did too. He was worth every penny of his fees, food, leash, bowl and currently unused bed down there on the floor against the wall. I slid into sleep.

I started awake when Rocky growled softly. I raised myself on one elbow and looked fearfully around the room. The moonlight had dimmed as the moon moved across the sky, but I could still see well. Everything looked normal.

"Shh, baby. Everything's all right."

He ignored me, his head cocked as he listened, a deep shadow against the lighter shadow of the wall. I listened too and heard nothing. I glanced at my bedside digital clock. Almost one. I lay down again.

I was almost asleep again when Rocky lunged from the bed and streaked from the room, barking and snarling.

"Rocky!" I scrambled out of bed and raced after him, my heart beating triple time. As I dashed down the hall, Meg's and Lucy's doors flew open, and they ran out, bleary-eyed and rumpled.

I stopped and spun around. Doors! My bedroom door had been open. I was absolutely certain I had closed it when I went to bed. I closed it every night. But it had been open when Rocky tore out of the room, when I ran out of the room.

I went cold. "It was closed. But it's open."

Meg and Lucy looked at me, uncertain what I meant.

"My door. Rocky ran out. He was growling and barking."

"He sure was. Still is." Meg smothered a yawn. "Why?"

Now his barking, though still snarly, was coming from a distance.

"He's outside!" I rushed into the front hall with Meg and Lucy right behind me. We stared in disbelief and growing discomfort at the wide-open front door. As we stared, a rumpled Gray stepped out of the night onto the porch and came inside.

"You're supposed to be sleeping on the sofa," I said inanely.

"Not with all the barking and yelling." He ran a hand through his hair, and I noticed a sleep crease on his cheek. "How'd the front door get opened?"

I rubbed my arms, but the chill was inside, unreachable. "You didn't open it?"

He shook his head.

"I locked it." Meg flicked the lock shut, open, shut. "I always check. I know I locked it."

"I know you did." Gray pulled her hand from the door. "I checked before I went to sleep, and it was definitely locked. Don't touch the knob, Meg. It might have a print."

Rocky was still barking, but now the sound seemed less furious. I stepped onto the porch. "Here, Rocky. Come here, boy."

"Anna!" Gray grabbed my arm and none too gently pulled me inside. "What are you doing, woman?"

I stared at him in surprise.

"You're making yourself an easy target!" He pushed the door almost shut, making sure I was tucked out of sight behind it.

My mouth went dry, and I felt weak all over, like I had a bad case of flu. I leaned against the wall for support. "But Rocky chased him."

"We hope, but we don't know."

I nodded. He was right.

The door moved, startling all of us, and Rocky sauntered in. His head was turned so he could bark over his shoulder, but the heat was gone from the sound. It was like he yelled, "And don't come back again!"

When he finally turned to us, he walked to me and wagged his tail. He sat and looked up expectantly, obviously knowing he'd done a good job.

I leaned down, fondled his ears, and showered him with kisses. "You are a wonderful boy," I assured him. "Now tell me. What happened, Rock?"

He opened his mouth, torn between smiling at the praise and panting from his exertions. I saw a dark color against the white of his teeth and the pink of his gums and tongue. I knelt and grabbed the dog's lower jaw. There, snagged on his lower left fang, was a piece of material. I pulled it free.

In my palm sat a piece of black denim.

# TEN

Dar had just opened the door to her bedroom when he heard what he first thought was a deep snore. Then, startled, he recognized it for what it was: a growl. He paused, frowning. He took a step backwards, then another and another, every nerve hyper-alert. His immutable rule of engagement was that if there was ever an unknown, he pulled back to reconnoiter, regroup, reconsider. Risk only got you in trouble.

Still, when the dog launched himself from the bed, growling and snarling, Dar had never been so shocked in his life!

As he fled through the house, out the front door that he had unlocked before venturing down the bedroom hall, and through the woods at the side of the house, the dog had been right behind him, snapping at his heels. One time he felt sharp teeth sink into his left calf, but he had kicked furiously with his right leg, catching the dog in the ribs several times. It had finally let go, but it hadn't stopped chasing him, though it kept its distance.

Where had that animal come from?

Sure, he knew there was a cat, a big, black, lazy thing. But a dog? He'd cased the place carefully after that near-disastrous encounter at the development. No dog, big or little. None. He was sure of it.

So he'd broken the lock on a basement window, climbed in, then made the window look as if it were still securely locked. He'd hidden in the closet under the stairs, behind all her sewing stuff in the little corner where the stairs turned. If there had been a dog, it would have heard him and raised a ruckus. He hadn't made any effort to be quiet since no one was home.

There was no dog!

He'd listened to a book on tape to pass the time while he waited for the chance to get the girl, and he hadn't heard barking. Of course he hadn't been listening either. He wasn't even sure he'd have been able to hear over the voice in his ears.

He hated dogs. Hated them! When he was a kid, old man Horton next door had a skinny gray dog, a Weimaraner named Adolph. The old man'd thought it so funny to name a German breed after the most famous German of all times. In tenth grade Dar—still Alex Kemper, his real name—had learned the joke was on Horton. Hitler wasn't even German; he was Austrian. Of course by then Adolph-the-dog was as dead as Adolph-the-non-German. Dar had taken care of that with a piece of meat laced with rat poison.

But when he was little Alex, Adolph scared the pants off him. It was a high-strung, nasty thing. Never stopped barking. Dar still had the scar on his thigh from the time it bit him. He was six, and all he did was lob stones at it. Sure, he tossed a couple pretty hard, but it was all in the spirit of fun. Who knew the snarling demon would break his lead and attack him?

The horror of that time came rushing back when the dog leaped from Anna's bed and went for him. When Dar reached the Taurus a quarter mile away, he threw himself behind the wheel and slammed the door shut.

He'd screamed like a girl when the boxer threw itself against his window, barking and snarling, raking its claws down the glass. He reached for his SIG Sauer P239. He loved this pistol. Small, concealable, deadly, and its 9 mm parabellum round was common as dirt, which made its user just about faceless, unidentifiable. He didn't care if someone heard the shot. Even if a do-good citizen called the cops, he'd be gone long before they got here.

He slapped at the small of his back. He slapped again. In desperation he searched all across the waistband of his jeans, felt down over his back pockets, patted his hips. He blanched.

The P239 was gone.

What was it with this job?

Well, he had to go find it. Granted the serial number was filed, but he'd heard that dilute nitric acid could etch the surface where the numbers had been and their shadow reappeared. That didn't worry him too much. Even if they traced the pistol, he'd bought it back when he was James Garnet. But his prints would be on it. He didn't think they had any on file to compare those on the pistol to, but he didn't want any to ever be on file. Anonymity was and always had been his watchword.

He simply had to beat the cops to the pistol, or, even worse, some kid. As if they weren't looking for him hard enough as it was. Let some kid shoot himself, and there wouldn't be a safe place in the whole world.

He looked at the slobbering dog, still balanced against the side of the car, eyes intent on him. He wanted to hurt it so bad. He rammed the key in the ignition, turned it, and hit the gas. The animal disappeared from view as he pulled away and into a U turn. His headlights picked out the creature, standing in the middle of the road watching him.

He aimed the car and floored it.

At the last moment the dog jumped nimbly to the side,

barking at him as if this were a jolly game of dodgeball. Dar slammed on the brakes and twisted the wheel, and took another pass. A third. A fourth. He turned for the fifth and saw to his intense disappointment that the animal was walking across someone's lawn, heading for the woods. Every so often it stopped and barked in his direction just like a kid who had to have the last word. He watched it until it disappeared into the darkness under the trees.

Filled with rage at the dog, at old man Horton, at Adolph, and at Anna Volente, Dar drove a quarter mile away, parked, and waited until he felt certain the dog was home. He pulled a penlight from the glove compartment and climbed out of the car. He'd have to walk a bit to get to the stretch of woods he'd escaped through, but it shouldn't take him long. He had to find that gun.

Fire shot up his left leg at his first step. The bite! Adrenaline had masked the pain until now. As he realized he couldn't walk back to the woods, and as he remembered how infectious a dog bite could be, rage gripped him anew. It wasn't fair.

And it was all her fault!

# ELEVEN

Two state policemen arrived at the same time as Sergeant Poole and Officer Schumann. All four looked sleepy, especially our stalwart Amhearst cops who had been rousted from their warm beds before they'd had opportunity to recover from their long day in the classroom. While four men in blue—or gray in the case of the state guys—were very comforting, I'd have been happy if they'd brought along four more.

The killer had been in our house! He had come to my room! I was so unnerved that I toyed seriously with the idea of calling my father and brothers and pleading with them to come, loaded shotguns and all. Let me tell you, *that's* unnerved.

As it was, I kept Rocky at my feet and stood as close to Gray as I could manage without climbing into his lap. Lucy and Meg hovered close too.

Our living room was bursting when we all sat down to tell the officers our story. Eight people and six seats presented a slight problem until I sank to the floor with Rocky at my side, and Lucy sat on the raised hearth.

First we told them of the man in black's visit at Freedom's Chase and gave them copies of the pictures I had sent as requested but which they hadn't yet seen. They grinned with pleasure when they saw the license plate in the one photo. Then we told the night's tale.

"I woke up when Rocky growled." I shivered at the memory. "Then the dog tore out of the room after someone."

"I woke up when Rocky came tearing up the bedroom hall, barking and growling to wake the dead," Gray said. "I heard someone race out the front door, Rocky on his tail. I pulled on my jeans and took off after them, but I couldn't catch them. They ran into the woods."

Meg asked the big question, the one that had us all wondering. "How did he get in through a locked door? Both Gray and I checked it when we went to bed, so we know it was locked."

"The back door?" Officer Schumann suggested.

We all shook our heads.

"We checked. Locked. The same with all the windows here on the main floor and in the basement." I shifted slightly and came to rest against Gray's legs. For a brief moment he laid a comforting hand on my shoulder. For a brief moment it eased my tension.

"Let's see if we can't find you an answer." Sergeant Poole rose, and so did the others. They split up and searched the house.

"Down here," Sergeant Poole called after a few minutes.

"Not you guys," one of the state cops told us as we civilians all trooped to the steps. "We don't want to accidentally contaminate the evidence."

We clustered at the top of the steps, listening to the low murmur of voices rise from below. When the four of them reappeared, I was on tenterhooks for more than one reason. I wanted to know what they had found, and I wanted to be assured that the things in my work area were unharmed. After all, I had a substantial monetary investment down there.

"He came in through a basement window," Sergeant Poole said when we'd taken our seats in the living room. This time Gray sat on the floor after insisting I take his place on the sofa. The sergeant sat in the chair I'd reupholstered.

"Which one?" Gray asked. "I looked down there."

"The one nearest the oil burner. It looks fine. It's only if you try to open it that the broken lock shows."

"The guy's good," one of the state cops said. "That's why I'm surprised he didn't do something to neutralize the dog."

I thought about the timing. "Maybe he didn't know we had one. We only got Rocky late today. If he checked out the house after he left Freedom's Chase but before we got home, he thought there was no dog."

"So it's reasonable to assume that he came in before you brought the dog home."

I was appalled. "He was in the house all evening? While we ate? While we watched the movie? While we got ready for bed?"

Lucy rubbed her arms. "That gives me the creeps."

Meg silently wrapped her arms about herself and looked uncomfortable. "So where was he all this time?"

Officer Schumann held out a tape cassette she grasped by one corner with a tissue. "Are any of you listening to this? It's part of an audio book, a detective story."

In concert the three of us all shook our heads.

"Where was it?" I asked.

"In the closet under the stairs, back behind the material and other stuff, in the cramped space where the stairs turn. It looks like he broke in, hid there, then settled down to wait until you were all asleep, passing time by listening to the book."

A literate killer. Wasn't I lucky.

"Is there a library name on the cassette?" Meg asked. "I get lots of audio books from the county library.'"

"Nothing to indicate any kind of ownership, which probably means he bought it himself," Schumann said. A state guy held out an evidence bag, and she dropped the cassette in.

Gray indicated the tape. "That's probably why he never heard the dog walking around. I was wondering about that. The snick-snick of a dog's claws sounds very different from a person's footsteps." He looked at the floor. "But I guess since most of the house is carpeted with wall-to-wall, he wouldn't sound all that different after all."

"Is everything else okay down in the basement?" I held my breath as I waited for the answer.

"That's your sewing stuff?" Sergeant Poole asked.

I nodded.

"Looked fine to me. We dusted for prints around the closet and found none, no surprise. This guy knows what he's doing."

I thought of all that grit and what it would do to my fabrics and my machines. I also thought of something else. "Gloves. Like at the Ryders'."

"So it appears," Poole agreed. "We won't dust around your work area unless we feel we have no choice. Since we have the cassette, the piece of fabric, and the pictures you took this afternoon—" he nodded at Lucy who beamed back "—we may not need to disrupt your things. However, you can't work down there until we're sure."

That was a lot better than I'd feared. Freedom's Chase could live without a few more pillows, and I had no more immediate jobs scheduled. I always kept the calendar clear at the end of August, beginning of September because of the new school year.

The state policemen rose and moved toward the front door.

"I doubt the hunk of black fabric will tell us more about who your intruder was," one of them said. "Of course we'll check, but odds are that it'll be from a pair of jeans like millions of other pairs. Levi's. Wranglers. Something like that. We'll need to find the pair with the matching hole to prove anything. But the pictures." He grinned and winked at Lucy who glowed like a solar flare under all the praise. "We'll get busy on them right away."

When they were gone, I immediately felt more vulnerable. My world had always been safe, secure and relatively mundane until two days ago. Skip Schumann was my worst "enemy".

Now I had a genuine I'm-going-to-kill-you enemy, and I wanted my old boring life back, Gray now included, of course.

Sergeant Poole looked at me. "Can't leave you alone for a minute, can I?"

I smiled at what I assumed was his little joke.

"You are a very fortunate woman, Anna." There was no humor in his face or voice now.

I nodded. "I know."

"I'd like to assign Officer Schumann to act as your bodyguard."

I was going to get my own bodyguard? Wow! I felt safer already.

Out of the corner of my eye I saw Natalie Schumann start and then frown. "But, Sergeant—"

Then again. I spoke quickly. "It's all right. I'm going to Seaside for the weekend, so I'll be fine. He won't know where I am, even if he dares come back."

*He won't, will he, Lord?* But if he was half the man we all thought he was, a man who stalked and killed innocent women, he'd be back. The very thought was enough to make me clammy all over.

"Are you going to Seaside by yourself?" Poole asked, his craggy face intent.

"With Meg and Lucy. Lucy's brother James has a house there."

"Will he be there?"

Lucy nodded. "He lives there year round."

"Are you going with them?" the sergeant asked Gray.

Now it was his turn to start and frown. "Uh," he said helpfully. Doubtless he was thinking of all the appointments recorded in his precious little PDA.

"Good," Poole said. "If you're along to watch over the ladies, and the brother is there, and of course the dog goes along, then Schumann can be in the wedding she's supposed to be in on Saturday."

Gray looked at Officer Schumann who looked back at him. Then they both turned to me. It was more than obvious that one of them was going to have an unhappy weekend.

I waved my hand like I was chasing away a bothersome fly. "You don't have to change your plans, either of you. I'll be fine."

Sergeant Poole shook his head at my naiveté. "Can you say wishful thinking?"

He certainly knew how to make a girl feel better. I swallowed, trying to force my fear back into my stomach where it belonged, doing cartwheels and trapeze stuff down there.

I was conscious of Gray's eyes on me, but I wouldn't look at him. The last thing I wanted was for him to come along and end up resenting me for interfering with his crowded schedule.

"I'll go with the girls," he finally said, voice flat.

The sergeant nodded approval, and Schumann wilted with relief. I scowled at Gray who looked stoic and noble. I wanted to tell him to keep his gallantry to himself, but I wanted the comfort of his presence more. It was amazing what fear could do to a girl's self-respect. I swallowed again and forced out a raspy, "Thanks."

"But I can't leave until tomorrow evening. I need to go to Dorothy Ryder's viewing."

Of course he did. Business was business.

I was immediately ashamed of myself. I hated the side of me that always suspected others' motives. It was all Glenn's fault, dastardly man. I may have been too blind, too naive to see any of the signals that must have warned that disaster lay ahead, but I'd learned my lesson. In fact I'd overlearned. Now I looked for hidden agendas and warped intentions too much, especially in men. Just because the Ryders were business acquaintances was no reason to assume Gray didn't feel a personal loss at Dorothy's death. After all, I felt one, and I didn't even know her.

Be honest, Anna. You're miffed because he didn't immediately jump at the chance to go with you for the weekend.

Too true. Way too true. It was hard to remember that I'd only known him for three days—now four, since it was almost three in the morning, Friday. He didn't owe me any allegiance or any assistance.

"No problem then, except for the heavy weekend traffic." At least the sergeant was clearly delighted with the way things were working out. "Natalie will stay here through the day, and you, Mr. Edwards, can pick Anna up when you're finished at work."

And so I passed the day with Natalie Schumann trailing me wherever I went—the grocery store with Lucy to get extra food for the weekend, school to make certain all was ready for the new year, the coin laundry since we couldn't go down to the cellar to use the washer and dryer. Together Natalie and I waved Lucy and Meg off for Seaside around one so they could beat the worst of the shore-bound traffic.

In the course of my time with Natalie, I discovered that she was everything that her little brother Skip was not. Of course Natalie was about twelve years older than Skip which might have accounted for her pleasant disposition and manner. Then again, Skip might just have gotten all the family's bad genes, sort of like Danny DeVito in the movie *Twins.*

Gray showed up shortly after five, all showered and shaved and looking good in summer slacks and a dress shirt with a carefully folded tie stuffed in his chest pocket. Natalie practically raced out the door to make it to her rehearsal dinner on time.

I served us a quick hot-weather dinner of taco salad and fresh fruit, and I liked eating across the table from him way too much. The chair in which he inevitably sat had too quickly become "his" chair.

"Did Lucy leave this for us?" he asked around a bite of lettuce and hamburger. "It's delicious."

"Thank you, I think."

He stilled a moment, studying me. "Oops. Sorry. You made it, right?"

I nodded.

He grinned. "Doesn't change a thing. It's still good."

Demoted from delicious to good. *Good* was sort of like *nice,* a polite way of saying the quality was so-so. Was he saying I cooked as well as I painted? If so, my matrimonial future looked dark indeed.

"Were you able to clear your calendar without too much trouble?" I asked as I washed the dishes.

He shrugged. "I've got my laptop in the truck. I can work in Seaside as well as here."

"And miss the beach?" I was truly horrified.

"The beach is sandy. And the ocean is salty."

"You're kidding, right?"

"About what?"

I shook my head sadly. "I'm afraid I'm going to have to rethink my opinion of you."

He grinned, but I wasn't certain that I was teasing. How could a shore lover ever hook up with an anti-shore philistine?

# TWELVE

Dorothy Ryder's viewing was one of the saddest things I had ever been to.

When Gray and I arrived at the funeral home Friday evening, the parking lot was nearly full. We joined the steady stream of people going inside even as I wondered where the people arriving after us would find space to park. The death of someone as young as Dorothy always brings a large response. Add to that the violence of her death and the splashy newspaper coverage, and it seemed all of Chester County had turned out.

Ken stood in the front of the room by the head of the closed casket. He had that shell-shocked look on his face that I had seen on my grandmother's face when my grandfather died and on my father's when Mom died.

Just beyond Ken stood a man and woman with silver hair. They wore the same disbelieving, lost expression, and I thought they must be Dorothy's parents, enduring the unthinkable pain of burying a child. Near them stood two couples about Ken's age. Dorothy's siblings, I decided.

The line was long, and as we moved slowly forward, I watched Ken. He shook hands with the men and hugged the women, who often kissed him on the cheek. As we approached, I could hear a woman telling Ken a story about Dorothy bringing her family meals when she was in the hospital.

"How old do you think she was?" I asked Gray. I stared at the large picture of Dorothy sitting on the casket. She had been a very lovely dark-haired woman with strength and purpose shining in her dark eyes.

Gray shrugged. "Thirty-five? Forty? Somewhere in there."

"So sad." I sighed for the abrupt and tragic ending of one who had apparently been a very nice woman as well as a successful businessperson.

When Ken saw Gray, he tried to smile. "Gray. Thanks for coming."

The men shook hands, and Gray patted Ken on the shoulder with that awkward show of affection men have. I hung back, not wanting to intrude.

"I can't tell you how sorry I am, Ken." Gray's voice was rough with emotion.

Ken's eyes filled with tears, making me blink against the burning in my own eyes.

Gray put his hand on the small of my back and pushed me forward. "This is Anna Volente, Ken. She was with me when we—"

Ken gave me the saddest smile. "I saw your picture in the paper."

I nodded and gestured helplessly toward the casket. "I'm so sorry."

"Yeah, me, too." Ken sighed, his shoulder sagging as he studied Dorothy's picture. Then he turned and introduced us to Dorothy's weeping family. I felt the tears pooling in my eyes, knowing how they hurt, remembering what it had been like when Mom died. I hadn't known what to do with all the love I'd still felt for her or how to fill that empty space in my heart where she had lived. In many ways I still didn't. I ached for these people struggling with their versions of those emotions.

We moved on to make room for the many behind us. As we walked toward the exit, Gray looked at me with a crooked smile. He pulled out a handkerchief and handed it to me. "I'd hate to see you at the viewing of someone you actually knew."

I wrinkled my nose at him as I blotted my eyes.

"You are such a girl." He shook his head as if in disbelief.

"Is that a compliment or a criticism?"

He just grinned.

"It reminded me of my mom's funeral."

"Ah." He slid an arm around my shoulders and gave me a comforting squeeze as we reached the front door. He was very good at comforting squeezes. All those sisters probably.

We stood back as a man and woman entered. The man stopped when he saw Gray.

"Edwards." Though he stuck out his hand, his manner was as friendly as a linebacker's as he faced his opponent in the Super Bowl. "Such a sad thing. And to think you found her?"

"Reddick, how are you?" Gray's manner was cool, too, and he ignored the question in the man's voice.

"Have you met my wife?" Mr. Reddick asked. "Josie, this is Gray Edwards."

"Hello." Josie didn't offer a hand, and she looked at Gray with barely concealed dislike. She was a tall, slim woman with a beautiful face marred by her cold, hostile expression. I expected arctic winds to start blowing despite the hot, humid temps.

After introducing me, Gray said, "Hal's a builder too."

Ah, Reddick Brothers, a name even I knew. Competitors. Cobidders on the downtown project. That explained the chilly demeanors. Reddick Brothers had lost. Edwards Inc. had won.

Hal looked toward the front of the room where Ken stood, momentarily alone. "I bought our last two cars from him, and she was a partner in the CPA firm that handles my business account." He shook his head. "Her death feels so personal. Josie and I have felt like a black cloud has been hanging over us ever since we heard."

Josie Reddick nodded agreement though no tears sat in her well made-up eyes. "We'll miss her."

Clearly about as much as I'd miss pneumonia.

"It's going to be a bear for Windle, Boyes, Kepiro and Ryder to replace her." Hal frowned. "She was so good at her job. Even looked over my stuff recently what with Bob Boyes struggling with chemo treatments."

Another couple came in the door, and the Reddicks were forced to move on.

"Lovely folks," I muttered as we again stood aside to let the newcomers in.

Gray raised an eyebrow at my sarcasm. "Insightful of you to peg them so quickly. Most people think they're charming."

"I'd say that he's nicer than she is. He's competitive like guys are, doing everything to win but moving on if he loses. While you'll never be his good buddy, he doesn't hate you. But Josie? Different story. She disliked me on sight simply because I'm with you. Going by that look in her eyes, she's never going to forget that you beat Hal. Never."

"So it's a good thing that our paths rarely cross. Is that what you're saying?" He sounded amused as he leaned past me to hold the door.

I turned to answer and found his face very near mine. I could smell his shaving lotion, a smooth evergreen fragrance. It made me think of tall trees and woodsmen, strong things, just like Gray. "J-just don't let her find you in a dark, empty alley." I looked over his shoulder at the Reddicks gladhanding everyone they passed. I looked back at Gray. "But I can tell that the best man definitely won."

Gray grinned, his dark eyes warm and pleased. "Thanks, Anna. That means a lot."

I gulped and hurried through the door. Talk about charm!

He took my elbow as we walked across the parking lot, and I liked the feel of his fingers on my skin. Since Glenn all those long years ago, I hadn't let myself be so attracted to a man. Sure, I'd dated. Sure, I'd enjoyed conversation with men. In fact I liked men's way of looking at life. But…

"You know, their house is my very favorite," I said to get my mind back on mundane things. "Ever seen it?"

Gray shook his head.

"Big barn with an addition. Huge. Wonderful landscaping. And guess what? They have my window treatments in all their windows."

"And Josie didn't even recognize you?" Gray shook his head.

"She never met me. She only dealt with the interior designer, not the lowly seamstress."

"I can't say that surprises me." He opened the passenger door for me. "But it was definitely her loss."

The intensity of his gaze made my breath catch. I was grateful for the few moments that I sat in the truck alone as Gray walked to the driver's side. By the time he climbed behind the wheel, I felt I had myself in hand. I sighed. I'd better, for the sake of my mental and emotional health.

We drove for a few minutes in silence. Gray seemed lost in his own thoughts, and I had no idea what they might be. It was a relief to reach home. Gray followed me in with the intent of checking out the house for intruders once again. He stripped off his tie and stuck it back in his pocket.

Rocky greeted us, delighted that I had come home. He

wiggled so hard it was a wonder he didn't dislocate something spinal. Tipsy lurked in the background, clearly still ticked at having to share his home with this interloper.

I leaned over Rocky, rubbing his ears and scratching his head. "Any visitors while we were gone?"

"I'm going to check the basement to be sure." Gray rolled up his sleeves as he headed for the stairs. Rocky abandoned me without a second thought for the fun of accompanying Gray.

"You're not supposed to go down there," I told both of them.

"We won't touch anything. Besides, there's no other way to be certain there's no one lurking," he said, the very soul of reason.

I couldn't argue with his logic. "I won't turn you in to Poole unless it's either you or me." I grinned. "Then it's you."

I leaned down and lifted Tipsy so he wouldn't feel totally left out. What an armload! At first he held himself stiffly, miffed that I'd loved on Rocky first. I kissed Tips on the top of his head. He turned, showed me his fangs, then melted against me.

I stared at him, struck by an unexpected thought. "Is all that fang-showing supposed to be a smile?"

Tips gave no answer, just settled more comfortably in my arms.

Gray came back upstairs, proclaiming all was well. Rocky ran over to me and Tipsy stiffened, the hair on his back rising. He hissed his displeasure and swatted at Rocky who by now had learned to duck. Tipsy pushed away from me with enough force to leave bruises, hit the floor, and headed for Lucy's room at a run. Rocky loped after him, clearly delighted with the game of tag. I hurried after both of them and saw Rocky trying to wriggle under Lucy's bed to join his new best friend.

Since Lucy used under the bed for storing all her out-of-season clothes, I didn't give the dog much chance. In truth, I found it amazing that Tipsy could find room under there.

I changed into something more comfortable for the trip to Seaside and was throwing the last of my toiletries in my duffel when Rocky joined me. "Couldn't fit under, huh?" Fifteen minutes later, Rocky and I were seated in Gray's truck, me in the passenger seat, Rocky in the second seat, all buckled into his restraint, clearly miffed at his lack of mobility. He wanted to sit in Gray's lap.

Sorry, dog. I get first dibs.

"You're sure you don't mind him in your truck?" I asked Gray again.

"Anna, I work on a construction site. Compared to some of the things I have to cart around in this vehicle, a dog is nothing, even a lug like Rocky."

I turned to the back seat. "He loves you, baby," I said, rubbing Rocky's ears again.

Gray snorted. "I don't think that's quite what I said."

I grinned at him. "But it's what you meant, I'm sure."

Apparently Rocky thought so too because he leaned forward and rested his chin on Gray's right shoulder.

We were well along the Atlantic City Expressway when Gray glanced at me, curiosity obvious in his eyes.

"What?" I asked.

"I've been dying to ask you this question ever since you fell on top of me the other night."

"Don't remind me!"

"I ought to warn you." He pulled into the left lane to pass a van stuffed to the gills with folding chairs, pillows, duffel bags, and kids. "I learned from my sisters that it's always wise to have something embarrassing you can hold over the head of anyone you have a relationship with."

We had a relationship? How cool was that! Of course, the fact that it was Rocky who rested his head on Gray's shoulder, not me, said something about the depth of our liaison. "So what's your question?"

"Why isn't someone as beautiful as you married?"

Beautiful? Me? I almost swallowed my tongue in surprise.

"Or is there a guy out there that I don't know anything about?"

"No guy."

"Never?"

I felt Gray glance at me, but I stared resolutely out the front window. I never talked about Glenn. It was too painful, too humiliating. Even Lucy and Meg didn't know about him.

"Mmm," Gray said. "What was his name?"

"Glenn," I answered before I could stop myself. "But I don't talk about him."

"That bad?" Gray's voice was sympathetic.

"Worse."

"He stood you up?"

"Is sending you a note as you're waiting in your living room in your wedding gown, all ready to get in the limo for the ride to the church, standing you up?"

"Ouch."

"Yeah."

"Was there someone else, or did he just change his mind?"

"My maid of honor. They've been happily married for five years now." I could no longer decide whether that fact made me happy for him or sad for me. I guess the fact that the I'm-going-to-die-it-hurts-so-badly feelings had eased into the-most-embarrassing-thing-that-ever-happened-to-me meant I had gotten on with life.

"You still miss him?"

I shook my head. "I miss what I thought I had with him,

but not him. I'm not dumb enough to miss a guy who was an unfaithful wretch." Honesty forced me to add, "Though it took me a while to get to this point."

"Yeah, I would think so." His voice was gentle, and it made me wonder.

"How about you? Is there some girl mad at me because you have to play bodyguard all weekend?"

"No, no one."

"But there was." I made it a statement.

He gave a little puff of bitter laughter. "There was." He fell silent.

"Hey, I confessed my humiliating story. It's your turn. What was her name?"

"Becky. She gave me my ring back about three years ago. 'Here, Gray. I don't want it any more.'"

"Because?" I prodded when it seemed that was all I was going to get.

"Because she said I spent all my time working."

Now there was a surprise. "How long were you engaged?"

"Three years."

I stared at him. "Three years? You're kidding!"

"What's wrong with that?" he asked defensively. "Is there a rule no one ever bothered to tell me about the accepted length of engagements?"

"For a man who grew up with four sisters, you didn't learn much about women, did you?"

"Look, a man's got to establish himself."

"I say you didn't love her enough, sort of like Glenn didn't love me enough. He turned to Mae, you turned to work."

"I thought your degree was in art, not psychology."

"Well, you do like to work," I said, ignoring the edge in his voice. "I see you sneaking peeks at your PDA and cell all the time. I should hide your laptop for the weekend and make you have fun." I wished I had the courage to follow through on my threat.

Apparently he gave me more credit for guts than I gave myself. He turned to me, eyes flashing. "What is it with women, always knowing what's right for everyone."

I blinked, taken aback by his genuine anger. He saw my reaction, seemed to hear himself, and muttered, "Sorry."

Talk about not meaning what you say. "Right." I knew his reaction was as much or more about Becky than me, but it still stung.

We didn't talk for some time. I fumed; he fumed. I knew we were being stupid, acting like a pair of six-year-olds. Besides, starting the weekend off mad at each other wouldn't ruin it only for us, but for the others as well. I decided I would show Gray how I could be mature and magnanimous. Maybe he could learn from my example.

My cell phone rang while I sought just the right words.

"Anna? It's Natalie Schumann. I've got good news!"

"I could use some good news," I blurted, looking at Gray. His brows arched in question.

Natalie's voice became muffled as she apparently covered the phone and called to someone near her, "Yeah, I'm coming, I'm coming." Her voice came clearly again. "We've got him."

"What? Him? Already?" I couldn't believe it.

"They got the man in black?" Gray looked as surprised as I felt. "How? Where?"

I waved him quiet as Natalie continued, "They picked him up in his car just a couple of minutes ago."

Through the phone I heard music swell and a voice call, "Natalie, you're up."

"I gotta go," Natalie said unnecessarily. "It's my turn to walk down the aisle with a bouquet of ribbons from one of

the many showers. Corny but fun. Not that they need me.
There are seven bridesmaids, can you believe it? And that's
not counting the maid of honor. But, man, do I partner with
a gorgeous guy. Makes wearing the puce gown bearable. I just
hope the marriage lasts as long as the wedding, though I have
my doubts. See ya."

"Wait, Nat—" But the line was already dead. With my
head spinning slightly at this very different Natalie from the
professional cop Natalie I'd previously known, I started
smiling. "They got him!" My voice bounced around in the
truck cab. Rocky barked his pleasure. "They got him!"

I looked at the ceiling and spread my hands. "Thank You,
God. Thank You."

Gray grabbed my hand and gave it a squeeze. "I am so
glad for you!"

I felt light, as flyaway as a tuft of dandelion fluff floating
on a warm breeze. Once again Skip Schumann was the worst
thing to blight my life. I couldn't stop smiling. Gray's smile
was as broad as mine.

We turned off the Garden State Parkway and drove
through Somer's Point and across the Ninth Street Causeway
into Seaside. I glanced at Gray. By this time his smile had
turned wry. "I guess my services aren't needed after all, are
they?"

Uh-oh. I'd been so busy rejoicing that I hadn't thought
about his original reluctance to come with me. Now he was
trapped at the shore for the weekend with no purpose but to
have fun, relax and lie in the sun. Poor man.

"Your services might not be needed," I said carefully, "but
you are." I pointed at him and became the voice of a million
TV giveaways. "You, Gray Edwards, are about to receive an
all-expenses-paid vacation at the beautiful Jersey shore,
courtesy of James Stoner, millionaire. Included in this

exciting package are gourmet meals served on the deck of the millionaire's beach-side mansion, exciting nights walking and shopping on the historic Seaside boardwalk, and unlimited use of the Atlantic Ocean and the wide sandy Seaside beaches as your own personal playground."

He looked as pained as my father when he suffered acute indigestion.

I sighed. Such a party pooper. That Becky was one smart girl to run while the running was good, but idiot that I am, I didn't want to run. I wanted to save him from himself. How delusional was that?

"At least spend the night, Gray." I pointed to the dashboard clock that read five after ten. "It's too late to drive all the way home now." It wasn't as if he really wanted to go, but I couldn't think of any other argument.

He grunted, a noise I took for assent. My spirits rose, and I grinned.

"Wait until you see James's house. It's amazing, all glass and glorious views of the sea. There's nothing like breakfast on the deck overlooking the beach and the water. Everything tastes like a gourmet restaurant. Turn right here."

He turned. "I'm sure it's lovely."

Can you say noncommittal? At least he wasn't negative. I thought that was hopeful.

"I don't know who designed it—not Hal Reddick, I'm sure—but he did a wonderful job."

"Hal's not an architect. He's a contractor."

"See? I was right. He didn't do it."

We stopped at a traffic light and Gray turned to me. He was almost smiling. "You are something else."

I fluttered my lashes at him. "Is that good or bad?"

"Neither. It just is," he said as we drove the last block. We were smiling at each other when we pulled between the pilings onto the cement slab that was the parking area under James's house.

We climbed out and gathered our stuff. Rocky pulled at my arm, determined to shed his leash and run. A couple of hours in the car had increased his already near-manic need for movement.

James, six feet, skinny, with the family's red hair—though on him it was more a rust than a red—met us at the door. I could never decide if this streetside door was the front door or the back door since the house was built to focus toward the ocean. James gave me a quick hug and shook Gray's hand, then stepped back to look Rocky over.

"Hey, handsome." He held out a hand, and Rocky slobbered happily over it.

"I think you're supposed to offer a paw, buddy," Gray said.

Rocky grinned, clueless. I didn't need a crystal ball to see canine obedience class in my future.

We walked down the hall toward the living room, a now-leashless Rocky galloping happily ahead. He ran right up to and into the floor-to-ceiling glass which looked out at the water. With a shake of his head to clear the effects of the collision, he sat and stared with longing at the stretch of beach that called his name.

The house, two rooms wide but quite deep, had six bedrooms and six baths on two floors, which were really the second and third floors since the first was the parking slab under the house. The open slab was designed for the sea to flow through if a hurricane or severe nor'easter hit. The theory was that the house itself would therefore escape damage. That premise had yet to be tested.

I hurried upstairs and dropped my things in the bedroom that was "mine". Lucy and Meg had rooms across the hall.

The ocean side of the top floor was a great office with more floor to ceiling glass and glorious views. James wrote and worked there, though I always wondered how he could concentrate on anything but the seething sea. Gray was given a room on the main floor across the hall from James's.

"Lucy and Meg are out on the deck." James slid a door open, and Rocky charged out to slobber a happy greeting to the girls. I managed to grab him and click on his leash. I stuck the end of it under the leg of my chair. He looked disappointed that he couldn't run wild through the sand.

James and Gray seemed to click, especially when the two pizzas James had ordered arrived, all hot and cheesy with onions, green peppers and sausage.

"Ah," Gray observed, giving me a sideways glance. "The gourmet meals I was promised."

I made believe I didn't hear. Besides, I could tell he was glad to be here, even if he'd never admit it. The house alone was enough to fascinate an architect/contractor. Maybe he'd stay the whole weekend after all.

The five of us sat on the deck, enjoying the food and the sea breeze that kept the mosquitoes away. Meg and Lucy were delighted with the news about the man in black, and James was properly appalled at the whole story. The susurration of the sea was a gentle rhythm that pulled tension from my shoulders as effectively as the ministrations of a masseuse. By the time we all called it a night, I was ready to sleep for the first time in several days, and Gray seemed at least resigned to trying to have fun.

I slept well with Rocky at my feet, wakening to a warm, sunny day, perfect for the beach. What fun it would be to have Gray diving under the waves with me, walking with me along the water's edge, throwing his PDA to the fishes while I applauded as the dying waves washed around my ankles and my feet sank into the sand. Alive with optimism, I walked into the kitchen to see him at the counter, brow furrowed as he typed away on his laptop. Both his phone and his PDA were clipped to his swim trunks like little tumors. Even Rocky's drooling dewlaps resting on the man's thigh didn't distract him.

Aurgh!

# THIRTEEN

"What do you want on your omelet, Anna?" Lucy asked from her place at the stove. "Gray?"

Somehow Gray heard. "Cheese and onions." He didn't look up.

"Me, too." I grabbed knives, spoons and forks, napkins and dishes, glasses and cups from James's very well-supplied kitchen. I began setting the table around Gray, taking care to make as much noise as possible.

He looked up now. "I thought we were going to have breakfast on the deck." His expression was way too innocent.

"You could work on the deck," I countered, knowing he couldn't.

He shook his head. "Can't see the screen in the bright sunlight."

I smirked. What a shame!

"I'll just go work in the living room." He stood, preparing to gather his things for the move.

Curses. Foiled again.

"Hey, Gray." Meg gave me a sly glance, then turned an innocent face to him. "Help us carry the table stuff outside?" She thrust a tray into his midsection so that he had no option but to take it. She and I loaded it with all the paraphernalia for the meal and followed him to the deck where we became enamored of the sea until he started to set the tray on the table.

"Oh, no, don't put it down," Meg said. "Just hold it while we work."

We very slowly set the table while he continued to hold the tray. By the time we were finished, Lucy had breakfast ready, and Gray had been away from his toys for almost twenty minutes. And he wasn't even foaming at the mouth. It gave me great hope about his workaholism.

As usual Lucy had done a magnificent job with the omelets and fresh cinnamon rolls. Rocky sat, his leash attached to a porch post, watching every bite we took.

"You did feed him, didn't you, Anna?" Lucy asked. "I feel as if a starving kid from a third-world country is staring at me."

"He's eaten. He just hasn't learned yet that it's impolite to stare."

A few minutes later Gray sat back, a contented look on his face. "That was great, Lucy. I usually have cold cereal. Thanks."

Meg rose and started collecting dishes. I rose to help. The deal here, as at home, was that Lucy cooked because she loved to, and the rest of us cleaned up. Well, Meg and I did. We let James off the hook because he gave us all these free weekends.

Gray rose and started for the kitchen and his trusty laptop. Granted he was carrying his dirty dishes, but I feared breakfast had been only a momentary reprieve. My thoughts were confirmed when he looked at his cell phone, still clipped to the waist of his swimming trunks.

"Gotta call back," he muttered.

I saw my dream beach day dissolving like a sand castle in the incoming tide.

James got to his feet. "Hey, Gray, let the girls worry about the dishes. Why don't you help me set up the volleyball net? I put one up on the sand every weekend."

Usually Meg, Lucy and I helped with setup, but I didn't mind one bit being passed over in favor of Gray.

I watched him turn from setting his dishes on the kitchen counter to look with longing at his laptop.

Don't be dumb! He's your host and he's asking a favor. Do it!

Apparently Gray agreed with me. "Let me close things down and jettison my phone." He put his computer on hibernate and set his cell on the table beside his laptop.

"Your PDA." I rinsed a dish as if it didn't matter to me in the least whether he wore it or left it. "Sand will ruin it."

"Thanks." He dropped it on the table beside his laptop and cell and went off with James to hammer poles into the sand.

After we women finished loading the dishwasher, Lucy and Meg went to supervise the volleyball-net project. I dried my hands on a paper towel and turned to go upstairs to get my beach towel. As I walked past the table, Gray's phone rang. I stared at it. Should I answer it for him or let his messaging service take over? If I was in someone's house and their land line rang and they weren't in the house, I'd answer for them and take a message. Was etiquette any different for a cell phone?

Besides, much as I hated to admit it, there might be a work emergency.

I picked up the phone and hit Send. "Hello?"

There was a little silence. Then a woman said, "I must have the wrong number."

"You probably don't. This is Gray Edwards's phone. May I take a message?"

"Is he nearby? I'd like to speak with him. This is his mother."

"Oh, Mrs. Edwards. Hi. I'm Anna Volente. I'm the one who saw the murderer and fell on Gray."

This time the silence was longer, and I felt my face glow red. Why had I thought that Gray would tell his mother about me and my problems?

"You saw a murderer?" She sounded appalled when she finally spoke. "And Gray did too?"

"Yes, at Freedom's Chase. Me, not Gray. But he was with me when I fell off my ladder and gave him a bloody nose. That was because the murderer shot at me. Then Gray and I found the body."

"My goodness, Anna! And I thought all he did was work."

I didn't comment. It's just not polite to say unkind things about a man to his mother.

"So tell me all about this adventure of yours. All the details. It's the weekend, and I've got unlimited minutes."

I took a seat and told her everything, ending with, "So Gray's here at the shore pretty much against his will, but he's being polite about it. He's helping James—that's Lucy's brother—we're staying at his house—put up a volleyball net on the beach." I walked to the windows and looked out. "In fact he's playing volleyball at the moment."

I hoped his mother couldn't deduce the cause of my sudden breathlessness as I watched him dive for a ball and smile in triumph when he made the save. Wow! His smile was gorgeous.

"Do you know what an answer to prayer you are?" Mrs. Edwards asked.

"Me?" I think my voice squeaked.

"Mm. I've been praying for him for years to have some kind of personal life. I think it's wonderful that he loves his work, but no one's life should be only work."

"That's just what I tried to tell him, but he didn't take it very well." I remembered his sudden anger last evening.

"Stubborn cuss, isn't he?" his mother said happily. "Can you keep him there for the entire weekend?"

I shrugged. "I think so. I'll do my best."

"That's all I ask. Tell him I called and ask him to return the call when he can." I was laughing when I hung up. There was a woman I could appreciate.

I was smiling as I went upstairs and collected my sunscreen, beach towel, and book. I found Gray and told him his mom had called. Then I joined Lucy and Meg who had staked a claim on the soft sand above the tide line. We read and chatted and enjoyed relaxing. About one o'clock we went to the house and made some sandwiches. James and Gray joined us on the deck as we ate. Gray seemed to have had a wonderful time all morning. When he wasn't playing volleyball, which he did with great enthusiasm, he was in the water or playing handball on the tide-packed sand. It was very obvious that the man couldn't sit still.

"Want a book to read?" I asked as we prepared to go back to the beach for the afternoon. "James has a great collection of mysteries." Not surprising since he wrote them.

Gray squinted at me like he'd never heard of a book. "Let's take a walk instead."

We headed south toward the far end of the island that was Seaside. The water was a warm seventy-five degrees, and we walked in the small waves slurping onto the beach.

"So you don't read much?" I felt as though I was stating the obvious.

He shrugged. "I'm a doer. Reading is just sitting. Sort of like architecture."

"Like architecture?"

"Yeah. All you do is sit at your computer or your drawing board. Sit, sit, sit."

"You're a licensed architect?"

He nodded. "A Drexel grad. Two years with a Philadelphia firm was more than enough. Dress slacks, oxford-cloth shirts, neckties." He shuddered. "Becoming a contractor was one of the smartest things I ever did. Now I'm in on the projects in a real way. I get to wear jeans, I get to drive a pickup and I get my hands nice and dirty."

Yup, this was a man who loved his job. He told me how he talked his father and several of his cronies into investing in Edwards Inc., and that none of them had any reason to complain about their return.

"He must be very proud of you. You've done very well."

"I hope he would be." Gray's voice was soft. "He died three years ago."

"Oh, Gray, I'm sorry." I laid a hand on his arm, patting him a couple of times. "I know how painful it is to lose a parent." I told him about my mother, and before I realized it, I was telling him about The Promise. As I heard myself talk, I marveled at the level of trust I was putting in a man I barely knew.

"So I was an art major at Kutztown University, and now I teach art."

"And you sew. How does that fit with The Promise?"

"It doesn't, really. I started doing it to help put myself through college. Remember I'm the last of five, and Dad was really sweating by the time my bills came due."

"So it's your painting that keeps The Promise?"

"Yeah."

He studied me a moment. "You don't seem very happy about it."

How did I explain my ambivalent feelings? "I'm not unhappy," I said carefully as I watched the water lapping around my calves.

He stopped, took my hand, and turned me to face him. "But?"

"But I'm not really any good."

"Are you sure you're not being too hard on yourself? The picture in your kitchen is very nice, very good."

I made a face. *"Nice. Good.* They're just kind synonyms for mediocre."

Gray nodded, not disagreeing. I sighed. We resumed our walk, our hands still linked.

After a few minutes of silence he asked, "So what do you really enjoy doing?"

I didn't even have to think about my answer. "Making my fabric mosaics."

"Making what?"

"You know those strips of material you saw?" And I was off.

By the time I finally ran down, Gray had stopped walking again. When I turned to him, I knew I probably wore a goofy grin.

"Have you ever thought that your mother asked more of you than she should have?"

My grin vanished. "Gray!" How could he challenge The Promise? It was sacrosanct. Not even Dad could budge me on it.

He held up a hand. "Wait a minute before you decide to eviscerate me. Do you think your mother would want you to be unhappy?"

I scowled. Stupid question. "Of course not. She even said that being an artist would give me joy."

"Were you making your mosaics back then?"

I shook my head.

"So she didn't know where your artistic talent would take you, did she?"

Again I shook my head.

"Did she make you promise to be a painter?"

"No," I managed to whisper. "An artist, but she meant painter."

"Only because that's all you had done to that point, Anna. But there are different kinds of art."

"You don't understand!" I was trembling. I knew he was only saying what my father had been saying for as long as I could remember, but I didn't have years of resisting his words as I did Dad's.

"Oh, I understand better than you think. When I decided to leave my job at the architectural firm and begin Edwards, Inc., my dad was not a happy man. 'You mean I spent all that money on your education, and you're throwing it away so you can hammer nails and chuck your necktie? Just because you worked construction in the summers doesn't mean you can start a business and make a go of it. You just stay put, boy!'"

I was fascinated. "Obviously you resolved your differences if he invested in Edwards, Inc."

"We did, but only after I agreed to take a master's in business."

"Great compromise."

He grinned. "It was and it worked."

We turned and began walking back toward James's.

He bent and caught a child's float that had gotten away from its owner and was riding the waves to shore. He handed it to the chubby girl chasing it. She grabbed it and rushed back into the water.

"Thank you," I called after her.

"Yeah," she yelled back over her shoulder.

Gray tugged on my hand. "Listen to me, Anna. What I'm trying to say is that sometimes parents don't know what's best for their kids."

Stated baldly like that, I couldn't help but agree. But a

dying promise had a special cachet, didn't it, even when it was an albatross about your neck?

I must have looked frayed at the edges because Gray said, "I believe that God has programmed each of us to love certain activities. We are born with certain talents, and for Christians there are extra gifts God gives us for furthering his Church. We're only truly happy when we work in these God-given strengths. Anything else, and we struggle, filled with a yearning we can't explain."

My mind raced as we walked in silence for a while. Was my problem that I was trying to work outside my strengths? Could I stop painting and have a clear conscience? Was I following Mom's will rather than God's—or rather my interpretation of Mom's will? What would she say if she were living today?

I was so buried in contemplation that I didn't see the large wave that was a precursor to the incoming tide. It broke against my side, sending me careening into Gray, then falling to land on my rump. The rush of withdrawing water pulled at me, dragging me farther into the surf. The next wave broke over my head. I struggled to my feet, sputtering and laughing, knowing I looked like a wet rat. I loved the ocean.

The rest of the day passed in games of volleyball—I'm really not very good—and swimming. I even got to read a couple of chapters in my book while Lucy and Meg napped beside me, Gray played yet more volleyball, and James acted as referee. It was seven o'clock when we finally gathered, red-nosed and pleasantly tired, to go out to dinner.

"I'm going to take you to Moe's," James said. "It's a hole-in-the-wall restaurant with cracked seats and dinged tables and the best seafood in town."

"Tell me where Moe's is," Gray said, "and Anna and I will meet you there."

Trying not to read too much into Gray's driving just the two of us when all five of us could have fit in James's Acura, I climbed into Gray's truck and rode with him to the center of town.

At Moe's the five of us sat in a booth for four, James sitting on a chair in the aisle and forcing the waitresses to detour every time they served the diners between James and the front window. No one including James seemed the least bit put-out at the arrangement. If the fire marshal had been dining at Moe's, it might have been a different story.

After dinner we walked through the quiet streets to the boardwalk. I savored that wonderful seashore flush of sunburn and satisfaction as we started up the ramp to the boardwalk. The real-life murderer was in custody, I was with friends and the ocean breeze ruffled my hair. My feeling of contentment deepened when Gray reached for my hand and laced his fingers through mine.

I grinned up at him. The warmth of his return smile made the flush of the day's sun pale in comparison. My blood sang, and I wondered if this was what it was like to fall in love.

But hadn't I been in love with Glenn? I had been prepared to spend my life with him, to promise to love, honor and obey, though I'd probably have kept my fingers crossed on that last bit, wanting to define the word my own way. Glenn was a nice man, a good man, but I suddenly realized that I'd always felt I had to be what he wanted me to be, not who I was.

I almost stopped walking at the shock of seeing what a walking-on-eggs experience being with Glenn had been. What would a life of trying to be what he wanted have been like? If Gray was right, and not living in your God-given strengths led to a yearning, though you might not know what for, I'd have been an emotionally quivering blob, like a dish of cherry Jell-O but not as tasty. I'd have spent my life longing for something I couldn't articulate, something I didn't understand.

At that instant any residual hurt and embarrassment about being left at the altar finally disappeared. I'd made the most fortuitous of escapes. *Thank You, Lord, that Glenn was smart enough to walk out on me.*

Gray was so different, urging me to find the real me, even if it meant breaking The Promise. He might be a workaholic, but somewhere he'd taken time to think things through and arrive at his own conclusions. Me, I'd just accepted what I was told about all sorts of things. I was a real genius.

"I want to go on the Ferris wheel," Lucy announced, walking toward the amusement arcade.

"Don't you think you're a bit old for that?" James asked, as offensive as only an older brother can be.

Lucy stopped and glared at him. "My perfect brother James, how did you get to be so stodgy?"

He grinned at her. "Someone in this family has to show some common sense. Since you aren't that someone, I'm elected."

Meg scowled at James. "I'll go with you, Luce. I love the Ferris wheel."

"We'll go too." I pulled Gray toward the great circle of swinging seats. "If we're lucky, it'll stop when we're at the top, and we can see Atlantic City."

The man opened the safety bar and I slid into the seat. Gray settled beside me. He slid his arm along the back of the seat. The wheel moved us slowly upward as more people got on and off. Then the real ride began. Up, around, down, around, and up again.

I leaned forward. "Do you see James?" I spied him and waved. He waved back.

"Sit still, Anna," Gray ordered. "The thing's swaying. And sit back."

I turned to him in surprise. He looked slightly green. The wheel continued to turn, taking us round and round. Gray became greener. His knuckles grasping the safety bar were white, and I bet the ones behind me were the same color where they grabbed the seat back.

Big, tough Grayson Edwards was undone by a Ferris wheel. I had to bite my lip to keep from smiling.

"Is it heights?" I asked, trying to sound empathetic.

"Equilibrium," he managed between clenched teeth. We reached the top and he actually groaned. "Anything that goes around. And I hate the going-down part."

Personally I loved the feel of leaving your stomach behind. "I bet you're dynamite on a roller coaster."

"I'd die first."

"Well, there goes your career as an astronaut. They have to ride those centrifugal-force machines. Round and round."

He managed another grunt.

"Why'd you get on here then?"

"It hardly impresses a girl when your stomach can't even deal with the Ferris wheel. I was going to guts it out."

How macho was that. "How do you do on the merry-go-round?"

"It's a circle."

Enough said.

As we descended, Gray shut his eyes.

"Does that help?" I asked.

"I always think it should."

Taking pity on his obvious distress, I waved at the operator. When our chair reached the bottom, the man stopped the wheel.

"Open those eyes." I stood and grabbed his hand. "We're getting off."

Gray stood with obvious relief and without a backwards

glance walked away. I trailed him, trying to decide what deficiency in my character made me find his problem so amusing. It was probably because he was so very competent in everything else he did that this foible seemed endearing.

When we reached James, I asked, "What about skiing? Can you ski?"

"Sure," James answered. "Love it."

"It's not heights," Gray said. "It's circles."

I noted that his color was returning. I took it as a sign that I could tease him some more. "No Tilt-A-Whirl?"

He held up his hands. "The very thought makes me nauseated."

I looked back at the Ferris wheel in time to see Lucy and Meg reach the summit and begin their downward drift. I waved and the girls waved back. Their car began to rock back and forth.

"She's crazy," James muttered.

I shrugged. "You should be used to her by now."

"You'd think."

"But Lucy's always up to something."

James's eyes were still on the swinging car. "Oh. Yeah. Her, too."

I looked at James with interest. Was that the way the wind blew?

Ten minutes later the five of us walked slowly along, slurping soda and eating clumps of sweet, crisp caramel popcorn. The secret was to eat it fast so that the humidity, always present by the sea, didn't make it all soggy and chewy.

I stepped around a little boy of about three who had plopped down on the boards. Arms crossed, he scowled at his parents.

"Come on, Tyler, honey," his mother coaxed.

Tyler glowered.

"Up, son," his dad said, more a suggestion than an order. Tyler glared.

"We're going," his mom said and took a few steps.

Tyler, who wasn't born yesterday, didn't move.

"I've got to see who wins." I pulled Gray to a halt and tried to watch without being obvious.

"Tyler wins even if his father picks him up and carries him off bodily," Gray said. "It's all about control. Tyler is the head of that house."

I had to agree as I watched the father squat down to reason with the little boy.

Tyler continued to shoot daggers.

Suddenly the father grabbed the boy under the arms and stood. Tyler's eyes went wide with surprise, but only for a second. Then he howled. People turned from all directions to stare accusingly at the parents whose faces turned crimson.

Laughing sympathetically, I watched the little family walk quickly toward the closest ramp, Tyler kicking and screaming all the way. As they walked past the ice cream window of a little store, my eyes skittered to the folks in line. Maybe I knew one of them. Lots of my students and their families vacationed in Seaside.

Terror washed through me when I realized I did know one, and it wasn't a student. The man in black stood fourth in line, waiting patiently for a cone.

# FOURTEEN

The shock was so great I couldn't move. Finally I found my voice though it sounded thin and wobbly. "Gray!"

"Yeah?" Then he saw my face. "Anna, what's wrong?"

"It's him." I stared across the milling crowd to the ice cream stand. "See him? The man in black? He's fourth, no, now third in line for a cone."

Gray followed my line of vision. "He's supposed to be in jail."

I nodded. "That's what Natalie said yesterday."

Gray reached for his cell, but of course, it wasn't there. I'd talked him into taking the weekend off, smart woman that I am. I didn't have my phone either since I didn't have my purse.

"James!" I grabbed his arm, then pointed to the phone on his belt. "Call the cops. The shooter's here."

"At the ice cream stand," Gray added.

"At the ice cream stand?" Lucy squeaked, though she sounded more excited than afraid. "I thought they arrested him."

"You think bad guys don't eat ice cream?" James pulled his cell off his belt and hit 911. "I'd like to report that we've spotted a man wanted for murder. We're on the boardwalk near the—" He turned and looked for a street sign.

"Tenth Street," said Meg.

"—the Tenth Street off ramp. He's standing in line at the ice cream stand."

At that moment the man turned from the concession stand, cone in hand. Maybe he felt our eyes on him; maybe he just happened to glance our way. Whatever the case, our eyes collided. We both froze for a couple of heartbeats.

"I don't think she believed me." James flipped his phone shut.

"You've got to admit, it sounds like a joke," Lucy said.

"So no one's coming?" Gray pulled me close.

"They're sending someone to investigate, just in case." James slipped his phone into its clip. "We're to remain here."

I heard this conversation, but it seemed a long way off. My attention was riveted on the man with the cone.

He recovered faster than I. His cone hit the boardwalk as he reached for the small of his back.

I turned to run, strictly a reflex action. I wasn't going to stand there like a paper target at a shooting range, daring him to hit my heart.

But he wouldn't shoot on a boardwalk full of kids and moms and dads, would he? But then again, maybe he would. How did I know what he'd do? All the more reason to run. Get him away from these innocent people before one of them got hurt.

"Go, Anna," Lucy ordered. "You, too, Gray. I know just how to take care of him."

"Lucy!" James reached for her, but she eluded him.

Granted I never knew what Lucy'd do next, but never in a million years would I have expected what she did do.

"Man with a gun! Man with a gun!" she yelled in a loud, authoritative voice that made me jump. She pointed at the man in the black clothes. She began striding down the board-walk toward him. "Get down! Get down! Man with a gun!"

Everyone stopped in their tracks, including the shooter, his hands stuck at the small of his back.

*"Gun!"* The word spread through the crowd. *"Gun!"* People began screaming and dropping to the boards. Many turned in the direction Lucy was pointing, trying to locate the danger.

"There!" Lucy shouted. "Over there!"

With hardly a second breath, James and Meg took up the call. "Gun!" they shouted, running after Lucy.

Gray and I sprinted in the opposite direction as fast as we could, sticking close to the storefronts as we went. I looked over my shoulder and saw the shooter whirl and point behind him.

"Gun," he shouted. "Look out! Gun!" He began running as if he was chasing someone.

"He's getting away, Gray." With a sinking heart, I watched the man limp toward the Ninth Street off ramp.

"Forget him." Gray tugged at me. "We need to get you to the cops and safety while he's occupied."

We tore down the first off ramp we came to, the one at Eleventh Street. The peace and quiet of the street after the roaring of the ocean and the shouting of the people was stunning. Unfortunately there was no one in sight, no one to call for help, no one to provide protection. Apparently everyone was up on the boardwalk, being terrorized as they tried to enjoy one of the last nights of the summer season.

"Here!" Gray pulled me into the parking lot at the foot of the off ramp. We dodged between parked cars, putting distance between ourselves and the chaos near the Tenth Street ramp. We almost ran over a guy standing beside an SUV.

"Hey!" he yelled as he pulled back in surprise. "Watch it!"

I slowed, but Gray kept pulling me onward. "He's trying

to break in," I shouted. "He's got one of those metal strips you stick down the door."

Without lessening his stride or speed, Gray yelled, "Let him. It's only a car. I'm more concerned about you."

You've got to love a man who has his priorities straight. I forgot the car thief and raced toward Gray's truck, parked just off Thirteenth on Ocean, which ran parallel to the boardwalk.

We stayed as close to the back of the buildings fronting the boardwalk as we could. The shadows were deepest there. I wished I had worn a black top or maybe navy blue instead of the white one I had on. I wanted to blend with the night and be invisible.

We snaked our way through two parking lots and around a dilapidated motel that advertised Beach Front on its partially burned-out neon sign, a clear case of false advertising if I ever saw one. Both the boardwalk and the businesses on the boardwalk were between the motel and the ocean. You couldn't even hear the breakers here, let alone see them or the beach.

We slipped into a bicycle rental lot. A long, low white building with a wide garage door housed two-wheelers, three-wheelers and bicycles built for two. In the morning the place would be alive with tourists renting the bikes to ride on the boardwalk, but tonight the place was dark and silent. We slipped along behind the building.

When Gray's truck came into view, I had rarely seen a more welcome sight. The panic siren blaring in my head lowered its volume by a few hundred decibels to nearly tolerable. I just might live through the night after all.

We peered cautiously around the side of the building. A row of Schwinns lined the edge of the lot, a heavy chain strung between the wheels with a padlock securing it to a huge metal hook set in concrete. Beyond the bikes across the sidewalk, parked cars lined the curb. Across the street a boardinghouse showed lights on the second and third floors. Voices and laughter came from the darkened porch of another.

"Looks good," Gray whispered.

I nodded. "I'm right behind you."

We crept to the line of Schwinns. I strained to hear any sound or see any unexpected movement. One of the lights on the second floor of the house across the street went out. Someone lit a cigarette on the darkened porch, the match flaring, the red tip glowing.

We straightened and had taken a step to skirt the bikes when I became aware of running footsteps somewhere to our right. Gray must have heard them too because he froze. I leaned around him to see who was coming our way.

A lone man ran down the sidewalk toward us. Though he was still a block and a half away, I could see in a pool of brightness thrown by a streetlight that he moved with a decided catch in his gait. He wore all black.

I went cold. "How did he manage to follow us in all that confusion?"

Gray grabbed my hand and pulled me down behind the Schwinns. "Maybe he's not following us. Maybe he's just trying to get away."

That made sense, and I immediately felt better. He didn't know we were here. Gray pulled me close and tucked my head into his shoulder.

"Head down," he whispered. "Don't let him see your face or the shine of your eyes. We'll just let him run past."

We huddled behind the bikes for the longest few minutes of my life. With my head bowed so my face wouldn't be visible and my eyes wouldn't mirror light like an animal's eyes reflected headlights, all I could go by were the footsteps which got louder and louder.

Doppler effect, I thought irrelevantly. I might not do jeopardy well, but maybe I could do *Jeopardy*.

*Please let him just run past, Lord.*

In the distance I heard the wail of a siren. Police responding to the excitement on the boardwalk? Then I heard a shout that curdled my blood.

"There he is!"

It was Lucy, calling from a distance, as if she had just sighted the man in black after following him off the boardwalk. Hopefully, Meg and James were with her.

The man in black heard the yell too, and he slowed right in front of us. I could hear his heavy breathing, the rustle of his clothes as he moved. I was a rabbit, my heart beating wildly, as I hid from the wily fox.

A shot rang out. I heard a scream.

I jumped and gasped, then clasped a hand over my mouth. Had he heard me? I tried to shrink to Tipsy's size.

He stood quietly for a moment as if waiting.

*Don't let him find us, Lord. Don't let him find us!*

He didn't. He limped off with amazing speed in the same direction he'd been going. When he was past us, I looked up cautiously. I had to see him go to believe we were momentarily safe, and I had to find out what Lucy's scream had meant.

I saw him pause for a moment beside Gray's truck, and my stomach plummeted. He knew Gray's truck. He'd seen it at both my house and at the model. But then the headlights flashed on a black Jeep about half a block beyond Gray's truck, and I realized he had hesitated as he pulled his keys from his pocket and hit the unlock button.

Neither Gray nor I moved as we watched the man reach his vehicle, throw open the door, and climb in. The engine turned over, and he pulled out, all without looking back.

When he turned the corner and disappeared from view, I felt like cheering.

We'd escaped.

We stood. Gray grabbed my hand. "Let's go."

I balked. "Lucy! I've got to find out if she's okay."

We left the Schwinns and stepped onto the sidewalk. When I looked back toward Tenth, I saw three silhouettes. Three. Lucy, Meg and James, all running in our direction.

Relief poured through me, mixing with the adrenaline already flowing. I waved wildly, and they waved back. When I turned to Gray, I was grinning like the latest lottery winner. He grinned back and clicked his key. The lights blinked as the pickup chirruped softly.

He stepped off the curb and walked around the cab to open the passenger door for me. "In you go. Then we find the police station."

"It's between Eighth and Ninth on Central."

I had a foot on the running board with my hip stuck out, all ready to sit, when a car, tires screaming, careened around the corner on two wheels. I turned to look and saw a black Jeep barreling toward us. Before I could even cry out, Gray pushed me into the truck and down. He jumped in and fell on me as two shots sounded.

I yelped automatically as he and I slid off the seat onto the floor, carried by the momentum of his dive. I landed face-down, my arms beneath me, my face inches from the accelerator pedal. He landed sprawled on me, or as sprawled as you can be in the footwell of a pickup truck.

I heard the Jeep speed past. Doppler effect again.

A drive-by, only I knew this wasn't one of those random things. The man in black had circled the block and come back. He had heard my gasp just as I'd feared, probably recognized Gray's truck too, and known we were somewhere near. He had given us time to emerge from hiding. Clever man, realizing we would never come out until we thought he had gone.

What if he went around the block again?

The panic sirens were blaring at full volume again.

"Gray." I tried to move but couldn't, squished as I was between him and the floorboards. "He might come back. We've got to get out of here."

Gray grunted, a sound I took as agreement, but he didn't move.

"Gray!" I tried hunching my back, pushing against him.

This time the noise he made was a groan, the sound of someone in pain. I felt something wet run down my arm.

"Gray!" I tried to turn over so I could see him, though I was terrified that I already knew what was wrong.

"Stay still and stop yelling in my ear," he muttered, his voice grouchy but thready.

Grouchy was good, I thought, but thready was a man barely holding on. "He hit you, didn't he?"

Instead of answering, he dropped his head to rest on my shoulder. I wrenched one arm free and reached to cup the back of his head. I twisted like a Cirque de Soliel performer, trying to see him.

*Oh, Lord, don't let it be bad. Please don't let it be bad!*

"Where are you hit?" I was proud that my voice was as calm as it was since I was shaking inside like a California bridge in an earthquake.

He raised his head a couple of inches, and my hand slid from the back of his head to his cheek with the move. My fingers were slick with blood, and my insides tight with apprehension. He gave me a crooked smile.

Then without another word, his head hit my shoulder again. This time he was unconscious.

# FIFTEEN

Dar screeched around the corner in his black Jeep and dropped his new pistol on the passenger seat. He headed for the Ninth Street Causeway. It was definitely time to get out of Dodge.

He seethed with resentment and fury. He felt like a volcano pulsing with gases and fire, ready to explode at any minute. He had to go somewhere and cool off before he did something fatal based on emotions instead of cool, logical thought.

What was she doing here in Seaside anyway? She was supposed to be in Amhearst, scared out of her mind, quaking as she waited for him to come finish her off.

Instead she was here on vacation, walking the boardwalk like a normal person.

What an insult.

Thursday when he'd left Freedom's Chase after the aborted attempt on Volente's life, he'd assumed that the snippy redhead had gotten a picture of his Taurus. He understood immediately that the days of that car were severely numbered. The phony papers and tags were for just such a contingency. That's when he decided that before he left Amhearst, he would take care of her. For good.

Instead he met that beast and lost his SIG Sauer. He decided he didn't care if someone found it. It wasn't like his identity was a secret any more. It was just a matter of time until they learned about Dar Jones, aka Jerry Como, aka Johnny Parson, aka Ronald Reegan, aka Bruce Springstern. By then he'd be someone else. Maybe Dom Cruise. Or Chad Pitt. Or Tony Blare.

The only good thing that came from that fiasco at Anna's house Thursday was knowing that the cops were busy at her house. He would have time to deal with the car problem and win himself time to get to Tuckahoe. Then the car could rot along with the old lady and her garage for all he cared.

He cruised the area, looking for another black Taurus. He found one parked under a large oak tree on Sterling Street. He pulled into a slot three cars down and waited, senses alert for any sound or movement. There were none. It was, after all, almost two in the morning. The neighborhood was asleep, the houses black, and the glow from the corner streetlight didn't penetrate the heavy canopy of leaves above the car.

He disconnected his car's interior light and climbed quietly out. He moved to the back, knelt by the trunk, and using a penlight held in his teeth for illumination, removed his license plate with a few deft turns of a screwdriver. He stayed crouched there in spite of the pain that tore through his leg and the sweat that coated his body, listening again for any noise.

Satisfied that he was alone, he pulled himself upright, then limped to the other Taurus. He smiled sourly at the Pennsylvania license with its blue top band, yellow bottom band, and dark letters and numbers on a white background. It was the standard plate, not a special like his warships. In less than a minute he had the screws loose, the plate removed and his plate attached instead.

He hobbled back to his car, blood flowing down his left calf and into his shoe as his movements tore the coagulating wound open again. Stifling a groan and the desire to be sick to his stomach, he knelt and attached the stolen plate. When he climbed back into the car, he rested his head on the steering wheel until the urge to vomit was gone. The four Tylenol he swallowed dry barely took the edge off.

When he finally headed for Tuckahoe and the nutty lady's garage, his leg throbbed in time with his heartbeat. He was buoyed by the thought of the other Taurus being stopped, the driver perhaps arrested as a murderer. Granted whoever it was wouldn't be held long, but he had to laugh at the picture of the indignant driver and the chagrined police.

In Tuckahoe he traded the Taurus for his black Jeep and headed home to Seaside for a good night's sleep. On the way he stopped at the hospital in Atlantic City to get the beast's bite treated.

"You were just standing there?" asked the young doctor who sewed the wound shut. "In your own yard?"

"Just standing there," Dar assured him. "In my own yard."

"You need to report it to the police. A dog like that can't be allowed to run loose. They may even decide he should be put down."

"It probably didn't recognize me in the dark, you know? It really has a bad case of protect-the-neighborhood."

"Still, it should be chained or fenced or something, not running free."

Dar agreed, flinching at the shot of antibiotics. At least his leg was blessedly numb for the moment. The bite had taken ten stitches. "I'll report the incident first thing in the morning."

"Check with your neighbor to be sure the animal had his rabies shots," the doctor said as he handed Dar the paperwork about follow-up care.

"Don't you worry," Dar assured him. "I don't want this to happen to anyone else. What if it's a kid next time?"

The young doctor flinched at the thought.

Dar drove straight home and poured himself a tall whiskey. After a day like today, he needed something badly. He sat on his deck in the dark and drank and brooded.

Anna Volente. Granted she was a pretty woman with her hair the color of a Sugar Daddy and her big brown eyes all wide and frightened, but she had to die. He sighed. Not that he minded killing her. He just hated that there would be no compensation for it.

As soon as she was dead and Dar Jones disappeared, he had to get a nose job. The thought made him shudder because he abhorred the thought of being unconscious and at the mercy of someone else. Still his beak was too identifiable. The pictures Anna had done for the police proved that. He limped inside as the sun rose and looked at himself in the mirror over the bathroom sink, studying its size and the bump where his father had broken it in one of his rages and then refused to let him go to a doctor to get it treated.

He finally went to bed and slept until midafternoon Friday. He sat on his deck in the sun the rest of the day, his bad leg elevated. He went on a DVD marathon of *Seinfeld* until midnight. He slept in on Saturday, then sat on his deck reading or napping all day, enjoying his house for one of the last times. When he left to kill her, he wouldn't be returning. He sighed. He had gotten addicted to the sea and sand. He felt free here, not hemmed in like when he was growing up in the Chicago projects.

Maybe the Florida panhandle should be his next address. Plenty of sea and sand there. Of course there were hurricanes too, more than New Jersey got. But he was a risk-taker. He nodded to himself, satisfied that he'd made a decision. The Florida panhandle it was, maybe somewhere around Destin.

He smiled as a warm ocean breeze flowed over his sun-heated body. He was only forty. He had lots of good years in him yet. His bank account was plush and would grow by a million or so when he sold this place.

Around seven he grilled the steak he'd bought a few days ago and ate it on his deck in the early twilight. It was a lovely evening, and he decided to go to the boardwalk. Normally he avoided the Saturday crowds, but he didn't have a choice if he wanted to wallow in the Jersey-shore thing one last time. His leg wasn't throbbing as much, and if he didn't walk too far, he could manage. He parked along Ocean at Thirteenth, pleased to get a spot so close to the boardwalk.

He hated that he limped. It called too much attention to him, but there wasn't anything he could do about it. He swallowed four more Tylenol with a soda he bought and decided he would get a cone for dessert. When he turned, cone in hand, and saw Anna Volente staring at him, he was so floored that he dropped his cone.

He'd automatically gone for his new pistol only to realize he couldn't draw it here. Then the weird redhead started toward him, yelling about a gun. The other friend and some guy joined her. After a frozen moment of shock watching them advance on him, he turned, took up the cry, and chased a nonexistent gunman off the boardwalk.

Running hurt so bad! He hadn't any choice, so he swallowed the pain and gimped along as best he could. He was on Ocean, nearly to the car, when that blasted redhead spotted him.

"There he is!"

He stopped, turned, and fired, knowing there was no accuracy from this distance. If he hit her, he wouldn't mind at all. Maybe he'd just take care of her after Anna for the pleasure of it.

Then he heard the gasp and spotted the white shirt crouched behind all the bicycles. He also spotted the silver pickup that belonged to the guy who'd made himself her bodyguard. He kept on going, knowing he'd have a much better chance of getting to her if she thought she was safe.

When he came roaring around the block, there she was, the perfect target. Too bad the boyfriend knocked her down.

So now he was going to have to ditch his Jeep. He began counting all that she had cost him: his beloved house, his well-established life, his cars, and most galling, his perfect record as a hit man.

One thing was crystal-clear to him amid all the havoc: he wasn't finished with her yet.

# SIXTEEN

"Gray!"

He didn't move. I couldn't move.

"Gray!" I began to cry, tears streaming all over the pickup's carpet. I gasped for air as I sobbed, his dead weight making it difficult for me to draw breath.

*Oh, Lord, please don't let him be dead!*

It was all my fault. If I hadn't gasped….

I felt light-headed as I struggled to inhale. "Gray! Please answer me!"

Through the ringing in my ears I heard running footfalls. My heart turned over. Was the man in black back? If that was the case and Gray wasn't already dead, he soon would be—and so would I!

"Anna! Anna! Are you all right?"

Relief washed over me. It was Lucy, Meg and James.

"Call 911!" I tried to shout, but tears and lack of breath clogged my throat. "Gray's been shot. He's bleeding badly."

The driver's door was wrenched open and Meg appeared. I recognized her by the initials on the buckle of her belt. I couldn't raise my head to see higher. She dropped down.

"Are you all right? Did he shoot you, too?"

"Not me," I managed. "Just G-Gray. He saved my l-life by p-pushing me out of danger." I was blubbering so hard I could barely talk. "Get him out of here. We've got to st-staunch the bleeding."

Even as I talked, I could feel Gray's weight shifting. I drew a deep breath and felt the dizziness recede.

"I've got him." It was James. Slowly he pulled Gray from the truck. As soon as the weight was lifted, I pulled myself onto my knees, bumping my head on the steering column in the process. I grabbed Meg's extended hand and climbed out the driver's door just as James half walked, half carried the semi-coherent Gray to the sidewalk.

Relief made my knees weak. He wasn't dead! *Thank You, Lord!*

Lights had come back on at the house across the street, and the people on the porch at the other house were running toward us.

"We called 911," yelled one young man.

I rushed over and took Gray's other arm as James lowered him to the curb. Lucy followed with her phone at her ear.

"Hurry!" she ordered.

When I glanced up, I could see a man at the window of the house across the street, a phone to his ear. Good. The more calls, the faster the response.

"That car just drove by and shot you!" one of the porch-sitters said, appalled and shocked.

"Better than TV," muttered another in what I thought a terrible show of callousness.

James pulled his T-shirt off and wiped it across Gray's forehead and face.

"There!" I pointed to where blood welled from a long scrape on the left side of his skull. James pressed his shirt against the wound, his other hand holding Gray's head steady.

I sank to the curb beside Gray and told myself to stop crying. I wiped my eyes with the tail of my shirt and sniffed.

Meg stuffed some tissues in my hand, undoubtedly for my use. Instead I gently wiped blood from Gray's face.

"Déjà vu," he muttered.

"Yeah. How do you feel?" I mopped more blood from his brow.

He just slanted his eyes at me.

"Stupid question. Sorry."

"I didn't realize it hurt this much to be shot," Gray groused. "In the movies they just keep on fighting or they ride stoically into the sunset."

"In the movies the blood isn't real either," I said.

"Yeah." He swiped at blood I had missed as it ran down his cheek. "You know, Anna, we've got to stop meeting like this. I can't afford any more blood loss."

At his humor my eyes filled with tears again, and I dropped my head to his shoulder. "Oh, Gray, I'm sorry. All I've brought you is trouble and pain."

"True. It's a good thing you're worth it." He slid an arm around me and squeezed. I began to cry in earnest. What if I had lost him? I couldn't even imagine how much that would hurt.

"Shh," he whispered. "I'm fine."

"Liar," I whispered back and kissed his cheek.

He smiled. Just when I decided I could lean on him forever, he pulled abruptly away. His face twisted in pain and he grabbed at his stomach. With a cry of "Urp," he lurched forward and was sick, just missing my sandaled feet.

"Concussion," James said.

I nodded. Poor Gray. Meg handed over another fistful of tissues, and Gray wiped his mouth with a shaking hand.

"Did you see him limping, Anna?" Lucy demanded, demonstrating as she paced back and forth between two telephone poles. "Rocky got him good, and he's limping!"

Meg nodded with satisfaction. "I bet having to run like that didn't help any. I bet he's in pain as we speak."

I hoped so, then felt immediately guilty. In spite of David's psalms where he asks God to take out his enemies, I wasn't sure whether my serves-him-right-and-I-hope-he-really-hurts feelings were something God would like. They sort of clashed with love your enemies; do good to those who persecute you.

Anyone who thought being a Christian was easy had no idea.

In a remarkably short time, the ambulance and the cops arrived, and our porch audience stood beside us as we watched the EMTs load Gray onto a stretcher and start IVs. They wouldn't let me ride with him in the ambulance even though I said please, and the police wouldn't let me take the truck because it was now a crime scene. James drove us all to the hospital in his Acura, right behind the ambulance which didn't have its siren on, a good sign, I thought.

It was several very long hours before we were allowed to see Gray, and the police helped us pass the time by interrogating us one by one about the "incident."

Finally they let us visit with Gray for a few minutes after he was all finished being scanned, X-rayed, disinfected, stitched and bandaged. He had antibiotic IVs dripping into his arm and an impressive-looking bandage wrapped about his head like a turban.

I started to cry again as soon as I saw him, lying there so pale.

"Don't worry," he said, sounding remarkably normal. "I'm fine."

"Your mom's going to kill me. I'm supposed to make sure you have a relaxing weekend."

"I'm relaxing," he said and proved it with a yawn.

I hiccupped and wished for a tissue to blow my nose.

"The bandage makes it look worse than it is," his nurse assured me as she checked the automatic blood pressure cuff on his bicep. "The bullet just grazed him. No penetration of the skull. He's a lucky man. He has a slight concussion, so we're going to keep him for observation overnight. He'll probably be released tomorrow morning. You can call to check on the time." She smiled reassuringly and urged us all out of the room.

James drove us home, and after a shower to clean off Gray's blood, I climbed into bed. Even though I kept the light on for the rest of the night, I had bad dreams about men in black chasing Gray and me, shooting at us. Every time we tried to call the police, we got a busy signal. Every door or gate we ran through refused to shut behind us, and the shooter kept coming, emptying who knows how many rounds into us. While it didn't hurt, I was furious that my clothes were torn and bloody.

Dreams are so ridiculous.

I woke at seven from a new nightmare about drowning, in which, no matter how hard I tried, I couldn't get to the surface. I was pulling Gray's inert body with me, and another second without air would kill us both. The man in black circled us in his black scuba suit, air bubbles from his gear floating upwards. He was laughing. I could hear him quite clearly. Distressed as I was, I kept admiring the way my long hair floated so gracefully in the currents. It mattered not that in real life my hair was a chin-length blunt cut.

When I woke with a gasp and a startled movement, Rocky momentarily stopped licking my face. I looked at his lolling tongue dripping slobber. With a happy whine, he resumed his licking. Apparently he liked the taste of the face cream I'd put on when I went to bed. No wonder I'd felt like I was drowning.

"Eeyew!" I pushed him away and climbed groggily to my feet. I looked out my window at the wall of the house next door, then angled my head to peer at the strip of beach I could see between the houses. No bright sun warmed the sand today. I looked up and saw a gray sky but thankfully no rain.

James and I went to get Gray at ten o'clock. When the nurse made him ride to the exit in a wheelchair, he was less than pleased

"With your turban and all," I said, "just make believe you're a potentate with servants to fulfill your every whim, including transportation."

The look he gave me showed he didn't think much of my idea. He was barely through the front hospital door before he jumped to his feet and strode to James's car.

Male pride.

We made it home in time for Lucy, Meg and me to leave for church. Gray decided that with his great swathe of white wrapped about his head, he'd be more distracting than was good for a worship service, and James decided that Gray shouldn't be left alone, so the guys stayed home.

I love church. I love the worship songs and the old hymns. I love to hear Scripture read. I love a good sermon, whether it teaches me something new or reminds me of a truth I had forgotten. I always leave in a mellow mood.

"Wouldn't it be wonderful," Lucy said, "if we went home to a nice lunch the guys had fixed for us?"

Meg and I just looked at her.

"Yeah, you're right. I forgot I was talking about my brother here. He may be pretty much perfect, but even he has limits."

It was a good thing we hadn't counted on the men coming through. When we got back to James's, they were glued to the television and an Eagles pre-season game. They ate the lunch Lucy fixed while staring at the tube. We girls ate on the deck in spite of the overcast sky and the steady wind off the water. We read and talked and napped in lounge chairs until the guys joined us, elated that the Eagles had won with a field goal in the last thirty seconds.

"I've got to go to Atlantic City to drop some clothes off at the mission over there," James announced as he stretched away the kinks of sitting on his leather couch for almost three hours. "Anyone want to ride along?"

Since he seemed to be asking everyone, and since the wind was driving the sand so that it stung like tiny BBs, we all said yes. We climbed back into his car, guys in the front, girls in the back, and drove over the Causeway, through Somer's Point, Longport, Ventnor and into Atlantic City.

"I'll drop you guys at the Boardwalk and be back for you in about an hour if that's okay with you," James said.

There being no objections, we waved to James as he drove away, turned, and walked up the ramp to join the folks walking the boards or hurrying from casino to casino. It soon became obvious that Gray wasn't yet up to strength.

"This is ridiculous," he said with all the intolerance for weakness of someone who is rarely if ever ill.

"You were shot, remember?" I pointed out helpfully. "There are consequences when that happens."

He looked down at me with one eyebrow raised. "Thank you for telling me, Anna. I didn't remember."

"Mock all you want, but I'm right. There's a bench. Let's sit."

We did while Luce and Meg continued walking and window-shopping.

An old lady with wispy white hair, black penciled eyebrows and red, red lipstick strolled past, followed by a trio of young teen boys in cammie pants, boots and olive-drab T-shirts. A couple in golf-bright slacks and tops argued their way down the boards while several high-school girls in bikini tops and board shorts giggled at them.

"I love watching the people," I said. "They're just wonderful! Take those girls. Are they laughing at the couple for arguing or for their clothes?"

"The clothes, definitely." Gray looked very Pirates of the Caribbean in his turban with one of James's baseball hats, the back loosened as far as it would go, sitting backwards on top of the bandage. "I didn't grow up with four sisters not to recognize the don't-they-look-ridiculous giggle."

I looked thoughtfully at him. "I wonder what those girls would say about you with your turban?"

"Handsome dude," he said smugly.

"Confidence is good, guy. Conceit is deplorable."

He grinned, but I saw the little lines of pain around his eyes and in the creases of his forehead.

"Headache?" I asked.

He didn't answer.

"I've got some Tylenol if you want a couple."

"Thanks, but it'll go away."

I rolled my eyes. "Eventually. In the meantime, there's nothing wrong with easing your discomfort. After all, you were shot last night."

"It's not that bad. People who get headaches a lot would probably say it was only a two on the one-to-ten scale."

"Where do you put it?"

He shrugged. "I don't know. I've never had a headache before."

"What?" Surely he was joking.

"I'm never sick."

"Really? Or don't you allow yourself to admit it?"

"Why would I be that foolish?"

"It's some guy thing to prove you're Mr. Self-Sufficient."

He looked provoked. "What's so bad about being self-sufficient?"

Good going, Anna. You've put your foot in it again. "Nothing, I guess, except maybe you work too hard trying to prove you are."

If anything he looked more provoked. "I do not."

"Sure, you do. Your mother told me so."

"My mother also told me my expression would freeze in an ugly snarl if I kept making faces at my sisters, so we'll leave her out of this discussion."

I laughed. "Okay, she's out. How about if I say so."

"Anna, you've known me how long?"

"And I've never seen you without your laptop, cell and PDA."

"I happen to enjoy my work. Is there something wrong with that?"

I shook my head. "It's a blessing. I don't mind teaching, but I'm only doing it to make a living." A lot of people hated what they did. At least I didn't hate teaching, and that was good. "You're really very fortunate. All I'm saying is give yourself time to enjoy life too."

"Look, if Edwards, Inc., is going to be a success, and it is if I have anything to say about it, I have to work hard. I have to be self-sufficient. Nobody's going to hand me an established reputation. I've got to earn it."

I nodded. "You do, but my point is that there's more to life than work, even work you love. When was the last time you took a weekend off? Or a week off? Besides, being too self-sufficient can make us forget that we need God."

He studied me. "Am I getting this morning's sermon secondhand? Or are you accusing me of a lack of spiritual depth?"

"No, no. I'm not quite that presumptuous." *Help me ar-*

*ticulate my thoughts, Lord.* "I just know it's been my lacks that drive me to the Lord for strength and courage and guidance, not my self-confidence. It's our holes that God uses to develop us into the people He wants us to be."

The corners of his mouth quirked up, and he slipped his arm along the back of the bench. "Then you don't have to worry, sugar. I may appear self-confident and try to be self-sufficient, but I'm all too aware of the many holes in me and my need for the Lord to fill them. I know that without Him I'm lost."

More than satisfied with his comment, I leaned comfortably back, letting my fatigue from last night make me slightly foggy, my pleasure that Gray was beside me make me much more than slightly happy. Many of the people passing in front of us carried cardboard tubs of coins as they wandered from casino to casino, hoping the slots in the next gave better returns than those in the last, never quite accepting that the house always won.

Hope springs eternal, I thought as Gray's arm moved from the bench to my shoulders. I jerked up straight. I blinked and stared. No doubt my mouth fell open.

"Gray, look!"

He straightened, his arm falling to my waist, pulling me closer. "Not the man in black again!"

I shook my head. "Stranger than that." I pointed.

Stunned, we watched as Ken Ryder stopped under the casino marquee directly across from our bench. He was smiling broadly at a glamorous blonde in a slinky black jumpsuit. Huge gold earrings the size of Hula Hoops dangled from her ears, and if her heels had been any higher, she'd have been standing on tiptoe. She leaned into him and kissed him. He kissed her right back.

# SEVENTEEN

For a few moments I was too surprised to move. When I finally turned to Gray, he looked as shell-shocked as I felt.

"Do you know who she is?" Not that I expected that he did. It was just that he'd known Ken and Dorothy, and I hadn't.

"Never saw her before in my life." He scowled ferociously at Ken who was happily oblivious.

I grabbed my little digital camera from my purse, aimed and shot. I got them kissing. I got Ken smiling at her, and I got her glancing at him coyly. I could practically feel the breeze from her fluttering eyelashes all the way over where we were.

We watched as Ken walked down the Boardwalk, his arm around the blonde's waist, hers about his. I took that shot too. I clicked on the photos I'd just taken, holding them out so Gray could see too. "Well, she's very pretty."

He shrugged. "If you like blowsy blond bombshells. I don't."

Interesting. I thought all guys did, at least to look at. My brothers sure did. I studied the picture of them walking away. "Maybe it's not Ken."

"Anna."

So I'm a wishful thinker. So sue me. "Maybe he's got a twin brother."

"I wish, but I doubt it."

"But he just buried Dorothy yesterday!"

Gray nodded. "In all my times with them, I never once got a whiff of something being wrong between them."

"Maybe he just picked the blonde up today. Maybe she's a convenience to help him cope with his grief."

"They looked pretty chummy to me."

"Yeah. To me too. There's an ease between people who have been together for a while, and they had it." Gray and I didn't, at least not yet, but we had a remarkable affinity and were more at ease all the time. I had great hope.

He sighed. "People can be so disappointing."

True words. I found myself irate at Ken for being unfaithful to Dorothy, and I didn't even know Dorothy. Sisterhood, I guessed. Girls sticking together.

"Makes me wonder if Dorothy had a large insurance policy naming Ken as beneficiary," Gray said grimly.

My breath caught in my throat. "Oh, Gray!" I looked at the facades of the casinos lining the Boardwalk. "Maybe he needed the money fast because he's in debt to some people who aren't good at extending credit when payment is due."

"He's got a thing about thumbscrews and torture."

"He fears being knee-capped." I jumped to my feet. "We should follow them."

But we didn't. Gray wasn't up to it, and I didn't know what good following them would do anyway. It just seemed we should do something if for no other reason than to let him know we knew.

I sighed as I sat back down. "He seemed so distraught!" Never had someone proven to be so completely different from my first impression of him.

"Well, no matter what we think of him morally, we do know that Ken couldn't have been the man who killed

Dorothy," Gray said. "There's no physical resemblance there. Ken's taller, leaner. The shooter is stockier, more powerfully built."

I agreed. "And the man in black is limping from Rocky's bite." My mind was racing. "So did Ken hire the man in black to do the deed? How would a car salesman know a hit man? Or even know how to contact someone like that? What did he do? Google Killers for Hire?"

"Hit men have to buy cars somewhere, just like the rest of us," Gray said.

"We have a paid assassin living in Amhearst?" Talk about a disconcerting idea.

Gray shrugged. "Maybe he lives down here somewhere. Maybe Ken made contact through his gambling connections, assuming that's what he's doing at the casinos."

"There's a logical assumption if I ever heard one."

"And the killer was in Seaside on the Boardwalk because he lives down here. In Atlantic City? In Seaside?"

We sat in silence, overwhelmed by what we'd just learned and by what we suspected.

"Poor Dorothy." I hugged myself in sympathy. "At least she didn't know she was killed by a paid assassin hired by her own cheating husband."

"*Maybe* hired by her own cheating husband."

"Maybe?"

"It's all speculation on our part, Anna. Just because he has a girlfriend doesn't mean he had his wife killed."

Gray was right, of course. Countless spouses, both men and women, were unfaithful, but they didn't kill off their mates. Still I found it a hard idea to dislodge once it had taken up residence. "We need to tell Sergeant Poole what we saw and what we suspect. We need to show him these pictures so he can find out who the woman is."

"We do. And here come Lucy and Meg, right on time. James should be waiting at the foot of the ramp."

The rest of the afternoon and evening, all I could think about was poor Dorothy Ryder, buying a wonderful new house with her louse of a husband, and all the while he was fooling around on her, maybe planning to get rid of her.

"I just can't believe it!"

"So you've said." Lucy turned around and looked at me as we worked our way through the crush of traffic waiting to pay the toll after crossing the Commodore Barry Bridge from New Jersey over the Delaware River to Pennsylvania.

"These people need to buy EzPass," Meg muttered as we drove slowly through the toll station without stopping. "It'd save them a lot of time."

We were on our way home, and it was almost nine o'clock, a good five hours after Gray and I had seen Ken Ryder and that woman kissing. Since Gray's truck was being held by the Seaside police, Meg was driving us all home.

"You should have seen him when Dorothy's body was brought out of the house the other night, or standing beside her casket at the viewing. He looked shattered." I elbowed Gray. "Didn't he?"

He nodded agreeably. "He did."

"An Oscar to Ken Ryder for his dual role as the devoted husband and the philandering spouse," Meg intoned.

Traffic eased somewhat as we hit I95 south, then 322, 202 and 30 west. It was good to be home. After we unpacked, we went to bed early, worn out from the weekend. Gray spent the night on our sofa again, though none of us expected the man in black to show. Still, a man in the house made me feel safer somehow.

"Not that I'll be much good if he comes," Gray said as he

watched me shake out a sheet and tuck it around the sofa cushions.

"Head hurting?"

"A bit. I'll take a Tylenol, Anna, if you're still willing to share."

I was. I was also glad to see the superhero had left the building. We all spent an uneventful night sleeping off the effects of the sun and sea and various degrees of nervous prostration. When I got to the kitchen for breakfast the next morning, Gray was showered, dressed and ready to leave for work, cell and PDA clipped to his belt, laptop open on the table. He'd taken off his turban and the non-stick pads that had covered his wound. I could see the shorn area and the crusting over of the injury. I couldn't help shuddering at what might have been.

*Thank You, Lord. Thank You, thank You.*

"Do you have a doctor to go to?" I asked, thinking about how new he was to Amhearst.

"Nope." He took the glass of orange juice I offered. "Just give me another painkiller, and I'll be fine. I promise to buy my own bottle today."

I looked at him in exasperation. "You sound just like my brothers. What is it with guys and the macho complex?"

He didn't bother to answer. He just put down his empty juice glass and picked up James's Phillies cap, adjusting the back closure to fit his head *sans* turban. The red in the cap clashed terribly with his orange T-shirt.

"What time is Natalie Shumann coming to take up bodyguard duties?" he asked. "I'm already late for work."

I glanced at the clock. Seven. "In about a half hour. You go on. I'll be fine until she gets here."

"She will." Lucy assured him as she put two slices of bread in the toaster and pushed down the tab.

Gray left, using my van, just as Natalie arrived to escort me to school. He pulled back into the driveway and followed her in.

"What was that about the killer being arrested?" he asked none too graciously, but I guess getting shot could be blamed for making him a bit snippy. "Anna nearly got shot Saturday night."

"And he hit Gray." The might-have-beens still made me weak-kneed.

Natalie paled. "I heard."

We waited, Lucy and Meg as interested as Gray and I.

"Apparently the killer, a man now identified as a professional hit man with more aliases than a redhead has freckles, exchanged license plates with another black Taurus. The arresting officer saw the license number we had a BOLO for, and brought the driver in. I heard that news just before the wedding rehearsal."

"That's when you called me," I said.

She nodded. "I had the weekend off, so I didn't know they had the wrong man until I signed in this morning, and no one at the precinct knew I had called you." She looked miserable. "I didn't mean to put you in danger."

"Of course you didn't," I assured her. "We never thought you did."

The others offered their assurances, Gray included. "We just wondered how the mix-up happened."

As color returned to Natalie's cheeks, Gray headed for the door. "See you all tonight."

"Dinner's at six-thirty," Lucy called. "Chicken parm."

As we gathered our supplies and purses, I asked Natalie, "Are you planning to stay with me all day?"

"Will you be alone?" she asked.

I shook my head. "Today there are meetings all morning and final prep in the afternoon. I'll be alone in my room, but surely no one would risk coming into the school with all the others around."

"Let me check with Sergeant Poole."

"Oh, I've got some new information and photos for him," I said.

Natalie opened her cell and relayed my comment. "What time is lunch?" she asked me. "He'll come see you then."

"The cafeteria's not open today. We'll have to meet off campus."

At lunchtime, Natalie escorted me to Ferretti's, one of Amhearst's better restaurants, where the sergeant waited in a booth. All that was left of his lunch was a smattering of crumbs on his plate. He looked at the prints I'd made of the pictures of Ken and Whoever with great interest.

"Do you know if he was much of a gambler?" I asked. I knew the spouse was always the primary suspect in a murder like Dorothy's and assumed they'd been doing lots of research on Ken. "Maybe he's in debt to the Mob or something?"

"Thanks." Sergeant Poole waved the pictures. "We'll check this out very carefully."

And I knew he wasn't going to tell me anything about the status of the investigation. I snarled mentally.

Natalie returned for me at three, and she stayed with me until Gray showed for dinner at six-thirty. She appeared again Tuesday morning to take me to school. When the students appeared, she disappeared.

The interesting and hard thing about teaching art is that I have all the students in the school at some time during the week. I knew almost everyone in seventh and eighth grades by name, but the sixth-graders, all one hundred and fifty of them, were new to me. It makes for a confusing time until I get them all straight.

Imagine my delight when I discovered that I had Skip Schumann's class the very first day of school. Welcome to the new school year, Anna.

It wasn't that Skip or the other kids in the class did anything overtly wrong. Oh, no. He was too clever for that, but his subtle disrespect poisoned the attitude of the whole class. I felt as if I were watching a union boss overseeing a work slowdown or as if I were living in a slow-motion film. Everything that took five minutes in real time took ten.

The smug look on his face when the passing bell rang and half the classwork was still undone drove me nuts. I showed great restraint and said nothing to him, but I wanted to pop him one. When he left, he practically strutted from the room, clearly king of his own small hill. I smiled sweetly at him just to let him know he hadn't gotten to me, though he definitely had.

We teachers are supposed to stand in the hall outside our rooms when the kids change classes or are at their lockers. We're supposed to prevent riots and control the chaos. With my typical luck, Skip's class was assigned lockers between my room and the next. At the end of the day the kids were clanging their doors, slapping their books, and talking at a dull roar. The girls' high-pitched squeals and giggles mixed with the deeper guffaws of the guys. A typical close of a school day.

In one of those lulls that sometimes happens in a crowd, Skip's voice carried clearly to me.

"Of course she's the murderer," he told the cluster of guys around him. "Why do you think my sister's been assigned to keep her in custody?"

I rolled my eyes. It took no brains to figure out who the "she" was that he referred to, especially since some of the boys shot furtive glances my way, glances I was careful to ignore. As the noise level increased once again, I moved closer to hear what other fabrications Skip was telling. He and his covey of pigeons were so busy concentrating on what he was saying, they never noticed me practically joining their circle.

"It was a very bloody crime, probably a crime of passion."

"You mean she killed the lady because she's in love with her husband?"

"Looks like it to me," Skip assured them. "And I've got inside information, don't forget."

Right. I could just see Natalie telling her kid brother all the details of the case.

"Boy, that makes A-TAG all the more important, doesn't it?" asked the largest kid in the group, a wonderful but somewhat slow boy named Jason.

Everyone nodded solemnly.

"Speaking of which," Skip said, "we still need some more supplies to finish headquarters since *she* messed us up the other night. Nine-thirty at the shed."

"I can't come," Jason said. "My dad's really mad at me since I took his riding mower for us to make into a tank. He watches me like a hawk."

"Well, you did steal the thing and hide it in the woods for three weeks," Skip pointed out. "He even reported it stolen to the cops."

"Yeah, but it was for A-TAG."

What, I wondered, was A-TAG? Maybe Natalie could tell me.

Skip patted Jason on the shoulder. "It was a good effort."

The boys all made affirmative noises.

"Nine-thirty." Skip shook his finger at them. "Don't forget."

More mumbling noises, though many sounded negative to

my ear. Skip seemed unconcerned. Apparently even if he was the only one at "the shed", he'd still get the supplies he needed.

"So why don't they arrest her?" asked Pete, a sharp kid with too little parental supervision.

I couldn't wait to hear Skip's take on this question, and wished Natalie were here. And then she was. She appeared beside me as if in answer to my wish, just in time to hear her brother pontificate.

"The cops are building their case. Nat says they can't act too soon, or she'll get off on a technicality when she goes to trial. I hate to say this, but we've got our very own murderer teaching right here in our school."

Over the kids' gasps and shivers of delighted fear Natalie's voice thundered with all the authority of her uniform. "Skip Schumann! What are you talking about?"

Skip jumped and spun, blinking wide-eyed but unrepentant. The other kids' eyes skittered from me to Natalie and back as they wondered how much we'd overheard.

"Hey, Nat!" Skip said. "Gotta go!" And the troops scattered.

Natalie's face was red, her mouth pursed. "I am so sorry, Anna!"

I held up my hands palms out. "Don't worry about it."

"You do know that I'd never discuss this case or any other case with the kid, don't you?"

I nodded. "Natalie, what's A-TAG?"

She groaned. "It's Skip's summer project. It stands for Amhearst Tactical Army Group. It's the boys' attempt to keep Amhearst safe 'from all enemies, both foreign and domestic.' That's a quote. They wear cammies, and they built themselves a headquarters in the woods behind my parents' house, and they skulk around in the woods training."

"They don't have any real weapons, do they?" It was so

sad that courtesy of Columbine and similar tragic incidents, I had to ask this question.

Natalie shook her head. "My father'd skin him alive if he thought they had guns." She grew thoughtful. "Of course they all have BB guns, and I did walk into the garage this summer to find Skip with a Molotov cocktail he'd just made using gasoline from the lawn mower."

I was shocked, though I wasn't certain why. My brothers had all been fixated on anything that went boom when they were Skip's age. One of them even made a bomb out of a piece of aluminum pipe he stuffed with match heads. He crimped the ends closed and using a nail, tried to hammer a hole for his fuse. The thing exploded. Because he'd used aluminum pipe instead of iron, the metal didn't shatter. No shrapnel, just a loud boom, a blinding flash, and one scared kid.

But I knew my brother, and he wasn't a nasty kid. Dumb, perhaps, but not nasty. Skip, on the other hand, was inclined to be nasty. I didn't trust him one inch.

"Don't worry," Natalie said, though she was clearly worried. "I'll talk to Mom and Dad. I'm supposed to have dinner there this evening. I go once a week to get a good home-cooked meal." She grinned. "I'm lousy in the kitchen." The grin faded. "We'll all keep a closer eye on him."

"You might set him straight on the question of my guilt while you're at it," I suggested dryly.

She nodded. "The curse of the late-in-life child. Everyone's too tired or too busy to train him."

On the drive home, she told me that they'd found out the identity of Ken Ryder's blonde. "Starr Goodnight."

"You're kidding." A laugh bubbled up. "That's her real name?"

"On her birth certificate."

"Sounds like something an exotic dancer would name herself."

"Her mother saved her the trouble."

I blinked. "She's an exotic dancer?"

"At a gentlemen's club in Atlantic City."

Dorothy, a partner in an accounting firm, sound, stable, reliable, and Starr Goodnight, an exotic dancer, exciting, sexy and uninhibited. Was Ken as schizophrenic in all his dealings?

We climbed out of the car and walked to the house. I could hear Rocky barking inside.

"Poor boy. It's a long day for him."

I opened the door, and he raced out, taking time to jump on me in greeting as he passed. He tended to nature's needs, then raced back inside.

"That was quick." I lugged my tote bag inside, Natalie on my heels.

Rocky ran to me but turned away when I reached out to pet him. He sat by the closed cellar door, quivering. Tipsy sat on the kitchen table, glowering at Rocky.

"Come here, baby." I pulled a treat from the cabinet and held it for him. He ignored it.

"Sergeant Poole, please."

I spun to Natalie. She was on her phone, her eyes on the cellar door, her easy manner gone.

"I think we've got a situation at Anna's. I need backup."

That's when I realized that Tipsy wasn't glowering at Rocky but the door. Both animals were telling us in no uncertain terms that something was very wrong.

# EIGHTEEN

Natalie and I waited on the front porch, Rocky pulling on his lead, desperate to be taken somewhere more interesting than a slab of concrete. Tipsy had taken himself to safety under Lucy's bed.

"Do you think he's down there again?" I rubbed at the goose bumps puckering my arms. Natalie's alert demeanor unnerved me.

She shrugged. "I don't know, but we're not going to find out by ourselves."

I stepped off the shaded porch into the sunshine, hoping the radiant heat would warm the chill inside. "Why won't he leave me alone?"

Natalie looked at me without speaking.

"Yeah, I know. I'm an eyewitness. But wouldn't he be using his time better trying to escape than chasing me?"

"Anna, do you seriously expect logic to be the strong point of someone who kills people for a living?"

I lengthened Rocky's lead so he could wander around the front lawn. "How does a person ever decide to become a professional killer? It's not a job they tout at Career Day."

"You'd be surprised at the evil men are capable of." Natalie looked both distressed and cynical. "I'm only a small-town cop and haven't even been on the force all that long, but I still have nightmares about some of the things I've seen."

I nodded. I hadn't seen evil up close like she had, but I read a lot. I knew of historical figures from Caligula to Hitler. I knew of Saddam Hussein and Idi Amin and other brutal dictators. I'd watched the Towers collapse on 9/11.

"Original sin gone mad," I said.

Natalie shrugged. "Maybe. All I know is that someone has to hold the line, and for some unfathomable reason, I want to be that person."

We watched the police cars swoop up the drive, lights flashing, though thankfully no siren blaring.

"Along with the help of several other armed people," she added with a slight smile.

Lucy and Meg arrived just after the police and had to park out on the road. They stumbled up the yard, faces full of concerned distress. I met them halfway.

"What's wrong now?" Lucy didn't even acknowledge Rocky's exuberant greeting, a telling sign of the depth of her anxiety.

"The animals were all upset and hovering at the basement door."

"He's down there again?" Meg was incredulous.

I shrugged. "We don't know."

After a brief consultation with the other officers, Natalie approached us. "Stand with your backs against the house," she ordered. "We don't expect any trouble, but just in case, the bricks will offer you protection. Just don't stand in front of a window."

While we were blinking at those words, she pulled her weapon, and with the other responders cautiously circled the house. As I watched the professional Natalie handle her firearm with intelligent ease, teaching intermediate art suddenly seemed like a safe and sane profession. In my own way, I might be holding the line too, but facing down Skip Schumann was vastly different from facing down a professional murderer. My respect for her and all those who worked with her rose.

We stood nervously, our backs against the bricks, waiting to hear what new threat lay in wait for me. I held Rocky by my side on a short lead. He seemed to sense something wasn't right because, alien to his nature, he sat quietly. When we heard the cops' cursing, their voices carrying clearly through the air, we looked at each other with trepidation.

The front door slammed open, and we jumped, waiting for the man in black to rush out. Instead it was a uniform.

"You can come in. The house is clear."

Thank goodness! We had just begun to smile at each other when he continued, his face carefully neutral, "Sergeant Poole wants to see you downstairs."

My stomach sank. My work. My sewing machines. My projects. My wave!

"Don't let the animals down there," the cop said when Rocky pushed his way to the cellar door, impatient to learn what had been concerning him for who knew how long. "There's glass all over the place."

I shut him in my room, and after making sure Tipsy was still under her bed, Lucy shut her bedroom door too. Then we went down to chaos, my heart crashing against my chest like storm waves crashing against the rocks.

Even before I saw the damaged machines, I saw the words on the wall, done in red spray paint that dripped impressively: You're dead. Believe it!

Then I saw the shattered sliding glass door. The ruler Gray and I had put in the track had held it shut, but a rock through the glass had circumvented our burglar proofing. The rock lay not too far inside the door beside a large stick used to finish the B&E. Shards of shattered glass crunched underfoot.

I groaned when I saw the yards of material that had been unrolled, tossed on the floor, and sprayed with the same red paint that marred the wall. Hundreds of dollars of fabric, spitefully ruined. The shelf for spools of thread that Dad had made me was ripped from the wall, the thread pulled from the scores of spools and knotted into a huge, useless tangle. My paintings that had rested against the wall at the far end of the basement had all been slashed repeatedly, the canvas hanging limp, the frames no longer square.

Most painful of all to see was what remained of the work I'd done on my wave mosaic. The part already stitched had been cut to shreds. The small squares waiting their place in the work had all been gathered in a pile and thoroughly sprayed with the red paint.

The devastation was so complete that I couldn't take it in. Lucy and Meg cried, but I stood stony-faced, the slashed mosaic bits hugged to my chest. I felt violated, invaded, shriveled by evil. I looked at the torn canvases and felt a wrenching pain as if somehow I hadn't properly kept The Promise. And the scraps of material I clutched were pieces of my heart ripped from my chest.

Melodramatic, I know, but true. And what scared me most was that there was no purpose in this violence except intimidation. The man in black wanted me afraid. He wanted me trembling, jumping at shadows, flinching at any sudden moves, unable to sleep. He wanted to dominate me as he played with me, the menacing cat batting around a helpless mouse for the fun of it before he took that first big fatal bite.

I have to admit that I felt like running home to Daddy. But choice doesn't have to be made on the basis of emotion. It can be made for other reasons like right and good. I could be

Marshal Will Kane standing for his principles against Frank Miller in *High Noon,* or I could run away like the good townsfolk of Hadleyville.

My decision.

"Anna! Anna! Where are you? What's wrong?"

"Gray." I heard the panic in his voice as his footfalls thundered across the floor over our heads.

He exploded down the steps, his eyes sweeping the room until he found me. "Are you hurt?" he asked as he grabbed my shoulders and studied my face.

I managed to shake my head, but the sight of him and his obvious concern started the tears and the shaking. I fell against him, my arms still clutching the mosaic pieces, sobbing out all the fear and pain of the past week.

He wrapped his arms around me and just held me, rocking me gently, making soothing noises. I cried harder.

"Take her upstairs," Sergeant Poole said. "You girls go up, too." He sounded very tired. "We'll be a while down here."

We went up, Gray helping me with an arm around my waist. It was a good thing because I couldn't see the steps through my tears. The four of us went to the living room and sat, Lucy and Meg in chairs, Gray and I on the sofa. He pulled me close with an arm around my shoulders. I let my hands fall to my lap, and the bits of ruined fabric I'd been clutching tumbled onto my hands, the sofa, the floor.

Meg made a distressed sound and began to pick up the bits. I watched without the energy to help. When she had collected them all, she held up a fist with fraying edges sticking out between her fingers. "Do you want them?"

I shook my head. "Throw them out."

"You can make another, Anna." Lucy sat forward, her face intent, her eyes wet. She swiped at a tear. "It'll be even more beautiful."

I managed a wobbly smile. What wonderful friends these two women were. By rights they should be asking me to leave their home before I got one of them killed or brought the literal roof down on our heads. Instead they were encouraging me to make another go at the wave. "Maybe."

"You must. Just so he doesn't win." Meg stood and gestured to the fireplace. "We'll hang it over the mantel."

I looked at the adequate painting I'd done that hung there now. A stone farmhouse flanked by evergreens, bathed in a brilliant sunset, very Chester County. I shut my eyes and let my head fall back against the sofa cushion. Gray made a little move, and my head rested on his shoulder instead. Bonier but much more comforting.

Meg left to dispose of the scraps, and Lucy followed. I think she mumbled something about starting dinner.

Gray picked up a slash of navy material Meg had missed and held it out. "Do you have any completed mosaics you could show me? I'm trying to imagine what it is you love so much, and all I can envision are Amish quilts."

I took the piece of fabric and crumpled it in my hand. I felt too tired to do anything as strenuous as walk to the bedrooms where the mosaics were. But he wanted to know, and somehow that was very important.

I pushed myself to my feet, swaying slightly. He steadied me with a hand on my waist. We walked down the hall, and the closer we got to my room, the louder Rocky's cries for freedom became. I glanced back to make certain that the cellar door was closed. It was, and I set him free. He lavished us with love, not seeming to recall that I was the one who had imprisoned him in the first place.

I decided to save my Noah's Ark for last and led the way to Lucy's room.

"I'm going to show Gray your cat mosaic, okay?" I called

to her before I opened her door. "And I'll let Tipsy out at the same time."

A muffled sound came from the kitchen which I interpreted as affirmative. I opened her door and pointed to the red, whimsical cat hanging over her dresser.

Gray didn't say anything for several seconds, and I began to fear hearing, "Very nice." He walked into the room for a closer look just as Tipsy stuck his head out from under the bed.

"Come here, Tips," I coaxed, holding out a hand. It was easier to talk to the cat than watch Gray as he studied my work. My heart beat like a flamenco dancer's castanets as I waited for his reaction.

"I've never seen anything quite like this before." He sounded amazed. At least I think it was amazed, not dismayed or what-can-I-say-that-won't-hurt-her-feelings. "Let me see another."

I nodded, abandoned Tipsy, and went to Meg's room. I pointed to the red rose over her desk. Again Gray studied the work carefully. I thought of the hours spent searching for the right fabric, the right shades of red and green, the hours spent piecing the tiny scraps, every hour satisfying, even when I struggled to make the reality match my inner vision.

"Another?"

I led the way to my room. Noah's Ark immediately drew the eye. Gray walked to it, even reached out to touch the lion's yarn mane and the porcupine's broom quills. He began to shake his head, and my heart plummeted. He didn't like them.

"Anna, these are absolutely amazing." His voice was warm with admiration.

"Really?"

"Really. They're creative and full of life and so unique. And so beautiful!"

Not *nice.* Beautiful. Unique. Full of life. I could have soared higher than any hot air balloon.

"Why aren't you hanging one in the model home?"

I blinked. "I never thought of it."

"Let the people coming through see what you can do, and you'll have more orders than you can fill." He grinned at her. "Your mother would have been so proud of you for keeping The Promise. These wonderful creations prove that you are definitely an artist big-time."

I looked from him to the Ark and back. I felt something tightly coiled inside let go. I began to cry again, but this time with relief. "I am, aren't I?" It wasn't the medium that made an artist. It was the heart married to talent. And the wisdom to recognize where the real talent lay.

Gray held me as I wept out all the years of frustration and failure and laughed with me at the sheer joy of being released to work guilt-free in my area of strength.

# NINETEEN

Dar Jones drove along the street by the rancher on the hill with a smug smile. Lights flashed on official vehicles littering the drive ahead, and people stood in the front yard. It didn't get much better than this, and he couldn't resist the opportunity to gloat, even if he was the only one who knew he was gloating.

He saw Anna Volente standing with the two who lived with her, the girl cop, and the monster dog. The only one missing was the Edwards guy. Dar couldn't understand this continual congregation of people around her. It was much more than the mere provision of protection. She was a people magnet, pulling people to her as surely as the sun drew the morning dew. As a loner by inclination and by profession, he simply couldn't comprehend why anyone tolerated, let alone wanted, such constant companionship.

It would make getting her alone and in close quarters a challenge, but what was he if not a man who loved testing his superior skills against the rabble?

He hit the brakes as if he was stunned by the activity he saw. He pulled off the road and climbed out of the car. It was a nice car, a black Volvo. The man who owned it lived a couple of miles away and was at the moment lying unconscious in his garage. The needle Dar had stuck him with had held enough to keep the man down for an hour. When he roused, he wouldn't remember what had happened. He'd wonder why he was on the garage floor and where the hour had gone, but that was all. By that time, Dar would have the car back in place and be long gone.

"What's going on?" he asked a young cop.

"Nothing significant, sir," the kid answered.

Dar eyed the kid. He looked about sixteen. No wonder they couldn't catch him if this was what they had to work with.

"Well, something happened." Dar looked significantly at the pandas.

"Vandalism," the kid said. "The coward's crime."

Dar blinked. Coward's crime? Coward? The burn began deep in his stomach, but he fought it. His face impassive, he managed a "Huh."

Someone should tell this kid that vandalism done right took nerve and skill. You had to case the place first, find the right time for the entry. Then there was a creativity and a vision in vandalism done right. Purpose.

Of course he knew that so many punks destroyed just for the fun of destroying that very few understood the demoralizing effect of vandalism, and fewer still used it in the battle of wits between quarry and hunter. Attack what the victim felt most strongly about. Strip her of her sense of security. Make her vulnerable, unsure, frightened.

And the kid dared call him a coward.

"So what kind of thing was done? And whose house is it anyway?"

The kid cop looked at him. Dar knew he saw a nosey guy with a backwards baseball cap pulled over unruly brown hair, a guy who wore black-rimmed glasses and a Mickey Mouse T-shirt, a guy who had chubby cheeks. Dentists used the absorbent pads to move a patient's cheek away from his gums and teeth as well as to absorb saliva. Dar used them to round his facial contours as well as to change his voice. He liked to think he sounded like Marlon Brando as Don Corleone in *The Godfather* when he used the pads. "Go to the mats." Stroke cheek.

"The house belongs to those three women," the kid said, pointing to Anna and her friends.

"How awful. Attacking helpless women."

"I hope they have good insurance."

With a wave to the kid cop, Dar walked back to the Volvo. Just before he climbed in, he looked back to the cluster of people in the yard. To his surprise Anna was looking directly at him. He smiled, then turned and paused just a moment so she could see his profile. Then he roared off.

He changed cars once again, driving his own black Jeep. He was confident that no one had gotten this plate number on Saturday night. Things had happened too fast. Whistling, he drove to a nearby bar, the kind that were so dark you could barely see who sat on the next stool, let alone the guy in the back booth. He ate a truly terrible roast beef sandwich which he washed down with a couple of bottles of beer. He was careful to sit with his back to the wall, his face angled from the door. He'd learned that you couldn't be too careful.

At nine forty-five he left for his ten o'clock meeting at Freedom's Chase.

"We need to talk. I'm getting nervous," the caller had said.

"She'll be dead in no time," Dar had assured.

"Yeah? Well, while you're at it, I have another job for you."

"Fifty thousand," Dar said, confident he knew who the second hit was to be—Edwards.

"What? That's extortionate."

"Take it or leave it. And I want half tonight."

There was a long moment of silence which Dar let stretch.

"Ten o'clock. Same place." The line went dead.

Dar grinned as he headed for the site. He loved his job.

# TWENTY

At eight o'clock I went down the cellar stairs and knocked on the doorjamb. "Excuse me," I called into the general confusion. At least it looked like confusion to me.

People milled around doing mysterious crime-scene stuff, and the noise level was low but steady as they consulted or spoke into recorders. I rapped harder and called again. One of the uniforms heard me on my fifth try.

"I need to speak to Natalie," I said. She was on the far side of the large open room by the walled-off area that housed the oil burner and water heater.

The uniform nodded. "Hey, Nat! The lady wants you." He jerked a thumb in my direction.

"Thanks." If I'd known yelling was the accepted method of attracting someone's attention, I could have done it myself and saved my knuckles.

Natalie looked up, as did everyone else in the basement. I smiled an apology at the interruption as I signaled her to come over.

When she reached me, she looked at me with concern. "Are you okay? You're awful pale."

I shrugged. What could I say? Well, Nat, I feel like the bottom has dropped out of my world, but on the up side, I know I can do what I love and still keep The Promise.

"I'm okay, I guess. But that's not what I wanted to talk to you about." I fidgeted because I wasn't certain she was going to like what I had to say. I glanced over her shoulder at all her co-workers. "Can you come upstairs for a minute?"

"Sure. Give me a sec." She walked to Sergeant Poole and talked softly. He glanced at me, and I offered him a slight smile. He turned back to Natalie and nodded.

We climbed the steps, pushing Rocky back as we opened the door at the top. Lucy and Meg had both left, Lucy for her first graduate class of the semester and Meg for her aerobics class and routine workout. Gray was working at Lucy's red table in the kitchen, so I went to the living room, Natalie on my heels.

"What's up?" she asked.

I cleared my throat. This was harder than I'd expected.

"Come on," she said. "Spit it out."

So I did.

"I think Skip was at Freedom's Chase the night Dorothy Ryder was killed."

Natalie just stared at me in stunned disbelief.

I pressed on. "Today before you got to school, he spoke of how I had messed up his opportunity to get more supplies the other night. He was speaking in that context of my guilt for her murder."

"Come on, Anna." Natalie waved a hand negligently. "You know what a trip he is. He'd have said something to me if he was there. He knows how important all information is in solving a crime."

"And reveal his guilt?"

"What guilt?"

"I think he might be the one taking supplies from Gray's building site."

"What?"

"Or maybe I should say A-TAG, not just him."

She looked at me, her expression hard and unhappy. "Why do you think these terrible things about my baby brother?"

"This afternoon he was talking to his cronies about meeting at the shed at nine-thirty tonight."

Natalie shrugged. "So?"

"So where's this shed? It's not the headquarters they're building. Skip said they needed more supplies for it. That's why they're meeting at the shed."

"And you think the shed's at Freedom's Chase?"

I nodded. I didn't like accusing her brother, but I was a firm believer in catching a kid in small crimes and dealing with the little wrongdoing so that he never went on to larger stuff. Dad always told my brothers and me that he hoped, even prayed, we got caught if we ever did anything wrong. He didn't want us to think we were clever enough to escape consequences because sooner or later they'd catch up with us. That philosophy made sense to me.

"I'll check on where he was the evening of the murder, but don't worry about tonight. My parents run a tight ship, and he's not allowed out that late on a school night."

She seemed confident enough to make me momentarily doubt my conclusions, but only momentarily. I was convinced Skip thought that whatever he wanted was his, and that he'd never met a rule he didn't want to bend or break to get what he wanted.

She saw my uncertainty harden into conviction. "Go on. Tell me what you're thinking."

"Where do the kids get their supplies?" I asked.

She looked at me blankly.

"The lumber? The nails? All that stuff."

She turned thoughtful. "I'd assumed Mom and Dad got it

for them since the headquarters is being built in their backyard."

"Can you ask?"

She sighed. "The kids even have a pack of shingles up there, though I'm not convinced they'll ever get to the point of putting on a roof." She fidgeted with the coins in her pocket. "They never heard of a plumb line. The thing will collapse before they have anything to nail a shingle to."

I could easily imagine the A-TAG headquarters because my brothers had built various clubhouses through the years. I, as little sister, was never allowed in, but every "secret" conversation was audible to anyone nearby, the sound leaking out through the many gaps between boards.

Natalie walked to the kitchen. "Hey, Edwards, what kinds of things have been stolen at your building site?"

Gray hit the save button on his laptop, then ticked things off on his fingers. "Wood. Nails. Screws. Shingles. Paint. A couple of guys are missing hammers and screwdrivers from their personal inventory. One's missing a power drill."

"In other words, stuff to build a headquarters." Natalie was fast becoming one unhappy woman.

Gray nodded.

"And you have a shed where you keep these supplies?"

"It's more like a small trailer that can be pulled where it's needed. The men come there to sign out tools they don't own or to pick up supplies. The wood itself is mostly scrap, left lying at the different sites, very easily taken."

"How does the thief get into the shed?"

"That's a good question since the padlock is always in place."

"And you don't have a night watchman?"

"He works midnight to six."

Natalie checked her watch, pulled her cell from her belt,

and dialed. "Hi, Mom. Yeah, I know I missed dinner. I'm sorry, but I won't be over tonight. I'm just getting off work now, and all I want is to go home and sink into a hot tub." There was a pause while Natalie listened. "Mom, you know being a cop does not mean regular hours. Could I speak to Skip, please?"

Natalie looked at me. "She says he's in his room working on his computer. His room's on the second floor." She thought for a moment. "Its windows look out over the roof of the back porch which has a lattice on the side."

Then Natalie's mother was back on the phone, and I could hear her almost as clearly as Natalie.

"Calm down, Mom. I don't think he's been kidnapped. He's just gone AWOL."

I swallowed a grin as I pictured someone kidnapping Skip. It'd be *The Ransom of Red Chief* all over again.

More agitated words flew through the air.

"Don't worry. I'll take care of it. Bye, Mom." She flipped the phone shut on her mother's voice and stalked toward the door. "I'll see you tomorrow, Anna."

"Where are you going?" I asked.

"To catch me a petty thief and slap him in juvie for the rest of his life."

Gray shook his head as he rose. "Not alone you're not."

"I'm not calling backup on my own brother."

"I meant that I'd go with you. Strange things other than your brother have been happening at the site as you well know. You shouldn't be alone." He looked at me. "I won't be too long. I just want to help scare this kid straight."

"You won't let Natalie go there alone, but you're going to leave me here alone?" I sounded as forlorn and abandoned as I could manage.

Apparently I wasn't completely successful because Gray

raised a skeptical eyebrow. "The basement's full of cops, Anna."

Minor issue easily circumvented. "And just how much longer do you think they'll be here?"

At that serendipitous moment Sergeant Poole opened the cellar door, pushed back Rocky who was delighted to see him, and stuck his head into the room. "We're out of here. Feel free to put some plywood over the shattered sliding door, but don't clean things up yet. Oh, and you need to call your insurance guy."

We nodded and Natalie said, "See you tomorrow, William."

"Right, kid. You've got Anna detail again." He glanced at Gray. "You're spending the night, right?"

Gray nodded. "The girls have a very comfortable sofa."

Satisfied, the sergeant disappeared down the stairs, firmly closing the door against Rocky, much to the animal's dismay.

As I comforted the dog with an ear fondle, I looked at Nat and Gray. "Well, that settles it, doesn't it? You'll just have to take me with you."

That's how we ended up in the trailer at Freedom's Chase on a cloudy, mostly moonless night, waiting in the dark. Both Gray and Natalie had parked their cars in the double garage of one of the almost-completed homes, so there was nothing to indicate anyone was on the property.

Gray's penlight showed shelves holding building supplies of all kinds, and I could see why Skip thought he'd found a treasure trove. Knowing him, he probably planned to have the biggest and best A-TAG headquarters in the whole of Chester County—as well as the only one. Gray flicked off his light, and we settled down to wait. I sat on the floor next to him, leaning against the back of the counter where the supply guy and the job foreman kept tabs on the millions of materials needed on a construction site the size of Freedom's Chase. The plan was that I stay out of sight when the kids appeared. Natalie and I agreed that if Skip knew I'd seen his humiliation, it would make matters between him and me worse than they already were. Gray would reveal himself at what seemed the right moment, but most of the action would be Natalie's.

After about fifteen minutes we heard stealthy footsteps and the low murmur of voices. Skip had at least one A-TAG guy with him. We heard them move around to the back of the shed. Bumps, knocks, an "Ow! I pinched my finger" and a hissed "Shut up, idiot" from their noble leader, and slowly a panel of siding slid open. I felt Gray shake his head as the mystery of entry was solved. How they'd managed to loosen the panel in the first place was something to learn another time. We moved so we could peer around the edge of the counter, any sound we made covered by the noise of the boys' entry.

A flashlight held by someone outside backlit the silhouette of a short, cocky kid standing just outside the shed.

"Follow me," Skip ordered, and he stepped through the opening.

Quick as could be Natalie reached out, grabbed his arm, and jerked it behind him. Skip yelped in fear and surprise and, at the sound, whoever was with him dropped his flashlight and ran. The abandoned light cast huge eerie shadows of Natalie and Skip onto the inner wall of the shed.

Nat wrapped her other arm around her brother's neck and pulled him back against her. "Got you, you little thief," she said in a deep, gruff voice.

Skip began to cry and struggle. "Let me go! Let me go! I didn't do nothin'! Help!"

"There's nobody here to help you, kid." Her voice was still not her own.

She loosened her hold on his neck, pulled her cuffs from

her belt, and slapped one ring of the restraint on his wrist. He began to struggle even more wildly.

"Stay still," Natalie ordered in her own voice. "Or you'll hurt yourself." I heard the click of the other half of the cuffs.

Skip stilled and looked over his shoulder. "Natalie?" He sounded incredulous. "What are you doing here?" Then anger without a trace of remorse laced his voice. "And what do you mean slapping cuffs on me? I'm your brother!"

"My thieving brother." She made no move to free him.

"Thieving? Me?" Innocence, thy name is Skip Schumann. "You think I'm here to steal?"

"You betcha."

"Aw, come on, Nat. Would I do something like that?"

"Then tell me why you're here, breaking into someone else's property." She stood, hands on hips, and glowered. When he wasn't quick enough with his answer, she snorted. "Don't worry too much about your predicament. Dad will probably bail you out tomorrow morning."

"Bail me out?" He squeaked on the last word.

Gray stepped forward, his penlight held to light his face. He looked fiendish, all weird shadows and angles, especially with the shaved spot on his skull. "Maybe I don't want him bailed out. Maybe I want him held for trial."

Skip bleated in shock and fear.

"Meet Gray Edwards, Skip." Natalie pushed her brother down into a chair. "This is his construction site. He's the man you've been robbing."

Skip stared open-mouthed. Gray looked back until Skip couldn't meet his eyes any longer.

"I want to hear why you think it's all right to steal from me." Gray leaned toward the boy, and I had to admit that I'd be intimidated if he stared at me like that.

Skip opened his mouth a couple of times, but no words

came out. He cleared his throat and tried again. "I'm not a thief!'"

"Then what would you call taking things that don't belong to you?"

Skip swallowed so loudly that I heard it. "We just, like, borrow them."

"Borrow." Gray let disbelief drip from the word. "That means you plan to return everything you took in the same condition it was when you took it?"

Skip frowned.

"You're a thief, Skip," Gray said. "Don't try and pretty it up. And there are consequences to being one." He looked at Natalie. "I don't suppose they still take prisoners at Alcatraz any more, do they?"

I bit my lip to keep from laughing. There was such a thing as pouring it on too heavily.

"We should have been satisfied with the stuff we already got," Skip said sullenly.

Natalie grabbed him by the hair and forced his face up. He squeaked in pain, but she ignored him. "You think you're only a thief if you get caught?" she shouted.

"Easy, Natalie," Gray said, putting a hand on her arm. "Don't let the big sister get in the way of the cop."

"Huh?"

"Big sisters pull little brothers' hair, cops don't."

She let go of Skip and stepped back, anger vibrating from her in waves.

Gray studied Skip for a long moment. "What do you think God thinks about what you did?"

Skip blinked. "God?"

"Yeah, God. What does He think of people who steal?"

From the uncomprehending look on Skip's face, it was obvious that he didn't think often, if at all, about God.

"You do know that one of the Ten Commandments is that you shouldn't steal, don't you?" Gray asked.

"Yeah, well—" He paused, thinking, and I could see the exact moment he had an answer for Gray. "But God always forgives, right? I bet that's even in the Bible."

Gray looked impressed. "Not bad, Skip, but God always allows for consequences, too."

Skip turned sullen. "What's that mean?"

"You have to pay for your crimes."

Skip slouched, frustrated and furious.

Gray studied the obstinate boy. "What if I'm willing to work a deal?" he offered.

I could see Skip's instant transformation, his cocky smile, his snotty smirk, in the dim glow of Gray's light. I couldn't help wondering how the kid actually felt inside. Surely he wasn't as arrogant as he appeared. At least I hoped not, or there wasn't much chance for him to grow into a decent adult. What he really needed was Jesus to change him, but I knew this wasn't the time or place to discuss that option.

"I'm offering you two ways you can work off the debt you owe me. If you cooperate and do both, maybe I won't press charges."

"What do I have to do?" he asked as if he were being imposed upon. He seemed to have no gratitude for the chance Gray was giving him.

"One, go to Sunday school every Sunday for the rest of the year."

Skip stared, wide-eyed. "You're kidding."

Gray shook his head. "I'm not. You obviously haven't understood the concept of right and wrong. Maybe a bit of teaching will open your eyes."

"That's mixing church and state. You can't do that." Skip's tone was smug.

Gray made a show of looking all around the shed. "I don't see the state anywhere here, do you? The whole idea of what I'm suggesting is to spare you the ignominy of dealing with the state and ending up with a record, maybe your name in the papers."

Skip slumped sullenly in his chair.

"As I was saying," Gray continued, "Sunday school. I'll even pick you up if you can't find a ride."

Looking disgusted, Skip muttered, "If I go, I'll find a ride."

"No ifs about it, Skip." Gray pointed a finger at the kid's nose. "You go under your own steam, or I take you and sit with you all during class."

"You wouldn't dare!"

"Try me."

I couldn't help wonder if Gray got that idea because his mom or dad had gone to Sunday school with him for a while in his younger days. The thought made me grin. I could just picture a young, scarlet-faced Gray slouched low in his chair, his parent seated beside him, smiling at the class.

"The second thing you must do is work for me every Saturday til the end of the year, organizing this shed and picking up any trash or mess around the construction site."

"Be a trash man?" Clearly Gray had offended Skip's tender sensibilities.

"Yeah, if you want to look at it that way. I think of it as site environmental control."

After ten seconds of silence from Skip, Gray turned to Natalie. "What time should I go to the station tomorrow to file—"

"How much do you pay me?" Skip cut in. "To be a—trash man." Scorn for the job went deep.

"Pay you? Kid, you're my indentured servant for the duration. You do not get one nickel."

Skip jumped to his feet. "That's not fair!"

I rolled my eyes. The kid hadn't a clue.

"You're sort of missing the point here, Skip." Gray leaned against a shelf filled with small boxes. "You're the one who wasn't fair. You took what wasn't yours."

"Yeah, well, you have plenty." He looked all around the shed at the full shelves.

"And that makes it okay?"

Skip shrugged and sat. "Well, yeah."

"Take off your shirt," Gray said.

Skip blinked. "What?"

"You heard me. Take off your shirt. I want it."

"You're crazy."

"Give it to me. You've got plenty."

"No way." He hunched his shoulders as if he would protect his ratty T-shirt.

Gray made an umm sound. "I bet you rode here on your bike, right?"

Skip nodded.

"I want it too."

"You can't take my bike." He sounded appalled.

"Why not?"

"It's mine."

Gray shrugged. "So get another."

"You can't take my stuff!"

Gray just stared at Skip, waiting to see if he got the point. After a few minutes, Skip lowered his eyes and nodded.

I felt myself relax. If the kid actually understood, maybe there was hope for him after all.

"Do we have a deal?" Gray asked.

"Yeah," Skip mumbled. "Deal."

After several seconds of silence Natalie spoke. "You were here the night Mrs. Ryder was killed, weren't you, Skip?"

He jerked at the unexpected question and refused to meet his sister's eyes.

"Answer me," Natalie ordered.

"I want immunity," he said.

I clapped my hand over my mouth to keep from hooting.

"You've been watching too much television, kid." Gray's voice was hard. "Immunity?" Natalie leaned down until she and her brother were nose to nose.

"Why, Skip? Did you have something to do with the murder?"

He jumped to his feet, for once scared. "No, never! We just watched. That's all, Nat. I swear."

They watched the murder?

Natalie's eyes narrowed. "What did you watch, Skip?"

"The cops at the house. That's all. We didn't see the murder or anything. We saw you, Nat. I was proud of you, being so important and all."

"Stow it, Skip." She pushed him gently back into the chair. "I'm not dumb enough to fall for a line like that."

"What else did you see?" Gray demanded.

"Nothing."

He's lying, I thought, and it was all I could do not to yell it out. But Natalie knew her brother.

"What-else-did-you-see?" she asked through gritted teeth.

He tried to stare defiantly, but when you're handcuffed, hulked over by two very angry adults, and only thirteen, you're at a disadvantage. He broke.

"Just the two people meeting."

"What two people?" Natalie demanded. "Where and when?"

"I don't know who. It was getting dark, and it was hard to see. I just know it was before the cops showed."

"Where were you when you saw these people?" Gray asked.

"Not too far from here, which, as you know, is at the opposite end of the development from where the cops were."

Natalie glared. "Watch the attitude, Skip."

Skip glared back.

"And what were you doing when you saw these people?" Gray asked.

"Sitting on the big dirt pile a couple of lots over, waiting for the guys to show."

"In plain sight?" Natalie was floored.

"Well, sort of. I was on the back side, digging a tunnel while I waited. I wanted to see if I could go all the way through without it collapsing."

Natalie stared at her brother. "Skip, what's your IQ?"

"My IQ? A hundred and thirty-four. What's that have to do with anything?"

"It didn't occur to you that if the tunnel collapsed, you'd be trapped?"

"Oh."

The kid didn't seem to get the concept of consequences. *Oh, Lord, help him reach his majority without inadvertently killing himself or somebody else!*

"Back to the people you saw that night," Gray said.

"Okay." Skip squirmed, trying to flex his shoulders. The cuffs must be making his arms stiff. "When I heard the car doors, I climbed to the top of the pile and peeked over. I was lying down so they couldn't see me, you know?"

"And you saw?"

"Two people. And two black cars."

"Okay, Mr. I-Can-Identify-Any-Car, what kind of cars?" Natalie asked. "Prove you're not just hot air."

"A Taurus and a Beemer," Skip said immediately.

"You're sure?" Gray asked.

"Positive."

My mouth went dry.
Ken Ryder sold BMWs.
Ken Ryder drove a black Beemer.

# TWENTY-ONE

$N$atalie uncuffed her brother and climbed out through the back panel of the shed after him. As I crawled out from behind the counter and came to stand by Gray, I could hear them talking.

"Dad's going to kill me," Skip moaned.

"I can only hope," Natalie replied.

"Do I really gotta go to Sunday School?"

"It beats spending time in juvie."

"Are you sure?"

"Very few guys want to beat you up in Sunday School."

"Huh. And I'm not getting paid?"

"Not one red cent," Natalie assured him cheerfully as they turned the corner of the shed and disappeared toward the garage that held Natalie's car.

"You and Natalie did a good job." I felt proud of both of them. "And I loved the punishments. Clever and constructive."

"Just so they work." He grinned. "I kind of like the cheeky little guy."

I blinked. "You do?"

"You don't?"

I shrugged. How did I describe how I felt about Skip?

"He's going to lead people his whole life," Gray said. "It's just a matter of who and where."

I grimaced. "That's a thought to make you shudder if he doesn't change."

Gray tapped a finger lightly on my nose. "You did very well, too, Anna. I know it couldn't have been easy keeping hidden and staying quiet."

I quirked a brow. "Is that a polite way of telling me I talk too much most of the time?"

"Not at all." He grabbed my hand and pulled me toward him. "In fact, I find you just about perfect, if highly opinionated."

I studied him through narrowed eyes, trying to decide if I'd just been complimented or subtly criticized.

"I meant that in the best possible way," he assured me.

"Yeah?" I said skeptically.

"Oh, yeah." His voice was soft as he leaned toward me. "The best possible way."

The air between us abruptly thickened as it did on a day with ninety-eight percent humidity when you felt you had to work harder than normal just to breathe. I willed myself to inhale. I couldn't tear my eyes from his.

He kept leaning slowly, slowly toward me, either suffering a very severe though slow-acting case of vertigo, in which case he'd keep on going until he was on the ground, or, more likely I hoped, giving me a chance to move away.

I was not moving an inch. My blood sang in anticipation. I forced myself not to close my eyes for the kiss I expected, wanted, longed for. What if he didn't give it, and I stood there with my lips pursed and my eyes shut? Talk about embarrassing.

When he was scant millimeters from me, his cell rang.

I sighed as he reached for his belt. So much for that kiss.

Was there a WA—Workaholics Anonymous—I could sign him up for?

But he only silenced the thing. He didn't even look to see who was calling. When his hand left the phone, it moved to my chin, lifting it. "Some things are more important than phone calls," he whispered. His other arm circled my waist.

And he kissed me.

My eyes definitely closed as I sank into him.

I wasn't an expert on kisses, having purposely limited the men I kissed. Certainly I'd kissed Glenn, but I'd decided a long time ago that kissing was too intimate to share with just anyone, at least romantic kissing. All around me I saw women who shared a lot more than kisses in what I considered an indiscriminate manner, creating appetites and memories that would make marriage more difficult than it should be, much poorer than the rich experience God meant it to be.

Kissing Gray made every other buss, even those shared with my former fiancé, seem like cubic zirconia instead of diamonds, the merest pretense compared with the splendid opulence of the real thing. Oh, my, I thought in the portion of my brain still thinking, I'm falling in love with this man.

When the kiss finally broke so we could both get our breath, Gray still had one arm about my waist and his other palm resting on my nape. I had my arms wrapped about his torso.

"Too good," he said, his voice deep. He gave my nose a quick kiss, then stepped back. "Way too good."

I knew just what he meant. Temptation for more had never been so strong. I stepped back too.

"We'd better go." He gestured toward the open back panel.

I nodded, wondering how many women got the kiss of their lives in a construction trailer. I have to admit that I'd dreamed of candlelight and soft music rather than hardware and tools, but I'd just learned that it wasn't where. It was who.

As I climbed outside, I couldn't stop smiling. He'd ignored his cell phone for me. Did it get any better?

Gray slid the panel closed. "Tomorrow we'll fix this so that if the kids try again, which I don't think they will, they won't be able to get in." He turned to me, hand out. I slid my hand in his, and we began to walk around the shed. I thought that I'd be happy to walk beside this man anywhere.

I glanced at him, strong and handsome, all that I'd dreamed of. Too good to be true? Did he truly care for me, or was it just the intensity of the night? Did he and I have a potential future, or was I just the woman he felt honor-bound to protect?

I thought it was more. *Oh, Lord, please let it be more! And let me mean more to him than his work.* But what if What's-Her-Name, his old girlfriend, came back? Would he leave me for another as Glenn had, and would I find myself once more embarrassed, alone and heartbroken?

The romantic music playing joyfully in my head began to sound off-key and tinny as it ground to a slow stop. Danger, danger, Will Robinson.

But the warning was too late. Gray had the power either to make me incredibly happy or to rip my heart out. And I knew that if he left me, the pain would eclipse the hurt of Glenn's defection as the brilliance of the sun eclipsed the light of the moon.

Gray stopped when we were still in the lee of the building, pulling on my hand to keep me in the deep shadows with him. My heart lightened as I turned to him. Another kiss?

"Do you hear that?" he asked.

I frowned. No kiss. "What?"

"Shh. Listen."

I listened as instructed and heard a car engine. It came closer and closer until it stopped not too far away. A door slammed.

"What's a car doing here at this hour?" I asked quietly. At least we knew it wasn't Skip returning for a second try at supplies. He wasn't old enough to drive even if he'd managed to escape his sister.

We peered cautiously around the end of the building and saw a tall, slim person leaning against the side of a car, waiting.

A black car, I thought, though I couldn't be absolutely certain in the darkness. A sedan as opposed to a van like mine or a pickup like Gray's. A BMW? Skip might be an expert at recognizing car makes, but I was the class dud. I needed to see the words written on the car to know for sure what any vehicle was.

Another motor purred in the distance, drew closer, and headlights cut the night before they were quickly doused. In that brief moment of illumination, I saw the waiting car was indeed black though I still couldn't tell if it was a Beemer or not.

"Is it a BMW?" I whispered.

Gray nodded.

In the brief flash of headlights I hadn't seen the face of the slim individual who waited because he looked toward the approaching vehicle and that meant looking away from us.

The second car parked, and another person climbed out, easily as tall as the first but heavier, bulkier. I could make out no facial features in the darkness, just the general body shapes. Both appeared dressed in black, which wasn't surprising for a night meeting in a supposedly deserted construction site. Even their body language suggested clandestine.

The two began to speak, and I felt incredible frustration because we were too far away to hear.

Gray breathed in my ear, "The two Skip saw?"

I nodded. I'd been thinking exactly the same thing. But why were they here tonight?

The stockier of the two turned and stalked toward the second car.

The slimmer one moved quickly, and the stockier one stopped. They talked again briefly. The slim one had his elbows sharply bent as if his hands were stuffed into jacket pockets. The stockier one stepped back quickly, reaching behind him.

I stiffened automatically. I'd seen that move before.

A shot tore the silence.

I jumped even though I wasn't surprised. Then I frowned. The stockier man's hands were still behind his back. The slim individual now had the gun out in the open, and a red light shone on the chest of the stocky man.

Another shot.

The stockier of the two began to go down as his knees buckled.

The slim one watched as the red bead appeared again, then fired a third time. Three point-blank hits, one apparently fired from the pocket for surprise, two sighted with a laser to the chest. By now the stocky man lay on the ground. The slim one reached down, straightened, then turned and climbed into the first car. He did a quick U-turn and drove away.

As Gray and I raced to the fallen man, Gray had his cell at his ear, reporting the shooting. We skidded to a stop beside the victim, and Gray shone his penlight.

It was the assassin, as I expected. His black hair was still neatly combed straight back, his jaw was slack below his beak of a nose, and he'd fallen awkwardly on his hands, still behind his back. Seeping slowly from three chest wounds was crimson blood turning his black T-shirt deep red.

Someone had cold-bloodedly shot the shooter, murdered the murderer.

My feelings were mixed. I felt horror that I'd actually witnessed a murder this time, not just the murderer leaving the scene of the crime. I felt relief that I didn't have to worry about every shadow, every unexpected noise. He was dead. I was safe. And I felt guilt that I could be glad a man was dead.

Gray knelt, and for the second time in a week felt for a pulse. The very lack of significant bleeding already told the tale, but we had to be certain. Gray shook his head.

I wrapped my arms about myself to ward off a bone-deep chill.

# TWENTY-TWO

"The police are on their way." Gray flipped his cell phone shut and grabbed my hand. "Come on!"

"Where are we going?" I yelled as I ran after him.

He dropped my hand at the foot of the drive three lots down. "Keep an eye on those headlights. Tell me which way they turn." He raced into the garage and got his truck. He backed out with a screech. "Get in!"

I did as he threw the shift into Drive and floored it. I grabbed my seatbelt and buckled up for what was going to be a bumpy ride.

"Where'd he go?"

"Left out the service entrance toward town."

Gray took the left out of the development at way too high a speed. I grabbed the dashboard to steady myself and bit my tongue to keep in my gasp of fright. We tore down the road, but we didn't catch the BMW. There were too many turns it could have taken, too many garages it could be parked in. After a few minutes, Gray's foot eased on the accelerator, and we proceeded at a sane speed.

"Was that Ken Ryder?" I rubbed at the tense muscles in my neck. "In the BMW, I mean."

"I don't know." Gray glanced at me. "Want to find out?"

I blinked. "How?"

"Go to his house. See if he's been anywhere tonight."

"You're not going to confront him, are you?" The last thing I wanted was Gray shot again.

It took him a long second to answer, and I started to sweat. "Gray, promise me."

He sighed. "I'm not going to confront him. If he is the killer, he's a dangerous man, too dangerous for me." As he spoke, he turned onto a tree-lined street with lovely but small homes, well-tended lawns, and window boxes filled with red geraniums and white petunias. Gray pulled to the curb and cut the engine.

"That white Cape Cod with the green shutters is the Ryders' home."

I looked at the house two down from where we sat. The azaleas lining the front would be a blaze of color in the spring, and a weeping cherry drooped leafy boughs almost to the ground. Light streamed from the living-room windows, reflecting off the dark, shiny surface of the black BMW in the driveway.

Gray turned off the interior lights of the truck cab before he opened the door. He looked carefully up and down the street and studied the houses between us and Ken's.

I slipped out my door and joined Gray as he walked hunched down the sidewalk. Quasimodo.

I walked as straight as I could, refusing to assume a dowager's hump before my time. We reached Ken's place and hurried up his drive.

"Down." Gray signaled to me with his hand.

We hunkered behind the car and crept carefully forward. I could feel the heat radiating from beneath the hood when I was back at the support between the doors.

Gray laid his hand flat on the hood, then drew it back

quickly, shaking it. "Hot. It's been driven very recently. Like minutes ago." He pulled out his cell and hit 911.

"They're going to be tired of hearing from us," I said.

"Right," Gray told Dispatch. "325 Sycamore." He hung up. "They'll be here shortly."

"They're probably at Freedom's Chase wondering where we are."

"Well, they know now."

I turned to Ken's place. "Gray, look!"

Standing right in front of the living-room window was Starr Goodnight. She was again wearing her Hula Hoop gold earrings, and her blond hair was gathered in a wilting ponytail on top of her head. She'd traded her black catsuit for the kind of jeans that cut off the circulation to the lower extremities and a red knit top cut so low it was a wonder she didn't get pneumonia even if it was the end of August. Her hands were gesturing wildly as she talked to someone out of sight, undoubtedly Ken.

The porch light flicked on, and the front door opened. We ducked, then raised up enough to peek through the windows. Ken walked out, a suitcase in one hand and a garment bag over his shoulder.

"He's running!" I hissed. I was almost glad Dorothy wasn't alive to see what a truly despicable person her husband was. Though philandering with Starr would never win Ken any points in my book, it seemed a mere peccadillo compared to the cold-blooded murders. "What do we do now?"

We watched Ken cut across his lawn to the car. He went to the trunk and lifted it.

Gray stood, rising from the shadows beside the car. "Hello, Ken."

Ken dropped his suitcase and grabbed his heart. He staggered. I thought for a minute that he was headed for cardiac arrest.

"G-Gray," he finally managed.

I popped up, and Ken once again and understandably looked startled, though a heart attack didn't appear threatening this time.

"You remember Anna Volente." Gray had the aplomb of a *maître d'* at a classy restaurant.

"Uh, yes." Ken nodded uncertainly at me. I nodded politely back.

"Wh-what in the world are you doing here?" he asked. "Were you hiding behind the car?"

"Going somewhere?" Gray asked, not bothering to answer Ken's questions.

"Vacation. I've got to get away. Too many sad memories around here." He managed to look the picture of sorrow. If the guy was going to Hollywood, an Oscar was definitely in his future.

"With all those suitcases?" Gray asked. "Guys usually manage to travel a lot lighter."

I peered over Gray's shoulder to look in the trunk and saw one mammoth red case, the size no woman can handle by herself once it's filled but that many use anyway, and two smaller ones.

"I, uh, I plan to be away for quite a while."

"A trip all by yourself?" Gray asked.

Ken shrugged, shoulders bowed down with despair. "I just have to learn to be alone, hard as that will be."

"Hey, Kenny."

We all turned to see Starr standing in the open front door.

"Do you have the tickets?"

Ken blanched. "My-my cousin. She's taking me to the airport."

Right.

"Hi, Starr," I called. "Where are you and Ken going?"

She started down the front steps in her stilettos. "Grand Cayman," she burbled happily. "Kenny's got a house there." She tiptoed across the lawn lest her heels sink into the ground and never come out. "Do I know you?" she asked, squinting at me.

"I'm Anna Volente."

"I'm Starr." She giggled. "But you already know that."

Gray pushed the lid of the trunk down and leaned casually on it. "Been out driving this evening, Ken?"

Ken, still reeling from Starr's inauspicious appearance and generously offered information, said, "Uh."

"There's been another murder at Freedom's Chase," Gray said.

Ken stared at Gray wide-eyed. He looked surprised, but he'd looked lonely too.

Starr was shocked. "Oh, no. Not another lady! I felt so bad about Dorothy."

"You knew Dorothy?" I asked.

"Oh, no." She flapped her hand as if Dorothy were a wisp of smoke she could wave away. "I just knew about her. Kenny told me stuff, you know?"

I nodded sagely. I just bet he did.

"Did you know her?" Starr asked.

"Starr, I don't think you should talk about Dorothy. It doesn't seem appropriate." Ken was sweating big-time. I eyed him with interest. Maybe they'd planned the murders together, and he was afraid Starr would spill the beans.

Starr smiled lovingly at Ken. "Oh, Kenny, you're just too nice." She turned to me. "Dorothy made his life a living—"

"Starr," Ken pleaded.

"Now, Kenny, you know she was a terrible person. Not that

I'm glad she's dead or anything, but she made you so un-happy." She turned to me again. "She just drove him right into my arms, and I was glad to love him." She beamed.

Gray pulled his cell from his belt and dialed.

Ken's look of apprehension disappeared, replaced by one of distrust. "Who are you calling?"

"The police," Gray said. "I thought they might like to talk to you before you leave."

Since Gray was leaning on the trunk, Ken pulled the rear door open and threw in his suitcase and garment bag. "You can't keep me here, and neither can they. I haven't done anything wrong." He glanced at Starr. "At least nothing the police are interested in."

"We'll let them decide that, okay? By the way, Ken, I know you and Dorothy had a hard time gathering the money for the place at Freedom's Chase. I can't help wondering where the funds came from for the house on Grand Cayman."

"None of your business!"

"It's okay, Kenny. Just tell him about your uncle's legacy," Starr urged.

Gray looked skeptical. "Must have been some legacy. Or did you borrow against the promise of collecting Dorothy's life insurance?"

Gray never saw the punch coming. Ken's fist got him in the nose, and Gray slid slowly from the trunk to the drive. I leaped forward to catch him before his head hit the ground. The punch was bad enough on top of his recent concussion. Slamming into the ground would have been terrible. I ended up kneeling with his head on my lap, watching as gallons of blood flowed down his cheek, under his ear and into his hair. And all over my slacks.

"I'mb bleeding again," Gray mumbled as he pushed himself up.

"Easy, Gray. Careful. Careful."

He pushed my hands away. "I'mb fine, Anna." He leaned forward so the blood ran onto the ground. He pulled his shirt from his waistband and pressed it to his face.

"Get your purse and shut off the living-room lights," Ken ordered Starr. "We're leaving."

I watched Starr as she ran to the house with little, wobbly steps. The woman would be so much happier in flip-flops. She tripped up the steps, somehow managing to make the denim plastered to her knees bend. Mentally I slapped myself in the forehead with the heel of my hand. What was I thinking? Starr would probably wear four-inchers to the beach.

Ken was staring at Gray in disgust. "You actually think I killed my wife? You deserve a lot more than a bloody nose."

"Men hab been killing wibes for money and love forever." Gray struggled unsteadily to his feet. I stood behind him in case he fell, arms ready to grab at him.

"Anna, I'mb fine."

"Right." I moved to his side.

"I don't even own a gun!" Ken shouted. "I hate guns."

"And I should believe that because?" Gray pinched the bridge of his nose.

"Because it's true."

The house lights went out, and Starr reappeared, a purse the size of Rhode Island slung over her shoulder. As she tippy-toed over the lawn, Ken climbed into the driver's seat. She stopped, hands resting on her hips.

"I can't even drive my own car?" she griped. "I love that car."

"You just drove over two hours to get here from Atlantic City." He turned the key and the motor purred quietly to life.

"Can I get another one in Grand Cayman?" Starr asked as she tripped her way to the passenger-side door. She paused. "Oh. Here." She threw a kitchen towel at Gray and handed a water bottle to me. "Not that you deserve it, accusing Kenny."

"I apologize." The fact that Gray's teeth were gritted may have undercut the sincerity of his contrition, but Starr seemed to be happy. She smiled and waved a few fingers, then climbed in the car.

Ken began to back out. Gray stepped forward and knocked on the driver's window. Ken frowned at him. Gray made a cranking movement. "Open your window."

With an aggrieved sigh, Ken lowered the glass.

Gray rested one hand on the roof of the car while the other continued pinching his nose. "We need to find someone with a black BMW. You're the sales manager at the only dealership in the area. Give me the names of tall, slim people who have bought from you."

Ken started to raise the window.

"Don't you want Dorothy's killer found?"

Ken hit the steering wheel in frustration, but he lowered the window again. He began reciting names, most of them people I'd never heard of. Every so often he mentioned the last name of one of my students, but one name leaped out like an off-sides lineman.

We watched until the taillights disappeared, then walked quietly to the car. I waited while Gray once again dialed 911 and told the dispatcher not to bother sending anyone to Sycamore Street. All was quiet here. Sorry for the call.

"Do you think having a wife who was an accountant helped him get the money for his Cayman house?" I held out my hand for the car's key.

"You didn't buy that convenient legacy as the source of the necessary cash?"

"I'll admit I can be pretty gullible, but even I'm not that dumb."

Gray dropped the key into my palm and climbed into the car where he rested his head against the seat back. "Dorothy was an accountant, not a financial planner or a stockbroker. She didn't make money for her clients. She kept track of where it went, largely for tax purposes."

"Maybe she helped him hide money from the IRS."

Gray thought for a few minutes while I turned the ignition and pulled away from the curb. "You'd need a forensic accountant to uncover something like that."

"When we get back to Freedom's Chase, we can tell the sergeant our suspicions. We can also give him that name Ken mentioned."

# TWENTY-THREE

The Sergeant was not happy with us when we arrived at Freedom's Chase.

"What do you mean calling in a crime like this and then disappearing?" he yelled, his craggy face one massive scowl.

"We thought we could follow the murderer." Gray shrugged. "He got away."

"But we know who it wasn't," I offered before the sergeant could yell at us some more. "It wasn't Ken Ryder."

"And you know this how?"

I squirmed under his irate gaze. "We went to his house."

The sergeant just closed his eyes and counted to ten. "Preserve me from amateurs."

I ignored his poor attitude. "You might be interested in knowing he's on his way to the airport with Starr Good-night."

"Going to Grand Cayman, is he?" Poole asked.

Gray and I looked at each other in astonishment.

"You know about his house there?" I couldn't believe it.

"As husband of a murdered spouse, he was our first suspect. He's been thoroughly investigated and is guilty of nothing more than being a two-timing louse."

"But the money? He bought here—" I swept my hand to

indicate Freedom's Chase, "—and he bought there. We're talking close to three-quarters of a million."

"Legacy from an uncle." Poole lifted his foot and looked at the hole in the sole of his shoe. "Wish I had an uncle like that."

"Me, too." I felt deflated and dumb. I'd been so sure Ken had been cooking the dealership's books.

"Now tell me exactly what you saw here tonight." The sergeant had his trusty notebook in hand.

We did, describing the two people, two cars, one of which, a black Jeep, was still parked against the curb. Crime scene guys were going over it, the scene brightly lit by the klieg lights once again.

Gray finished his recounting of what we'd seen with, "So we tried to follow the car, but we lost it."

"Mind telling me why you were here in the first place?" Poole asked.

"Checking the supply shed," Gray said. "You know we've been having trouble with petty theft."

Poole studied Gray for a minute. "Not too smart bringing Anna here, was it?"

"I couldn't leave her at home. Both Lucy and Meg were out for the evening. I didn't think the killer would be looking for her here."

If the sergeant suspected there was more to our being here, he didn't pursue the topic. "You two go home. There's nothing more you can do here tonight."

"We've got a name for you to check out," Gray said. "We asked Ken who had bought black cars from his dealership recently, and he gave us a list of names, at least those he could recall."

The sergeant looked mildly interested.

"Hal Reddick."

"The builder?" Skepticism laced his voice.

I nodded. "Black BMW, slim individual like was here tonight, used Windle, Boyes, Kepiro and Ryder as his accountants."

"Boyes was his regular CPA, but he's got cancer, so Dorothy was filling in. Maybe she found something criminal," Gray suggested.

Poole shook his head. "You two watch way too much TV. First of all, owning a black BMW, being slim, and using a certain accounting firm aren't grounds for an investigation. Secondly, I've got real clues to deal with." He looked around the crime scene. "I think I'll stick to them." He turned and started away, then stopped and looked back. "Be careful, Edwards. Accusations like that can sound very personal and vindictive."

I knew he was referring to Reddick Construction and Edwards Inc, duking it out for the Amhearst reconstruction job. "But Gray won."

"Still." He turned away and waggled a hand negligently in our direction. "Good night. Glad you're free, Anna."

"I guess he told us," Gray said, a quick laugh escaping. "And he's right about it maybe looking vindictive on my part."

"But you won!"

"Still, I think we'd better give up any PI aspirations and stick to sewing and building."

I nodded and climbed into Gray's car for the trip back home. I felt all kinds of weird, my emotions tumbling and churning, about as stable as the water at the base of Niagara Falls.

On the one hand I was free from the stalking fear I'd lived with for a week, and that felt terrific. I didn't have to worry about someone shooting at me or attacking me or one of my friends. I could sleep soundly and go places without a police bodyguard. I could clean up the basement and get back to work without worry that someone would strike again.

On the other hand I'd gotten to like having Gray around. What if he didn't feel anything for me but his Sir Galahad tendencies? Now that I was safe, he could move on with a clear conscience. He could bury himself in his work, live with his cell glued to his ear and his PDA attached permanently to his palm. He could wash his hands and his T-shirts of the woman who made him bleed all the time.

We rode in silence for a while until my favorite house appeared. Outside spotlights lit it. I pointed. "That's where the Reddicks live."

Gray slowed and studied the place briefly. "Quite a showplace. With all that property it must be worth a million to a million and a half."

"I didn't realize contracting was so lucrative."

Gray shrugged. "We do all right."

Silence fell again as I brooded.

"Well, it's all over," Gray said as he pulled up our drive.

Exactly what I was afraid of! He parked, turned and gave me a friendly smile, an I'm-your-good-buddy smile. I wanted to weep.

"You don't seem very happy, Anna. I expected you to be jumping up and down now that this mess was over."

"That's Lucy's style."

"True." He rested his arm along the back of the seat. "Come on. What wrong? Are you upset about the sergeant blowing off our suggestion?"

I shook my head.

"Then what?" He lifted my chin so our eyes met. "You should be all kinds of relieved."

"Oh, I am." Even to my ears I sounded forlorn.

"Come on, sugar. Give."

Sugar. Surely that was hopeful? I studied his handsome face, his beautiful dark eyes. Did I have the nerve to express my inner heart, to bleed on him emotionally? I mean, telling a guy that you think you love him is very risky when he's just said it's all over. But what if I never said anything? What if I just let him walk away? I'd kick myself forever, wondering what might have been. I closed my eyes and semi-leaped.

"Will I see you any more?"

"What?"

I heard the disbelief in his voice and my eyes snapped open. He looked almost angry.

I pulled back until I was leaning against my door, the handle digging into my back. "I'm sorry. I—I didn't mean to put you in a bad position. I appreciate all you did for me. You were great." I turned to grab the handle and let myself out.

He grabbed my arm and swung me around. I studied the pocket on today's T-shirt, forest-green mottled with crimson.

"Look at me." It was an order.

"I need to go in," I mumbled. But he now gripped both my arms, holding me firmly in place.

"Look at me, Anna. Now."

Taking a deep breath and figuring I couldn't possibly humiliate myself any more, I looked at him. I wanted to shut my eyes again against the heat and intensity of his gaze. His displeasure cut me deeply.

"What makes you think I don't want to see you any more?"

I blinked. "You said it was over."

"Sure, with the threat, thank God. But not with me."

"Not with you?" Had I heard him right?

"My name is not Glenn. I am not leaving you."

"Probably because I don't have a maid of honor waiting in the wings," I mumbled, making light of what he said because I was afraid of the hope that unfurled in my chest. It was either be silly or cry.

"Because I know a good thing when I see it." One hand released my arm and moved to cradle my neck. "I find I've fallen for you, Anna Volente. I'm not certain where all this is taking us, but I know there's something very special between us. Since I met you, I've bled more than ever in my life, I've been shot, and I've worked less than any time in recent memory."

The tears were moving in. I could feel the tightness in my throat and the burning behind my eyes. "You sure know how to woo a girl."

"Actually, I do. Four sisters, remember?" He smiled. "How about if you and I go out for dinner tomorrow night to celebrate your liberation?"

"Really?" The tears now sat, ready to overflow. I sniffed. "I was so afraid you'd want to cut and run. Four brothers, remember?" And Glenn.

He bent and kissed me softly. "Tomorrow night? A real date?"

I wrapped my arms around him and leaned my head on his chest. I listened to his heart beat while mine soared and the tears flowed. "I'd love a real date with you."

He handed me a very rumpled but clean handkerchief, and I mopped at my face. "I'm taking you someplace very special," he whispered in my ear.

"No bloody T-shirts allowed?"

"None. Dress up for me."

And I did. I wore my favorite jacket dress, a deep periwinkle, and my black sling-backs. I slipped on a string of pearls that had been Mom's and wore the earrings that matched. When Gray came for me wearing a navy pinstriped suit and a blue-and-red rep tie, I had to swallow fast so I wouldn't drool. The only thing that saved him from perfection was the lopsided haircut and the still-healing bullet crease on his skull.

During the drive to one of the classiest restaurants I'd ever been to, we talked about our brothers and sisters, telling funny stories and favorite traits. At dinner where the waiter actually wore a tux, we talked about our parents, especially Mom and her early death and Gray's father and the hole he'd left. When the waiter came with the little tray holding the check, it seemed impossible that so much time had passed.

"You know what?" Gray said, his eyes bright and fixed on me even as he fished for his wallet. "I think it's a very good sign that we have plenty to talk about even when there's not a life-threatening emergency hanging over us."

"A whole evening without calling the police or ducking bullets. Wow!"

"Look, Mom." He held out his hands. "No blood."

The waiter who had come to take Gray's card, looked at us strangely. We didn't bother to explain.

"I'm going to run to the ladies' room," I said.

Gray nodded. "I'll meet you in the lobby."

The ladies' room was huge, lit for making you look great in the mile-long mirror over the sinks, and full of some glorious fragrance piped in from somewhere. As I washed my hands, a stall door opened and a tall, slim, very well-dressed woman emerged. Our eyes met in the mirror as she set her purse on the counter. She seemed unconcerned that the flap holding it shut wasn't gripping and that some of the contents slid out. She was too busy frowning at me.

"Well, I wish I could say it was a pleasure to see you again." Her voice was clipped and hard. Gray wasn't even with me and the woman sill harbored such an intense dislike for me? How pathetic.

"Hello, Mrs. Reddick. How are you?" Not that I really wanted to know. I just wasn't about to fall to her level. I looked down to make certain the soap was all gone from my hands, and I couldn't help seeing the contents of her purse.

Among the usual paraphernalia of wallet, keys, makeup case and cell phone, she carried a small revolver, one where you could see the cylinder that held the bullets, sort of a small, women's version of the old cowboy guns used for the shootouts at high noon or the OK Corral.

I looked up quickly, studying her carefully made-up face, her huge diamond ear bobs, the great gems on three of her fingers. Nah. She was just an ill-tempered, spiteful rich lady.

"I love your house, by the way."

She merely inclined her head ever so slightly.

"The fabric in the window treatments in your living room is among the most beautiful I've ever seen." And it was, a soft mix of greens, lavenders, soft pinks and creamy yellow.

If I'd thought she was hostile before, she was positively glacial now. "How do you know what my living-room drapes look like?"

I smiled sweetly. "I made them for you."

I thought she might choke.

"In fact I did all your window treatments."

"Well, I'm sure replacements will be easy to find."

As I cranked the papertowel machine, I wondered if she'd actually be petty enough to makes those changes simply because I was the needlewoman who had sewn what was currently hanging. No wonder she carried concealed. Half the people she knew were probably gunning for her.

"I take it you're still seeing what's-his-name? Edward Grayson?"

"You mean Gray Edwards, the man who got the contract for the huge downtown Amhearst job? Yes." I grabbed my purse and escaped before I got pneumonia from the arctic winds blowing in my direction. As I hurried to the lobby, eager for the warmth of Gray's company, I tried to feel bad about that last jab, but I couldn't.

*Oh, Lord, I'm as petty as she is. I'm sorry. And I'm sorry that I'd probably say it again in similar circumstances.*

When I got to the lobby, I found Gray in conversation with Hal Reddick. The two men were doing much better at civility than we women had.

"You guys look like twins." I pointed at their dark pin-striped suits.

"The successful man's uniform," Hal said.

"Except for the ones where the stripe is too broad and the guy looks like a member of the Mob," Gray said.

The three of us made pleasant small talk for a few minutes while Hal waited for his wife. "She must have gone out to the car when I wasn't looking," he finally said. "Excuse me and good night."

I watched him walk out the door. "I don't care if his name was one that Ken mentioned last night. He can't be the one who hired the man in black."

Gray raised an eyebrow. "Why not? Because he has good taste in suits?"

"Works for me."

Gray took my arm and escorted me outside. We halted in surprise under the front awning. It was raining quite heavily. Hal Reddick stood there, staring at the deluge.

"When did this begin?" I asked, as a bolt of lightning flashed and long rumble of thunder followed in about three seconds.

The slightly chill wind blew the rain just enough that it slipped under the awning about the legs. I could feel my ankles and feet getting more moist by the second. I looked at the guys' trousers with longing. They probably weren't even aware that the rain was intruding.

A great bolt of lightning sizzled very close by, followed immediately by a crash of thunder. The restaurant lights went out. So did the lights in the parking lot, and the night suddenly became very dark.

I moved closer to Gray, and he slid an arm around my waist. "It's okay, Anna. Don't be afraid."

"I'm not, not really." But I was, just a bit. Sort of my version of post traumatic stress syndrome.

We stood quietly for a few minutes, waiting to see if the lights would go back on or the rain would let up. When another bolt struck nearby and the thunder followed immediately, I knew the storm was going to be here for a while, and I doubted that the electric company had only the restaurant to worry about.

Gray must have reached the same decision because he said, "Let me go get the car. Otherwise we'll be here indefinitely."

"I'll keep her company while you're gone," Hal said. "Josie must still be in the ladies' room because she sure isn't running around in this weather."

I thought of the immaculately coiffed Josie in her blue silk dress and just-so hair and had to agree.

Gray took off at a run, dodging puddles as he went.

"He's a fine young man," Hal said, watching Gray's shadow disappear into the gloom and heavy rain.

"He is," I agreed.

"I'm sure we'll bid against each other on other jobs." He grinned at me. "Hopefully I'll win some of the competitions."

Thunder cracked, and Hal's grin disappeared. Thunder cracked again, making me jump. Twice so close together!

Hal's back arched, and he began to topple toward me, his face twisted with shocked surprise.

A third crack sounded as I reached out to catch him. The corner of the brick beside me exploded, sending stinging bits of clay and mortar into my face.

"Hal!" I screamed. "Hal!"

A couple pushed the restaurant door open, bumping into Hal and me as he sagged in my arms. I struggled to hold his weight.

I turned a terrified face to the couple. "Call 911. A man's been shot!"

With horrified looks they disappeared back inside.

Hal and I collapsed in a heap on the small porch.

"Hal!" I screamed again. I could see blood forming a puddle on the concrete.

A car rounded the line of parked vehicles and screeched to a halt by the edge of the awning. Gray erupted from the driver's seat, leaving the engine running and the headlights shining.

"Anna!"

But I barely heard him. I was too busy staring at the bedraggled vision illuminated by Gray's headlights.

Josie Reddick stood in the rain, her little revolver dangling from her hand as she stared wild-eyed at what she had just done. "Hal?" She ran toward the little porch. "Hal!" She fell to her knees sobbing. "Hal!"

But he never heard her.

# EPILOGUE

I thought the second Saturday in June would never come, but finally, finally it did. My wedding day.

Again.

Stop that, I ordered my unruly self as I stood in the living room waiting for the limousine to take me, Dad, Lucy and Meg to the church. Do not think about before. This is now! This is Gray! This is not Glenn.

And while I agreed with myself mentally and knew the correct answer to the will-he-show-up question, I found myself feeling very nervous. My hands were clammy as I clutched a handkerchief Mom had carried when she married, and I couldn't stay still.

"Anna!" Lucy stood with her hands on her hips, scowling at me. "How are we supposed to arrange your veil if you keep stalking around like some caged animal in a zoo?"

I looked at my housemate, cute as could be in her bright navy bridesmaid's dress, her red curls a soft halo under the coronet of daisies and bachelor buttons with the navy streamers falling down her back. Meg stood behind her, staring in a mirror, trying to make her coronet of flowers stay on her glossy black hair.

"I'm going to need a dozen bobby pins, and it's still going to slide off," she moaned.

"Just don't move your head all day," Lucy advised.

I was going to miss these women who had become such wonderful friends. I didn't think Gray was going to want to sit up all night in his pj's and talk about the deep issues of life while munching on cold pizza or Rocky Road ice cream. I was fairly certain he wouldn't think giving me a manicure was a fun job or spending an hour in Bath and Body Works smelling everything was a good way to spend a rainy Saturday.

These women had been with me through the whole man-in-black situation, the unexpected finale, and all the legal aftermath. Of course, so had Gray. I guess it came down to the Lord giving me the best of both worlds, something for which I was deeply grateful.

The night Hal Reddick was murdered revealed much about what was going on below the surface, much that even Sergeant Poole and the Amhearst police didn't know.

When Bob Boyes, the accountant from Windle, Boyes, Kepiro, and Ryder, became ill and Dorothy Ryder filled in for him on the Reddick account, Dorothy became suspicious. Like me, she had always admired the beautiful Reddick house and understood its value. She also lived in Amhearst and noted in the paper the amounts of money that Reddick Construction gave to civic and social service organizations and agencies. She knew about the house the Reddicks had at Nag's Head, North Caroline, a very plush resort. When she saw the figures Hal Reddick was reporting for tax purposes, she became very suspicious.

Added to these more or less public observations was the fact that Dorothy and Ken Ryder had mutual friends with the Reddicks. Through the unintentionally damning gossip of these friends, Dorothy knew of Josie's visits to extremely expensive health spas for a month at a time, of her trips to New

York for all the spring and fall fashion shows and her costly purchases of designer clothes.

All it took was her whisper in the ear of the IRS, and Hal and Josie Reddick became subjects of great interest to the IRS Criminal Investigation Division. As one of the WBK and R accountants told the paper, "Cash-based payment and income flourishes in this country, and there's no way accountants can trace it. We can deal only with the figures we are given."

But the IRS can trace such non-compliance, and their agents began a detailed investigation of the Reddicks for tax evasion and tax fraud. Bank records were subpoenaed and assets evaluated. The possibility of offshore accounts and hidden monies was probed.

Not that Hal and Josie were aware at this point. Neither were the Amhearst police. However it is assumed that Dorothy asked enough questions to somehow reveal that she was suspicious, and her sudden overt interest got back to Josie. Bob Boyes, the Reddick accountant of years' standing, didn't live in Amhearst, he had no interest in local goings-on, and he never asked about or suspected assets other than those reported to him. Dorothy was not so obliging.

Josie became very nervous.

The *News* quoted her as saying, "I loved my husband and I *loved* our lifestyle. I was willing to do most anything to preserve it."

On one of the frequent gambling trips she and Hal took to Atlantic City where they were treated like royalty by the casinos, she made contact with the man in black who called himself Dar Jones at the time.

"I hired him to kill Dorothy Ryder before she learned too much," Josie freely admitted. "Then *that girl* got involved and messed everything up!"

When the reporter from the *News* called me for a reaction to that quote, I told her, "All I did was look out a window."

When Dar Jones couldn't manage to kill me, Josie decided he had become a liability. The police were chasing him, and what if they caught him? He could implicate her. So she met him at Freedom's Chase and killed him with her trusty little revolver.

Sergeant Poole, Natalie and the Amhearst police investigated the murders completely unaware that the IRS was conducting the investigation that provided the motive for the killings. Had Amhearst law enforcement known, perhaps Hal wouldn't have been shot. Who knows? Certainly if he hadn't been killed, he would be spending a considerable amount of time in jail, as Josie was doing.

The night Gray and I bumped into the Reddicks having dinner at the same restaurant we were, Josie was reveling in how easy it had been to take care of the Dar Jones and Dorothy Ryder problems. Maybe she should also take care of the Gray Edwards problem so he could no longer provide the most serious and potentially financially devastating competition Reddick Construction had ever had. The fact that she mistook her husband in his navy pinstriped suit as he stood with his back to her while talking to me on the restaurant porch for Gray in his pinstriped suit is one of life's ironies. Whenever I try to feel sorry for Josie for killing the man she loved, I remember that if she had hit her intended target, I wouldn't be getting married today.

I heard the limousine pull up in front of our little brick house. The next time I entered here, I'd be Anna Edwards. I'd have two first names, but no one would mix mine up as they did Gray's. I grinned to myself.

The doorbell rang, and my father hurried to answer. The limo driver slouched there, wearing a tux and a cap pulled low, sunglasses swathing his face. He handed my father a note.

I thought I might be sick.

Dad handed me the note. With a trembling hand, I opened it.

> Sugar, I know this is when it all went wrong before.
> It's not going wrong today, and I'm here to see to it.

I looked up, and there stood the limo driver, cap and glasses gone as he smiled at me.

"Gray!" I ran to him and threw myself into his arms.

"Anna!" Lucy called. "Your veil!"

"Gray!" Meg sounded appalled. "You can't see her before the wedding!"

Like I cared.

Gray held me close, and I could feel his heart beating against mine. Over his shoulder I could see his silver pickup behind the limo.

"I'm so glad he never showed," he whispered in my ear. "But I'll be here for you always. I promise, Anna." And he kissed me.

Society page of the *Amhearst News:*

> Anna Marie Volente became the bride of Grayson Hamilton Edwards on Saturday, June 12, at Calvary Church in Amhearst. In an unusual twist to the otherwise traditional wedding, the groom drove the bride to the church in his silver pickup while the bride's father and the bridesmaids followed in the limousine.

\* \* \* \* \*

*And now, turn the page for a sneak preview of
the beloved classic CAUGHT IN THE MIDDLE
by Gayle Roper
On sale in April 2007 from
Steeple Hill Love Inspired Suspense.*

*Check out all the classic Merry Kramer mysteries!*

*April 2007: CAUGHT IN THE MIDDLE, #50
May 2007: CAUGHT IN THE ACT, #54
June 2007: CAUGHT IN A BIND, #58*

*And on sale for the first time ever in August 2007:
CAUGHT REDHANDED, #64*

"It was a dark and sleety night," I muttered as I slid behind the wheel and slammed the car door, grateful to have reached protection without drowning. I tossed my briefcase onto the seat and shook the water out of my hair.

"Merrileigh Kramer, what have you done?" my mother had asked in horror when I'd had my waist-length hair drastically cut at summer's end on the new-look, new-person theory.

I looked in the mirror and wondered the same thing myself. I hadn't cut my hair, except for its annual split-ends trimming, since ninth grade. For a woman who hated change, I did a drastic thing when I entered that beauty parlor. And it had been step one.

Now I sighed and reminded myself that it'd grow eventually. The one trouble was that I didn't know what to do with it while it grew. Somehow women routinely got from Halle Berry short to Halle Berry long and looked good in the process. I feared there wasn't enough mousse in the world for me to accomplish that feat.

I eased my way across the parking lot, uncertain how slippery the millions of needles of icy rain had made things. The others who had been attending the Wednesday evening Board of Education meeting with me moved just as slowly.

What had begun as a cold, nasty rain had turned to sleet when we weren't looking.

When it was my turn to pull out onto the road, I stepped slowly on the gas. The wheels spun for an instant on the thin layer of ice, then grabbed hold.

I hated ice. Every time I drove on it, I thought of my mother and the winter's day in Pittsburgh years ago when she had been driving me and four friends from Brownies. I remember the terrifying spin across the other lane and the oncoming cars scrambling to avoid us. I remembered the thud of our car as it hit a utility pole. I still felt my heaving stomach and tasted the fear. Mostly I remembered the screams and my mother's white face and the blood from the bashed noses. The fact that no one had been badly hurt then did not ease my fluttery heart tonight.

I drove carefully, watching for trouble. At Manor Avenue and Lyme Street I detoured slowly around a pair of cars half blocking the intersection as they sat with their left headlights locked together. Their drivers stood in the rain doing a good imitation of their cars, noses mere inches apart.

I couldn't help grinning at them, but I gripped the wheel more tightly. My heart throbbed in my temple.

With relief I turned onto Main Street where traffic was moving more quickly, keeping the road from freezing. When I passed *The News* office, the lights were still on, and I felt a surge of belonging. I beeped my horn in greeting to whoever was working so late. Don, my fearsome editor? Mac, his lecherous but charming assistant? Larry, the sports guy?

I turned into Oak Lane and felt the wheels slue.

Hang on, I told myself. You're almost home.

I took my foot off the gas, gritted my teeth, and proceeded slowly between the rows of cars parked against each curb.

Suddenly a car on my right roared to life like a lion

scenting its prey. Without looking, it sprang from its parking spot, barely leaving the paint on my fender. I instinctively did exactly what I'd always lectured myself about not doing. I hit the brakes on ice.

Of course I went into an immediate skid. My headlights raked across the offending car as it pulled away, briefly revealing a man, hat pulled down over his eyes, collar up against the weather, staring intently ahead, completely unaware of me or anything else.

My stomach became mush and my heart thumped wildly in my ears as I skidded helplessly toward a new blue car parked on the left. I whipped my wheel into the skid just like everyone said you should, but still the shiny blue door panels with their navy-and-red racing stripes rushed at me. My headlights blazed on the chrome; the black windows loomed darkly.

But my real terror was for the man who had suddenly materialized at the front bumper of the blue car, standing like a pedestrian waiting for a clear path to jaywalk. I had no idea where he'd come from.

"Please, God, don't let me hit him!" I was a Brownie again, panic-stricken.

His features were indistinct through rain-washed window, but I could see the O of his mouth as he saw me rushing toward him. He turned to run.

I closed my eyes involuntarily against the crash, shoulders hunched, face screwed up in apprehension. I was probably screaming, but thankfully I don't remember. Screaming has always struck me as a sign of weakness, and I like to imagine that I react with style even when I'm afraid. And I was afraid.

After a very long, slow-motion moment, my car shuddered to a silent halt. I cautiously opened my eyes and found myself mere inches from the blue car's front fender, the two cars neatly side by side and too close together for my door to open. I could not have parked so well had I tried.

I slid across the seat and flung open the far door. I didn't think I'd hit the man—I had neither heard nor felt a thump—but I had to make sure he wasn't crushed beneath my wheels. I pressed a hand against my anxiety-cramped abdomen and climbed into the downpour.

The man wasn't lying broken on the road. I fact, he wasn't anywhere, lying or standing, broken or whole. He had completely disappeared.

I leaned against my car, weak with relief, and took deep breaths. I barely felt the icy sleet running down my neck. Finally I was able to move enough to get myself back into the car, and with a strange shaky feeling, I drove the few remaining blocks home.

It was still somewhat strange to me that this *was* home. Here I was, all alone in Amhearst, working as a reporter at *The News,* responsible to no one but God and Don Eldredge, the newspaper's owner editor.

I don't *have* to do anything, I had understood one evening during my first week in Amhearst. I'm completely on my own. If I want to eat and pay the rent, I'd better go to work, but I don't have to. And there's no one here who cares enough to make me.

It had been a strange, lonely, and frightening realization. There were no family, no friends, no acquaintances here. It was just me, making my own choices.

Leaving Pittsburgh and home had been hard for me. I like to think of myself as independent, but the truth is that I like to be "independent" surrounded by familiar things.

I'd gone back home after college, moving in with my parents, content to be where everything was known and comfortable. I hadn't had to find a new doctor or a new dentist or a new church. I'd become a general reporter at the paper where I'd worked for three of my college summers, and I'd done very well, even winning a couple of minor journalism awards.

And, of course, Jack was in Pittsburgh: handsome, personable, accomplished, irresponsible Jack.

I had expected to live at home one, maybe two years at the very longest. After all, I was an independent spirit. I was amazed and appalled when I woke up one day and realized that I had been there four years, waiting for life to happen. Waiting for Jack.

"Just a little more time, Merry," he'd say. "That's all I'm asking. Just a little more time."

Eventually to save myself from drowning in despair, I came to Amhearst, and my first weeks here were terrible. I hated all the new people, the new streets, the new stores. I got a toothache, probably from grinding my teeth all night in fear, and I had to find a dentist. I hated him. too.

But I made it. I learned to like my job, and I slowly remembered that being alone isn't the worst thing in the world. I might not be laughing much yet, but I was slowly regaining some self-respect.

"Forgetting what is behind," Dad said one night on the phone, quoting St. Paul. "Straining toward what is ahead. Pressing on toward a new life. We're proud of you, Merry."

Jack spoke to me on the phone a few times, too, and even came to visit me once. I agonized over that visit, filled with equal measures of hope and dread. The reality was dull compared to my nightmares and daydreams.

"Come back when you're ready to get married," he told me when he left.

"I'll come back when I have a ring on my finger and a date on the calendar, not before," I replied. Then I went into my apartment and cried myself sick.

And so summer became fall, and fall a nasty, sleety early December night with icy roads, and I was finally home.

I parked, climbed out into the cold and wet, and hurried to my trunk, where I'd stashed a case of Diet Coke. The dim light by the walk barely illuminated the area.

I looked uncomfortably over my shoulder. It was dark and spooky back here even on a nice night, but in the rain and sleet, it was worse than usual. The large lilac at the edge of the house was especially eerie tonight, with its branches creaking and complaining about their icy bath.

I eyed the dripping tree, trying to penetrate it to be certain it wasn't hiding someone. Come May, those blossoms had better be beautiful and fragrant to make up for my heart palpitations the rest of the year.

Although, I told myself with false bravado, no bad guy in his right mind would be lurking behind a lilac tree on a night like this.

Even so, the last thing I expected to find when I raised the lid of my trunk was a dead body.

Dear Reader,

You're holding in your hands my first book for the Love Inspired Suspense line, though this isn't my first book. It is my sincere wish that with my titles coming from Steeple Hill Books, I will get to meet many new readers like you.

Since one of my great loves is reading a good romantic suspense, that's the pleasure I want to give you. I want you to fall in love with Anna and her friends, drool just a little bit over Gray and root for the dastardly Dar to be caught. Most of all I want you to be aware that though *See No Evil* is fiction, the characters model for us just how God interacts with us in the crunches of daily living.

It's this showing us patterns of living that makes fiction so exciting to me. Sure, nonfiction is good as it tells us how we should live, but stories show us how. We see characters choose certain actions and reactions, and consequences follow.

"Whoops," we say. "If I make that bad choice, what happened to that character might happen to me, but if I choose well and follow the Lord, good stuff will happen." I'm not saying that hard times never come when we make wise choices, but the chances are that life will be less complex and more pleasant. Certainly the presence of the Lord makes all our experiences richer.

Drop me a line at gayle@gayleroper.com. I'd love to hear from you.

Warmly,

*Gayle*

# QUESTIONS FOR DISCUSSION

1. When Anna sees the murderer, her life takes an unexpected turn. Have you ever had surprising things happen to you that have taken you places you didn't expect to go?

2. Anna has the misfortune of being hurt deeply by her former fiancé, and consequently she finds trusting another man difficult. Has someone (not necessarily a man) hurt you badly? Does that situation affect you still? How do you deal with the hurt? How do you think God would have you deal with it?

3. Gray struggles with workaholism, and the perks of modern communication help him fall ever deeper into that pit. Colossians 3:23–24 reads, "Whatever you do, work at it with all your heart, as working for the Lord, not for human masters, since you know you will receive an inheritance from the Lord as a reward. It is the Lord Christ you are serving." What do you think these verses imply about our work ethic?

4. Dar Jones has the interesting affectation of making all his aliases almost famous names, e.g., Dar Jones=Dow Jones. What does this show about him as an individual? Is he yearning to be famous like his namesakes? Is he thumbing his nose at them? What are your thoughts on fame, especially from a Christian perspective?

5. Anna promises her dying mother that she will always remember that she is an artist. She finds this promise as she interprets it difficult to keep. What is our responsibility when we make promises?

6. How does God treat his promises? Jeremiah 29:11–12, the verses found at the beginning of this book, make promises. Is God breaking his word when we have difficulties and pain in our lives? What do you think is God's ultimate goal for us?

7. How do we find God's specific will for us? One clue: when Anna realizes her fabric mosaics are God's plan for her, what emotion does she feel? When she makes the mosaics, what does she feel?

8. Josie Reddick begins her slide with a combination of ambition and love for her husband. Are either of these emotions wrong? If not, how do they get warped? What marks the difference between her ambition and Gray's?

9. Why does Ken Ryder's duplicity seem less terrible than Josie's? What are your thoughts on degrees of sin? Are there always consequences to wrongdoing? What happens to consequences when we go to God in confession and accept his forgiveness?

10. If any of these characters could come to life, which one would you pick and why?